MISTLETOE *between* FRIENDS

—*The*—
SNOWFLAKE INN

SAMANTHA
CHASE

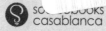

SOURCEBOOKS
casablanca

Published by Sourcebooks Casablanca Sourcebooks, Inc.
P.O. Box 4410, Naperville, Illinois 60567-4410
(630) 961-3900
Fax: (630) 961-2168
www.sourcebooks.com

Printed and bound in Canada.
MBP 10 9 8 7 6 5 4 3 2 1

For my favorite U.S. Marine

Not a day goes by that I'm not in awe of you and completely proud of all you've accomplished in your life. Thank you for your help and for just being awesome.

Love you, Justin Ryan.
Semper Fi!

Contents

MISTLETOE
between FRIENDS

Chapter 1

STAYING UP ALL NIGHT ON THE PHONE WAS NOTHING NEW for Lily Cavanaugh. If someone was in a crisis, she was the go-to girl to help out. Now, snuggling deeper into her bed, Lily did her best not to laugh.

"So was it Bitsy, Mitzi, or Kitten they tried to set you up with?" she asked, barely containing her mirth.

"You are *so* not helping."

An unladylike snort escaped before she could stop it. "I can't help if I don't have all of the information. So? Details, please!" Lily sensed more than heard Cameron's frustration growing on the other end of the phone.

Cameron Greene and Lily had known each other since before they could walk. Their families were the best of friends, and since Cam and Lily were so close in age—less than a year apart—it was only fitting that they continue the tradition.

"I'm telling you, Lil," he began, "I'm thinking of moving overseas just to get some peace and quiet."

"Oh, come on. How bad could it have been? Was she pretty?"

"In a Barbie-doll kind of way."

"Not a problem for most guys! Okay, so what about the rest? Did you have anything in common?"

"I don't have anything in common with most people, Lil. You should know that." Cameron had a near-genius IQ and was a little awkward socially. It was hard for him to find common ground with most people when he spent his days in a laboratory, studying the secrets of the universe.

"So what did you talk about?"

He sighed. "After I got the not-so-condensed version of her modeling aspirations, I started talking about what I do."

Uh-oh, Lily thought. That was normally the kiss of death. "How long did it take for her eyes to glaze over?"

Cam laughed. "Less than two minutes."

"Wow," Lily said with mock enthusiasm. "I think that's a new record."

"We never even made it to dinner," Cam said, sounding like that wasn't a bad thing.

"What excuse did she give? Headache? Family emergency? She thought she left the stove on?"

"Headache."

"It is a classic." Now it was Lily's turn to sigh. "I'm so sorry, Cam. Are you okay?"

"Sure. I didn't want to go out with her. My parents orchestrated the entire thing, and I didn't want to disappoint them—again. I just wish they'd find something else to obsess about. I'm not interested in the empty-headed beauties they've been setting me up with."

"They are depending on you to carry on the Greene family name, Cam. This isn't new information. They hassled your sisters just as much until they found acceptable husbands."

"That was different. Neither of my sisters had an issue with dating. They're smart and outgoing and enjoy socializing. Why can't I just be left alone?"

Lily's heart broke for him. Cameron had always been

painfully shy, and because of his intelligence and fascination with science, most of the population couldn't begin to understand the subjects he found enjoyable. "It's not healthy to be alone all the time, Cam. You need to get out once in a while and be around regular people. Go to a movie, eat a hamburger…live like us regular folk for a little while," she teased.

He chuckled. "Do you have any idea how bad ground beef is for you? Even with the stringent safety—"

"It was just a suggestion!" she interrupted. "I don't need the lecture—again—on how bad most foods are. You've all but ruined my fast-food habits."

"I worry about you. Is that a crime?"

She smiled. "No, it's not a crime. I just wish you could relax your standards a little bit and, I don't know, have some fun." Shifting her position in bed, Lily turned on her tablet and kicked up a game of solitaire. She knew that she and Cameron could talk all night, but sometimes she needed a little distraction to keep her going. "So what's new at the lab?"

"Nice change of subject. Have you already started a game of solitaire?"

"Damn," she muttered. "How do you do that?"

"I know you better than you know yourself, Lil. Is talking to me so painful that you have to play a computer game at the same time?" His tone was only partially teasing.

Immediately Lily put the tablet down and sat up. "What? Why would you even say that?"

"Look, we're friends and you never lie to me, so don't start now, okay? If you can't even stand talking to me, what hope do I have of anyone else wanting to?"

Lily felt ready to cry. "Oh, Cam," she said, hand to her chest. "I love talking to you. You know that. Honestly, you're the only one who actually talks to me and listens to me without treating me like I'm an idiot."

"That's not true and you know it."

"No, I don't know it. No one in my family takes me seriously. Every time I try to talk to them about what's going on in my life, I feel like I'm just being patted on the head and pacified. It's beyond insulting."

"They never did understand your creative side," he said soothingly.

"Neither did Biff," she replied with a dramatic sigh.

Cam was silent for a moment. "I'm sorry… Did you say Biff?"

"Oh, did I not mention my wonderful dinner companion this evening?"

This time it wasn't a chuckle but a full-bodied laugh that came through the line. "Come on, Lily. No one names a kid Biff. It's cruel."

"Well, I think that's what his name was," she said, reflecting on the evening.

"You went to dinner with this guy and you aren't sure what his name was?" Cam asked with disbelief.

"Like you, we didn't make it to dinner. As a matter of fact, we never even made it to the restaurant."

"Why not?"

"Let's just say that while we were in the car, he asked me about what I did. By the time I got through talking about my pottery classes and dog walking and that short stint as a nude model for an art class—"

"Wait. What? When did you take a pottery class?"

Lily burst out laughing. "Out of those three things,

you latched on to the pottery class to be upset about? What about the nude modeling? You'd think that would be a red flag for someone sensible like you!"

"Okay, never mind about the pottery or…the modeling. What happened next?"

"He literally turned the car around and brought me home. He claimed that he had a business call that had slipped his mind, but I think that my Asian-fusion cooking class was the last straw for him." She sighed. "Not that I wanted to go out with him much either. Also like yours, it was parent-orchestrated. But still, I was hungry."

"I cannot believe Biff just turned the car around and took you home."

"Maybe his name was Jeff…" Lily said, racking her brain for at least a hint of what the guy's name was.

"Biff, Jeff, it doesn't matter. That was incredibly rude of him. I'm sorry, Lil. You deserve to have someone take you out and treat you like a princess."

"I'd just settle for someone to take me out and talk to me like I had a brain."

"You have a brain, Lil. You just intimidate people with your creativity."

"Nice try, Einstein," she deadpanned. "I think you have me confused with you. You intimidate people. People just think I'm weird."

"Well, then they're not worth knowing."

Lily settled back against her pillows and got comfortable again. "I'm so lucky to have you, Cam. You know that, right?"

"Nah, we're lucky to have each other."

"I wish you were here right now. I could make grilled cheese sandwiches and popcorn, and we could watch a movie and just relax." She toyed with her tablet and contemplated going back to solitaire.

"While that sounds nice, wouldn't it interfere with your game of solitaire?"

"Dammit! How do you do that?" she asked, looking around her room for hidden cameras.

"Like I said, I know you better than you know yourself."

"We certainly are a pair, aren't we?" she said wistfully.

"A pair of what?"

"A sad pair. We can't even find people to have a meal with. If you won't come over and have grilled cheese and popcorn with me, then I'm in real trouble. You were my last hope, Cameron Greene, and even you don't want to share a midnight snack with me!" Her tone held just a hint of mirth and theatrics, and she added a long-suffering sigh for good measure.

"And you know what's worse?" he asked, ignoring her.

"That I got kicked out of acting classes?"

Cam sighed. "Thanksgiving is right around the corner."

"And you've suddenly lost your love of turkey dinner?"

"Focus, Lily!" he snapped and then immediately apologized for his tone. "The holidays are here, my friend. That means there will be a steady stream of parties and get-togethers we will be forced to go to, and potential spouses will be thrown at us from every angle."

"Personally, I'm waiting for our parents to just position us at the foot of our driveways with mistletoe over our heads and signs taped to our chests that say 'Please marry us.'" The thought sent a shiver down her spine because she was only partially kidding. Lately, her mother had kicked up the campaign to marry her off.

Rarely a day went by when Lily wasn't asked if she'd met anyone decent.

Dealing with her mother was an exhausting, full-time job in itself.

"I think it's safe to say," Cam began, breaking into her train of thought, "that neither of us is looking forward to another holiday season spent ducking and weaving to avoid the matchmaking patrol. Agreed?"

"Agreed. But what choice do we have? Other than packing our bags right now and *both* of us moving overseas to get away from the insanity."

"I'm being serious here."

"You're always serious, Cam. I'm trying to get you to break that habit." When she got no response from him, she sighed with annoyance. "Okay, what do you have in mind?"

"We take ourselves off the market. If we're involved with other people, they can't marry us off."

"But we're not involved with other people. That's the problem. Isn't that what we've been talking about for the past hour? I'm so confused…"

"You're not confused, Lily, and don't play the ditzy card with me," he said patiently. "I'm saying that we pretend that *we* are involved. We. You and me."

Another snort of laughter broke free before she could stop it. "Are you crazy? Have you completely lost your mind? No one is going to believe that for a second!"

"Why not?" he huffed.

"We've been friends for, like, *ever*, for starters. If anything was ever going to happen between us, it would have happened by now. You know it, I know it, and they know it. Pretending to be a couple will never work."

"Just…hear me out, okay?" he asked. "I have a conference in New York next week. Come with me."

Lily sat in silence, wondering where her levelheaded friend had gone. When he didn't elaborate on his plan, she finally spoke up. "What will that prove?"

"The day we're due back is the official beginning of the season, at least according to my mother. You know how our families map out the party strategies and travel plans. We can show up together and announce our newfound romance, and they'll be so thrilled that they'll leave us alone. We can break up after New Year's, and then they'll be too heartbroken over the whole thing to upset either of us and we can milk the breakup angle for another month or two. If all goes as planned, we can be off the radar for about four months."

"Cameron Greene, I always knew you were a genius. I just never realized you were an *evil* genius!" Lily said excitedly. "It's brilliant! They love us both, so they're not going to have an issue with us dating! They'll get all giddy at the thought of merging our families, and while they're busy picking china patterns, we'll have a relaxing holiday. I'm telling you, you've done me proud."

"Aw…I'm blushing," he teased. "So what do you say? I leave Monday morning for New York."

"Wow, that's quick," Lily said, mentally going over her calendar. "I don't know, Cam. That's only three days to get someone to cover for me at the coffee shop, and…"

"When did you start working at a coffee shop?"

Lily growled in frustration. "You need to keep up, Cam! If we're going to be all in love and dating and whatnot, you are going to have to keep up with what's going on in my life."

"Maybe try doing a little…shall we say…less with your life for the next couple of months?"

"What would be the fun in that?"

"We leave for the airport Monday morning at seven. I'll make all of the travel arrangements. All you have to do is show up."

"What am I supposed to do all day while you're at your conference?"

"Seriously, Lil? Do you think you'll be bored in Manhattan?"

"Okay, you've got a point." She stopped and thought of all the possibilities. "I do have one request as your girlfriend."

"Already?"

"I've only just begun," she teased. "Can I get an afternoon at a spa? You know, manicure, pedicure, facial, massage…the works?"

"Is that all?" he asked suspiciously.

"And can I eat food from the street vendors without getting a daily lecture from you?" Lily waited for Cam's response. And waited. And waited. "Cameron?"

"You're going to be the death of me. You realize that, right?"

"Me? After your traumatic date with Kitten?"

"Her name wasn't Kitten," he laughed. "And it wasn't traumatic."

"Okay, maybe it wasn't traumatic, but you've got to admit that I'll be way more fun to date than the other women you've dated."

"That is certainly true," he agreed and then paused. "I'll be in meetings during the day and we have a couple of dinners to go to, but maybe we can take a night to just go sightseeing. What do you say?" Lily was quiet for a moment. "Lil? What's the matter?"

"Maybe this isn't such a good idea," she said quietly. "I mean, this conference is a big deal for you, and I don't want to do anything to embarrass you."

"Why would you even think such a thing?"

"Because you're you—this super-genius guy—and I'm…me. A twenty-six-year-old woman with no real job, no real talent, and no idea of what I want to do with my life. I don't want your colleagues looking at you like you're an idiot for dating someone like me. I mean, you can go to the dinners and all that, and I can hang out at the hotel. You don't have to take me along."

"Are you kidding me?" he asked, more than a little offended. "Lily, I am tired of you putting yourself down. I know your parents have made you feel inferior, but let me tell you what I see. I see a beautiful woman with an amazing smile and the greatest laugh, who always makes me feel better. You have a way of making everyone around you feel special, and I am going to be the envy of every man at that conference because I'll have the most beautiful woman in the world on my arm."

"Thank you," she finally whispered.

"Get some sleep," he said softly. "I'll call you on Sunday and let you know our itinerary."

"Cam?"

"Yeah?"

"Thank you for asking me to be your pretend girlfriend," she said, her tone relaxed. "I promise that I'll be the best pretend girlfriend you've ever had. You may never want to let me go."

"Good night, Lil," he said in a near whisper. "Sweet dreams."

"Night, Cam." Going to sleep with Cam's voice the last thing she heard would make those dreams very sweet indeed...

Chapter 2

LILY COULDN'T FALL ASLEEP.

Fake dating Cameron was the closest she'd ever get to seriously dating him. Something was better than nothing, she supposed, but still. The thought of them being a couple—even if only for show—had her wondering what it could be like if Cameron really gave them a chance.

Growing up, Lily had seen Cam as her pal, her buddy. But one fateful night when she was seventeen and feeling rebellious, he'd become her hero. After a particularly harsh fight with her parents over her poor grades in school, Lily had climbed out her window and gone to a college party that she and her friends had been forbidden to attend. Once there, she'd had too much to drink and found herself being hit on by a guy that she really didn't want anything to do with.

With no way to get home other than walking—and scared that the boy from the party would follow her—she'd called Cam. Sneaking out of his own home and taking his father's car, he'd come to her rescue. Lily had made it home safely thanks to him, and her parents had never realized she'd left. Cameron, however, was not so lucky. When he'd arrived home, his father had been up waiting and wanted to know why Cam had snuck out. He'd refused to share Lily's part in the story and ended up being grounded for a month.

When Lily had asked why he hadn't just told his father it was her fault, Cam had simply shrugged. "What's the point in both of us getting in trouble?" he had said, and in that instant, Lily saw him as her white knight. It wasn't the first time Cam had helped her, but it was the first time he'd had to pay a price for doing so.

Unimpressed with her walk on the wild side, Lily had changed her habits and begun spending even more time with Cam. He was the perfect guy, but he was so engrossed with his studies and planning his future that Lily kept her newfound feelings to herself.

"I am *so* in trouble," she said as she punched her pillow to try and get some sleep. "How am I supposed to *play* the part of the girlfriend when I just want it to be real?"

⁓

Monday morning came way too soon for Lily. She'd given herself multiple pep talks and reminded herself how important it was to do the right thing for Cam.

It just sucked that the right thing for Cam was going to be torture for her.

Ever on time, Cameron arrived to pick Lily up at exactly 7:00 a.m. Knowing he was a stickler about time, she'd made sure that she was ready and waiting for him. But she could tell by the look on his face when she opened the door that he was surprised she was ready.

"What?" she asked.

Cam looked her up and down and then at the suitcase beside her. "You're ready," he said with just a hint of disbelief.

A shy smile crept across Lily's face. "You told me

you'd be here at seven, so I was ready for seven. Actually, I was ready at six forty-five. Impressive, right?"

His eyes narrowed slightly. "You're never ready when I tell you what time I'm coming to pick you up. I build a cushion for Lily time."

The smile shifted to playful annoyance as Lily cocked a hip and crossed her arms over her chest. "If it would make you feel better, I can change clothes and decide that I want a bowl of cereal before we leave."

"No, no," he said with a slight chuckle. "I'm sorry. I guess I should have just said thank you, right?"

"No," she corrected. "You should have offered to put my suitcase in the car because all this chitchat will make us late." Without another word, Cameron reached beyond Lily and grabbed her case while she locked up her condo. "I watched the Weather Channel last night while I was packing, and they said it's going to snow while we're up there. Won't that be beautiful? We can see snow in Central Park!"

Cam shrugged; he'd never given much thought to snow in Manhattan and didn't care about it now. They lived just outside of Raleigh, so it wasn't as if they'd never seen snow before. But that was just one of the things about Lily he adored—that the little things in life made her happy.

Lily had a bigger heart than anyone he'd ever known. He knew that even though she made light of it, she was easily hurt by her family. It didn't help that her parents always made her feel like she wasn't living up to her full potential, or that she had an older sister everyone seemed to think walked on water. Cam knew the real Lily. If anyone took the time to get to know her and saw beyond her inability to find a career, they'd see a person who'd give them the world.

For as far back as Cameron could remember, he'd been in love with Lily Cavanaugh. While everyone else around them treated him like a freak because of his intelligence, Lily always considered him Cam, her friend. He'd never once thought about telling her how he felt because the last thing he wanted was to lose her as his friend. Most days, she was the only one who kept him sane.

And now he was going to have her to himself for nearly a week.

Once they were on the road, Cam glanced over at Lily and saw the serene smile on her face. "What are you thinking about right now?" he asked.

"Actually, I was wondering if we were going to play the part of boyfriend and girlfriend during your conference or if we were waiting to kick it into gear when we got back."

He nodded and then pondered the situation. "I suppose it wouldn't hurt to try out the act around my colleagues before we return home." His tone was rather cut-and-dried, like he was talking about a root canal.

"How about a little enthusiasm, champ?" she asked sarcastically. "This was your idea, remember? And if we're going to pull this off and get four months of freedom from our parents, you can't talk about our relationship like it's a chore."

Cam turned to look at her as if she were crazy. "Talk about our relationship? It's seven fifteen in the morning, Lil. We haven't been around anybody except each other. What do you want me to do?"

She sighed. "You'll need to show a little more excitement if you're going to be believable as my boyfriend."

What had he gotten himself into? "Why, exactly, do I have to do that?"

"Cam, everyone who knows me knows that I'm a fairly happy-go-lucky person. You and I are complete opposites. I'm going to have to tone it down a little, but on the flip side, you're going to have to kick it up a notch. You know, crack a smile or a joke once in a while. Laugh." She looked at him quizzically. "You have no idea what I'm talking about, do you?"

Honestly, he didn't. When he had devised the plan to have a make-believe romance with Lily to survive the holidays, Cam had simply thought that by saying they were involved, people would get off their backs. But as Lily explained the complexities of the situation, he realized he was greatly unprepared.

And that was simply unacceptable.

Taking a fortifying breath, he said, "Okay. It's not like we have to play twenty questions to know each other better. We already know everything about each other. What do you suggest?"

"Well," she said, "it would probably help if we held hands when out in public."

Cameron considered her suggestions and—without reacting in any way, shape, or form—decided that this wasn't going to be such a bad thing after all. He'd finally have the opportunity to touch Lily, to kiss Lily, and it was all her idea. He really was brilliant.

"Seems simple enough," Cam said. "Done." He reached for her hand and held it while he focused on the road and drove one-handed. He wouldn't normally do that because safety dictated that he drive with his hands in the ten-and-two position. It took all of thirty seconds for him to start to squirm.

"This is physically painful, for you, isn't it?"

"What? No," he denied, although he was lying through his teeth. He wanted to concentrate on the feel of her hand in his but couldn't when they were on the road.

Lily pulled her hand away and almost burst out laughing at how quickly Cam's hand went back to the steering wheel. "Okay, baby steps. We'll only hold hands when we're walking. How does that sound?" She smiled at the annoyance on Cam's face.

"Safety isn't something to take lightly, Lily."

"Of course it isn't," she agreed. "I mean, driving twenty miles *under* the speed limit and one-handed? What was I thinking?"

"It's a little early for all of this sarcasm," he said dryly. "So other than hand-holding, what am I supposed to do?"

Was he kidding? At this rate, she could probably convince him to act out every one of her fantasies that she'd ever had about him. But that would be wrong.

Wouldn't it?

Yes, yes, yes. *Bad Lily! What were you thinking?*

"Kissing," she said before she could stop herself. "We'll probably have to kiss in front of people from time to time. And none of that buddy-buddy, on-the-cheek stuff. Like…real kissing."

Bad, bad Lily!

She saw him considering the idea from all sides as usual. He never agreed to anything without thinking it through. "I guess I can," he said, seeming bored with the idea.

"That's the spirit," she said and was relieved to see them turning onto the exit ramp for the airport. If all went well, within a matter of hours, she would be walking around Manhattan with Cam and presenting the image of a happy couple.

Project Girlfriend had begun!

Snow was falling when they landed at Kennedy Airport, and Lily was practically bouncing in her seat with her eagerness to get out and walk in it.

"It's just snow, Lil," Cam said teasingly. "This isn't something new."

She punched him in the arm playfully as they walked off the plane. "Yes, but this is my very first New York snow! I'm so excited!" Taking a chance and more than ready to jump into character, Lily took Cam by the hand and headed toward the baggage claim. Walking hand in hand felt wonderful and more than natural. Why had they never done this before? "I'm not crazy about the crowds, but I'm sure I'll get used to it." Truth was, she actually loved the crowds because they were forcing her to stay super-close to Cam who, interestingly, wasn't looking all that uncomfortable either.

"Hopefully we'll get our bags quickly and grab a taxi. I'd really like to have a little time at the hotel before my first meeting," he said.

"What time do you start?"

"Two o'clock. We'll check in at the hotel, have

lunch, and then I'll need to go." That was all said very matter-of-factly, much like everything Cam said.

"Oh, okay," Lily replied, her mind racing with thoughts of how she was going to spend her first afternoon in the city. "And there's a welcome dinner tonight, right?" Cam nodded. "What time is that?"

"It starts at seven thirty."

"Did you still want me to go with you?" She hoped that she sounded casual about it, but deep down, Lily was terrified that she would do something to embarrass Cam and let him down.

He was about to reach for her suitcase on the carousel when Lily asked the question. "Why would you even ask me that?" he replied. Lily noted with surprise that he let the suitcase pass. Missing it was unlike him, though he did grab his own as it went by.

"You know, it's your first night and maybe you'd rather just have the time with your colleagues without me tagging along," she said lightly before muttering, "and ruining it."

Cam set his suitcase at his feet before taking Lily by the shoulders to face him. "Listen to me," he said in a stern but loving way. "There's nothing you'll do to ruin anything for me. I asked you to come with me, and I want you there with me tonight and all the nights that we're here." When she still didn't look convinced, he added, "Besides, you're my girlfriend. What would people say if I left you alone in the room while I went out on the town?"

That made Lily laugh. "You are *so* not going out on the town. You're a group of scientists with big brains. You'll sit around and debate the universe until you realize the night is over." She said it lightly, but there was more than a hint of truth to it. Without thinking about it, she leaned in and hugged him. "Thanks, Cam. I needed that." For the first time in the history of their friendship, Lily broke their embrace first. She was just about to comment on that when Cam motioned that her luggage was coming around again.

Maybe it was for the best. If Lily started analyzing every touch and look, she'd make herself crazy. Cam was pretending to be in love with her. That was it; end of story. She might have to remind herself of that several times a day because they had only been playing the part for a few hours and she was already blurring the lines.

Their hotel was right in the middle of the Times Square neighborhood, and Lily couldn't help but gape at the flurry of activity going on around her as they arrived. "Oh my gosh," she gasped when the taxi came to a stop. "You didn't tell me we were staying right in the heart of everything!"

Cam simply shrugged and paid the driver as they got out of the cab. Once in the hotel, Lily stood silently while Cameron checked them in. As he was signing the paperwork, he said, "I booked us a suite so that you can have some privacy and I'll have a little more space to work."

"So there are two bedrooms?" she asked as she looked around in awe of her surroundings.

"No, but the living area has a sleeper sofa. I'll take that and you take the bedroom."

Lily didn't want to put him out. "Cam, you need your

rest more than I do. You take the bedroom and I'll take the sleeper."

He thanked the front desk clerk as he took their room cards and paperwork and then turned to Lily, who had her roller case by her side. "Let's just get to the room and we can argue logistics later, okay?" Cam took his luggage in one hand and Lily's hand in the other and led them toward the elevators. He was really starting to get the hang of this, Lily noted with delight.

Once they were in their suite, Lily went right to the windows to check out the view. "Cam, this is amazing! Between the lights and the buildings and the crowds and the snow..." She stopped and took a breath. "I just can't believe that we're here." She turned to see him standing on the other side of the room, simply looking at her, and wondered at the expression on his face.

"Do you want to go downstairs and eat or order room service or walk outside and see what we can find?" Lily asked as she collapsed on the living room sofa and motioned him to sit beside her.

"I want to go over my notes once more before two, so if it's all right with you, I'd rather just order lunch up here."

"That's fine," she said and kicked off her shoes. She scooted closer to him on the couch and placed her head on his shoulder. Looking up into his dark-blue eyes, Lily beamed. "I promise to keep quiet so you can study."

Since she was so close, Cam took off his glasses and closed his eyes before resting his head against hers. "You don't need to keep quiet on my account. And if you want to go exploring, please don't let me stop you."

They were both silent for a long while before Lily finally spoke. "Um, Cam?"

"Mmm…"

"I think that if we're going to eat and you're going to study, we need to get up from the sofa." She hated even suggesting it because they didn't just sit quietly and enjoy being near each other often enough. They'd sat and watched more than their share of movies together at either his place or hers, but just sitting in the silence was something new and Lily found that she liked it.

"Are you sure?" Cam asked lightly. "Maybe if we both think really hard, lunch will appear at the door."

"That is the dream," Lily said with a quiet chuckle as she reluctantly moved away from the warmth of his body and stretched. "I'll get the menu and order while you go through your notes. How does that sound?"

‑‑‑∞‑‑‑

Lily had everything set up on the coffee table and was watching Cam expectantly when he finally looked up from the paper he had been reading. "What?"

"In case you hadn't noticed," she said, motioning to the coffee table, "lunch is served."

When he put his papers aside, he looked at his standard turkey club and her bacon cheeseburger with fries. One dark brow arched at her as he looked from her entrée to her.

"No lectures, remember?"

Cam nodded and reached for his sandwich. "That only applied to food vendors on the street. I made no such promise concerning anyplace else that we dine." He was teasing her, and she knew it. They ate their meals while they talked about what was on the schedule for Cam's first meeting in the afternoon.

Though she always listened and tried not to let her eyes glaze over, Lily was glad for the distraction of food. She knew the appropriate places to nod and had gleaned enough information over the years to make elementary comments on his work, something that Cam seemed to appreciate.

"So are you ready for your presentation?" she asked as she dipped the last of her fries in ketchup.

"I believe so. I always feel like I need to prepare more, but once I'm up there, I don't really use the notes."

"That's because you know this stuff like the back of your hand. You're going to be great." She gave him an encouraging smile. "What time will you be back to get ready for dinner?"

Cam looked at his watch. "We should be done by five, so I'll be back here by five fifteen to five thirty and then we'll get ready. We'll need to head out around six fifteen." He finished the last of his sandwich and turned back to Lily. "What are you going to do with yourself this afternoon?"

Reclining on the sofa with her hand on her full belly, Lily thought about her options. "I had thought that I'd just walk around, but the snow is really coming down out there and it's nice and toasty in here and I'm pretty full so…"

"You're just going to hang here and nap, aren't you?"

She made a face at him. "Maybe," she said defiantly.

The phone in the room rang but Cam barely glanced up. "Can you get that, please?" Hopping up, Lily crossed the room. She noticed that Cam was doing his best not to smile.

"Hello? Yes, this is Lily Cavanaugh. Wait… What? Um… No, I wasn't… Oh, uh… Are you sure?" She paused and glanced over at Cam, who seemed deeply engrossed in his notes. "Yes, thank you. I'll see you then. Bye." Hanging up the phone, Lily turned and saw that Cam was finally looking at her. "Cameron Greene, what have you done?"

He placed a hand on his chest and did his best to look as if he had no idea what she was talking about. "Me? What? What did I do?"

Lily strode across the room and collapsed on the sofa next to him with a bounce. "You booked me an afternoon at the spa!" she cried excitedly. "I can't believe you did that!"

"Why? You said you wanted to do that, so I made sure that I scheduled it."

Her shoulders sank and she pouted slightly. "You don't get it, do you?" Cam shook his head. "You didn't have to do it. I was joking with you when I said it. Well, not exactly joking, but I would have taken care of it myself." When he started to speak, she held up a hand to stop him. "It was very thoughtful of you, and it was a wonderful surprise. Thank you." She leaned in and kissed him on the cheek—and had to remember not to linger, even though that was what she wanted to do most. "You are very sweet."

Just what every guy wants to hear, Cam thought to himself. Before he allowed himself to obsess on that statement, he stood and began gathering his papers. "I'm going to get changed and then head downstairs. I'll meet you back here at five thirty." He did his best to not look at her, but when he walked toward the closet to grab his suitcase and toiletries, he turned and saw that she was still sitting on the sofa and smiling at him.

Words escaped him. Lily always managed to take his breath away. Others merely saw it as Cam being shy or socially awkward, but the truth was that most times when he was around Lily, he simply kept quiet to keep from ruining everything by blurting out how he felt about her.

And the last thing that Cam wanted was to risk losing Lily.

Chapter 3

LILY FELT COMPLETELY BONELESS WHEN SHE ARRIVED back at the room three hours later. She had been pampered from head to toe and felt as if she could sleep for a week. But duty called and she had to make sure that she did her best to wow Cam's colleagues tonight.

Going to her luggage, she pulled out her cocktail dress and was thankful it had traveled so well. She decided on a quick shower so that when Cam got back to the room, he'd be able to do whatever he needed without her being in the way.

The hot water felt heavenly, and it was a real task to force herself out of the shower. Soon she had her hair done and her makeup applied, and all that was left was to get dressed. A quick glance at the clock showed that it was just five fifteen. The thought of sitting around for an hour in her dress was not the least bit appealing. She was racked by indecision, so when she heard Cam's key in the door, she breathed a little sigh of relief.

Cam wasn't sure what he'd expected when he got back to the room, but Lily all dolled up and wearing nothing but a silky, pink robe that barely came to her knees was not it. Her long, blond hair was softly curled and covered her shoulders, and she had done something smoky with her eye makeup that had him wondering if taking her to dinner with a room full of scientists was really such a good idea. After all, they could order dinner in the room and just be done with it. Then he wouldn't have to share her time with anyone.

And he'd get to find out what she was wearing under that silky, pink robe. His mind wandered to the image of nothing but silky skin and maybe, just maybe, a hint of lace.

"How did your presentation go?" Lily asked, thoroughly breaking his train of thought about locking her in the room for the night for himself.

Forcing himself to look away from the beautiful sight she made, Cam gave her the basics of the meeting and his presentation as he walked around the room putting all of his things in specific places. The strawberry scent she favored had permeated the room, and he found himself inhaling deeply, trying to draw her into his lungs.

"Do you want to take a shower? I made sure that I was done before you got back so that you could have the bathroom to yourself."

"The suite has two bathrooms, Lily," he said. "There wasn't a need for you to rush."

She smiled at his thoughtfulness. "Yes, but the second one doesn't have a tub or a shower. Anyway, I cleared out all of my girlie stuff so that it won't get in your way."

Cam didn't want to think about her girlie stuff. He didn't want to think about lotions and lingerie and God knew what else she had that always made Lily so... Lily. To get his mind away from that direction, again, he asked how her afternoon of pampering had gone.

"Oh, Cam," she said as she walked across the room and sat on the bed while he took his suit out of his case. "It was amazing, absolutely the best. I almost needed someone to carry me back up to the room because I was like a wet noodle."

She was sitting in the middle of the bed with her legs tucked to the side, and Cam could see from his vantage point that she'd had her toes painted a fiery red and that her legs—which looked amazing—were so smooth they glowed. "I was so relaxed when I got back here that I almost took a nap."

"You should have. We have time."

Lily shook her head. "I never would have been ready, and as your girlfriend, I am determined to be prompt. I know how important that is to you."

He shook his head at her as he walked toward the bathroom to put his things in there so he could get ready. "While I appreciate the effort, I don't expect you to morph into a complete stranger. I'm used to the Lily who makes me wait and is laid back and relaxed. If you get all punctual on me, I'm not going to know what to do," he teased.

He watched her intently while Lily teased him back as he walked around the room collecting his things. More than anything, Cam wished that he knew how it felt to just let himself relax like that. He'd been serious and studious his entire life because that was what was expected of him. What would it be like to break free, just for a while, from this mold that he had created for himself and to simply feel?

And with that thought, he closed the door to the bathroom to get himself ready.

Lily sat back and relaxed as she listened to the water from the shower and did her best to not think about Cam naked there. That would not be a good thing. Well, it would be a good thing, but not good for her as she was trying her best to keep to the role of *pretend* girlfriend.

Figuring that she had some time, she opted to get dressed while Cam was getting ready. Knowing him, he probably would be completely showered, shaved, and dressed in fifteen minutes or less. Hopping up from the bed, she took her dress off the hanger and laid it on the bed. Stripping off her robe, Lily stepped into her dress, zipped it up, and grabbed her stilettos before checking her reflection in the mirror.

The red cocktail dress was a risky choice, but she wanted to be festive. It was strapless and clung to her in all of the right places, and the pumps were just the right combination of sweet yet sexy. Reaching into her bag, she pulled out a pearl choker with a diamond clasp that matched the earrings she had put on earlier. She was admiring herself in the mirror, thankful for the fact that her panties didn't leave a line, when Cam opened the bathroom door. The look on his face stopped her cold.

He was dressed in nothing more than his black trousers, and Lily couldn't help but stare. His hair was still damp from his shower and uncombed, and all in all, he looked incredibly…yummy. The scowl on his face, however, was not.

"What the hell are you wearing?" he demanded.

Lily looked at herself and mentally cursed. She had been so worried about saying something to embarrass Cam that she'd never thought about needing to dress more conservatively than her normal style. Whenever Lily got nervous, she made jokes. "It's a dress, Cam," she said with a little laugh. "What does it look like?"

She saw him take a deep breath before he spoke. "I know it's a dress, Lily. I'm not blind. But isn't it a bit much for a business dinner?"

"Oh, well," she stammered, then walked over to her suitcase and pulled out an ivory cashmere sweater and put it on. "I was going for festive with the red and figured the sweater would tone it down a bit. If you don't like it, I can skip tonight's dinner and shop tomorrow for something a little more appropriate." She was nervous and sorting through all of her clothes to see if her other dresses were more subdued in style, so she never heard Cam's approach.

Gently placing his hands on her shoulders, he stopped her and simply said her name. When she didn't make a move, Cam turned her around to face him. "Hey," he said softly. "I'm sorry. I guess I'm used to being in stuffy, conservative mode, and I never really gave a thought to how a woman would dress for one of these events. You look beautiful, and I don't want you to skip dinner tonight. I want you with me."

His words warmed her, and she began to feel like her old self again. "Only if you're sure, because I would completely understand if…"

Cam placed a finger over her lips to silence her. "I want you with me," he repeated and smiled when she nodded. "Okay then. Let me finish getting ready, and we'll head downstairs for drinks."

"You wouldn't happen to have a red tie with you, would you?" she asked hopefully.

"Are we just meeting?"

Rolling her eyes, she shrugged and went to hang up her belongings, something she should have done when she got in. "I'm sorry. What was I thinking?" Lily went back to the task at hand, and five minutes later, Cam walked out of the bathroom looking like something out of *GQ*. His black suit fit him perfectly. The snowy-white dress shirt was pressed within an inch of its life, and the black silk tie looked immaculate against it. His hair, which was always styled to near-military precision, was impeccable, and his black wire glasses were the perfect accessory.

"You look incredibly handsome, sir," she said and brushed at imaginary lint on his jacket just so that she could touch him. She turned them toward the mirror so she could see how they looked side by side and then frowned.

"What's the matter?" Cam asked, thoroughly confused because he was smiling at how they looked.

"It's all wrong," she said, walking over to the closet. "I have a black dress with me. I'll change into that one, and then we'll look more coordinated." Then she mumbled, "If only you had a red tie."

Cam sighed loudly. "This is all over a tie?"

"And maybe a hanky for your pocket."

"What do you suggest that I do? I don't have anything red."

"I have a pair of red panties that I can stuff in your pocket," she said with a sexy grin—and nearly burst out laughing at the shocked look on Cam's face. "Relax, relax, I was just kidding."

Cam looked at his watch and then her. "Don't change, Lily," he said as he walked into the living room, picked up the phone, and called the front desk. Two minutes later, he was back in the bedroom. "It's taken care of."

"What? What's taken care of? Who did you call?"

Without answering her, Cam did his share of unpacking, placing his clothes in the closet beside Lily's. "Cam? Come on. Who did you call?" She was hot on his heels with every step he took until he sat on the sofa to wait. "You are the most frustrating man I have ever met," she huffed, sitting beside him.

Five minutes later, there was a knock at the door and Cam went to answer it. When he turned and walked toward the bedroom, he had a small bag in his hand and a smile on his face. Lily quickly jumped up to see what he was doing. Just as she walked through the double doors, Cam pulled a red silk tie and pocket square from the bag.

"Okay, I take it back. You are not frustrating; you're adorable."

"Good," he said as he tucked the pocket square in place. "That's what I was going for—adorable." Lily walked up to him, and before he knew what she was doing, she had his tie undone and was pulling it from around his neck and wrapping it around her wrist. He arched his brows in surprise. "Nice trick."

She smiled a saucy smile. "There was this belly-dancing class. You'd be amazed at what I can do with a silk scarf." Before Cam could respond, she had the new red tie in place and was tying it in a perfect Windsor knot. Standing back, she admired her handiwork. "There. Now we're perfect." Turning them both toward the mirror, she smiled brightly at their reflection. "Right?"

Cam had no words. Lily stared at him for a moment before he nodded and stepped away, clearing his throat. "Ready to go?"

Lily trailed after him and grabbed her purse. Cam was waiting by the door and held it open as she walked through. She murmured her thanks and waited for him to close the door. Silently they walked toward the elevator, and once they were inside, she forced him to face her. "Okay, what's the matter?"

"What are you talking about?"

"You got all quiet and sullen back there. Is this because of the tie? I mean, if it's going to make you so uncomfortable that you won't even talk to me, you can change it back. It's not worth all of this." She stood and crossed her arms defiantly and waited for his response.

"I'm fine, Lily. It's just that you... Well, you took me a little by surprise back there," he said, his voice croaking slightly.

"Me? What did I do?"

"Wanting to put red panties in my pocket, whipping my tie off and wrapping it around your wrist while telling me you do stuff with silk scarves... That's just a...whole other side of you that I... We... Well, we never discuss. It's just taking me a little longer than you to wrap my brain around this whole new phase of our friendship."

Lily had really wanted to stay mad at him, but his honest admission and the embarrassment on his face were more than she could bear. With a laugh, she stepped in, wrapped her arms around him, and gave him a hug. When she felt him stiffen, she immediately stepped back and smacked his arm. "Stop doing that!" she said loudly.

"Now what did I do?" Seriously, the woman needed to come with a manual because he couldn't keep up with her. If this was what most women were like in a relationship, then moving overseas was definitely the better option because the up-and-down mood swings were beginning to make him dizzy.

"You are going to have to get used to me touching you and hugging you and acting flirty with you, or nobody—not our friends or our family—is going to believe this nonsense that we're trying to feed them, and this will end up being yet another exhausting holiday season! Now unclench a bit," she demanded as the elevator indicated that they had arrived on the floor of the banquet hall, "and take my hand and let's go mingle."

Cam did just as she instructed, but he had a sense that he was in over his head. Even though the room was full of his peers, he was most definitely out of his element.

———

Four hours later and back at the room, Cam was a man with a major conflict. All night Lily had been the perfect date. She was friendly to everyone and spent time speaking to all the colleagues he introduced her to. When they were seated for dinner, she actively participated in all the conversations, even if just to ask a question—which all of the men at the table were more than willing to answer for her. She seemed to be completely in her element. Some of the other wives or dates had seemed bored or impatient, but Lily's gift was bringing her genuine interest in people to every conversation. She had dazzled his colleagues, and he'd felt proud and possessive.

And then they'd danced.

Cam wasn't sure what had happened. They'd danced with one another dozens of times over the course of their lives, and yet tonight was…different. As they'd swayed to the music, the way Lily had felt in his arms was simply amazing. There were at least four different times when he'd wanted to pull her even closer than they already were and just keep her there.

And then there were the times when they had gotten too close and all he'd wanted to do was take her back up to their room and say to hell with their friendship and finally—finally!—make Lily his own.

And then there was the mistletoe.

It still boggled Cam's mind how a simple Eurasian parasitic shrub could turn his mind to mush. Well, not so much the plant but what happened under it.

Lily had kissed him.

Not a small kiss, mind you. Oh, no. Apparently she wanted to act the part of girlfriend for all the room to see. When someone pointed out that they were indeed standing under a sprig of mistletoe, Lily had smiled saucily at him and silently dared him to kiss her. When Cam hadn't acted fast enough, she had simply grabbed him by the lapels and pulled him to her. He had expected a quick, sisterly kiss. That was their thing; that's what they did whenever the occasion called for a kiss. But the deep, wet, seductive kiss that she had given him? Cam had no idea where that had come from.

And he really wanted to try it again when he was more on board and not so shocked by the kiss that he spent most of the time it was happening trying to figure out *why* it was happening. Was it any wonder that he didn't have a steady girlfriend? If one kiss from Lily could stupefy him this much, Cam wasn't sure he'd make it through the next couple of months.

He was shaken from his thoughts when Lily asked if he wanted anything to drink. She was walking across the room as she took her sexy stilettos off, and that was a shame, in his opinion. After tonight, he'd have to consider taking her out to more functions so that she would have to wear the sexy footwear again. Now she was standing in the doorway between the bedroom and living room, looking at him expectantly. "Cam?"

"What? Oh, um…no. No thank you. I'm fine." Pulling his tie loose and making his way across the room, he slid the curtains closed and removed his jacket before kicking off his own shoes.

"Want to watch a movie?" Lily called from the bedroom.

What was she doing in there? The door was wide open; surely she wasn't getting undressed with him right here in the connecting room without closing the door! "Uh, no. I have another presentation in the morning. It's getting late, and I need to go over my notes and get some sleep. It's been a long day." He could hear hangers shifting and did his best to focus on his presentation instead of the slinky red dress shimmying down her body and over whatever tiny bit of lingerie she was wearing underneath.

Over the years, he'd seen Lily in everything from a snowsuit to a bikini. But now? He was dying to know what she was going to sleep in. He ran a weary hand over his face and sighed. For something that was supposed to be such a good idea, this pretend relationship was slowly making him go mad—and it was only the first day! They easily had another six weeks to make this completely work to their advantage, dammit!

Doing his best to keep his back to the open bedroom doorway, Cameron searched through his briefcase for his notes on his presentation for the following morning. Once he had them, he yanked the red silk tie off, unbuttoned the top two buttons of his shirt, and rolled up his sleeves, making himself a little more comfortable. Had it gotten hotter in the room? He was about to check the thermostat when Lily suddenly appeared beside him.

"Are you sure you don't want to just kick back and relax for the rest of the night? I'm sure you know this stuff by heart. Why don't you take tonight to unwind?"

Unwind? She wanted him to unwind? She was wearing a pair of red flannel boxers with snowmen on them and a white cami with the outline of a snowman right in the middle of her chest. Was she trying to kill him? "What is with all of the red today?" he asked suddenly, unable to remember if he had ever seen her wear the color this often.

Lily looked at herself and wondered at Cam's odd question. "Um, we're going into the holiday season. I always go a little overboard with the festive wardrobe at this time of year. I know it's silly but I can't help it. Even though my mother does her best to ruin the holidays for me with her barrage of potential husbands, I can't help but get into the spirit with my clothes. Surely you've noticed that about me over the years."

Had he? Cam couldn't remember. Maybe there had been a funny sweater or two or the occasional sweatshirt with some sort of holiday design on it, but she had been fully covered in those. Never in all of their years as friends had she pranced around half-naked like this— and the holiday decorations adorning the skimpy getup did nothing to dampen his growing arousal. He had to get her to go into the bedroom and close the door before he lost his mind.

"Maybe," he said distractedly. "I don't really pay

attention to that sort of thing." He looked around the room, desperately searching for anything to focus on rather than her. "Um, listen, I have a lot of work to do, so why don't you watch a movie and get some sleep? I know you don't really have anything planned for tomorrow, but I have to go over this stuff and get a good night's sleep. I need to be downstairs by nine for breakfast."

"Oh," Lily said with a pout. "I thought we'd have breakfast together before you headed off to the conference."

Great, now he had guilt. "I suppose I could," he said, although it would really be an inconvenience. "All the more reason for me to get through these notes tonight, Lil." Taking a risk and touching the bare skin of her shoulders, he gently turned her in the direction of the bedroom and gave her a little nudge. "I'll see you in the morning."

"I get the feeling you're trying to get rid of me," she said over her shoulder. "I get it, I get it. You've got work to do and I'm bothering you."

Cam hung his head and counted to ten. "Lily…"

"Relax, Cam, I'm just kidding with you. I know you have work to do. I promised not to get in your way, and I'm sorry I'm still standing here talking to you. Don't stay up all night reading. Make sure you get some sleep too." When he simply nodded, Lily wished him a good night, walked into the bedroom, and closed the door with a little wave and a smile.

<hr />

Two hours later, Lily was still awake and still questioning how much she appealed to the opposite sex. All night while they were at dinner, Cam was the perfect date. They'd laughed and talked and danced, and when he'd held her close, she'd felt confident that what she saw in his eyes was definite interest. Anytime another man had paid her too much attention, Cam had pulled her close as if staking his claim.

And then there was the kiss.

Lily wasn't sure what had come over her, but the fact that Cam had simply stood there contemplating what to do had hit a nerve. So, since impulsiveness was one of her strongest attributes, she'd done what any woman would do when there was an attractive man under the mistletoe with her. She'd kissed him. She had put everything she had into that kiss, and although he'd taken a little bit longer than she had hoped to get on board, the kiss was over way too soon.

Sigh.

Wasn't that just her luck? She had finally taken a chance and kissed the man who had captured her heart years ago, and they had to have an audience around them. The room was dark now except for the TV. Fortune had been on her side when Lily had found a channel with a marathon of some her favorite holiday classics. Glancing over at the clock, she saw it was nearing 1:00 a.m. The light was still on out in the living room, and she had a feeling Cam was probably asleep on the sofa with a pile of paperwork in his lap.

Quietly climbing from the bed, Lily paused as the announcer said *Frosty the Snowman* was up next. That was an all-time favorite of hers. Torn between going out and waking Cam so he could sleep properly on the sofa bed or curling back up in her own king-size bed so she could watch the best talking snowman ever, she envisioned Cam trying to do his presentation with his back aching from sleeping sitting up. Lily would never be able to forgive herself if she caused a problem for him with his morning meeting.

Opening the door, she found he wasn't asleep but pretty darn close. Without a word, she walked over to him and took the papers out of his hands even as he protested. She placed them by his briefcase and then came back over to him and held out her hands. "What?" he asked, but still she stood with her hands outstretched toward him. He placed his hands in hers and stood when she started to pull him to his feet. "Lily, what are you still doing up?"

"*Frosty* is about to start," she said by way of explanation. "Go and get your pajamas on, and I'll open the sofa bed for you. It's late."

"I can do this. Go watch your special," he said gently, not wanting to prolong his exposure to her in her tempting sleepwear.

"The faster you do what I say, the faster I can watch it. Now go." Cam knew Lily had a stubborn streak so he simply nodded and headed to the bedroom to get flannel pajama pants and a T-shirt to change into before heading to the bathroom. Lily made fast work of the sofa bed and turned down the lights before jumping back into her own bed just as the special started.

Cam came out of the bathroom and smiled at the picture she made. "I can't believe you're still awake."

"It's a holiday special marathon. How could I possibly sleep through it?"

Unable to help himself, Cam sat beside her on the bed. "You know they'll play this a dozen times before the end of the year, right?"

Lily nodded but didn't look away from the television. "Yes, I'm aware, but it's just so exciting to catch it the first time it's on." As the opening credits and song began to play, she reached out and pulled him beside her so that he was lying close. "Stay and watch it with me, and then I promise to go to sleep."

The bed did feel good after sitting hunched over the coffee table for the last several hours, so rather than object, he simply made himself more comfortable. For the next twenty minutes, they laughed together. The show was almost over when Cam realized that Lily was curled toward him, her head on his shoulder, a hand on his chest. Somehow his arms had gone around her. As he hugged her a little closer, he noticed that her eyes were definitely beginning to droop.

"Hey, sleepy girl," he said softly. "I think it's time to go to sleep." Lily sighed and snuggled even closer and then seemed to fidget a bit in frustration. "What's the matter?"

"You're on top of the blankets and I can't move," she said and then yawned. Cam was just about to speak when Lily nudged him. "Get under the blankets with me until *Frosty* is over." Looking up, she saw his hesitation. "Please?"

Knowing there was no point in arguing, Cam climbed under the blankets and nearly groaned when Lily immediately wrapped herself around him and sighed again. "Thank you," she whispered. Cam wrapped his own arms back around her, and together they watched the last five minutes of the cartoon.

"I do love that one," she said sleepily. "Thank you for watching it with me."

Cam kissed the top of her head. "My pleasure. But it's

very late and we both need to go to sleep." He looked around and found the TV remote and turned it off. But when he tried to get up, Lily held on tight.

"Not yet," she said quietly. "Don't go yet."

They had often sat together on her sofa with her head on his shoulder while watching a movie but this was the first time they were in a bed and she wasn't letting him leave. Part of him wanted to be strong and just do the right thing by getting up and leaving. "Lil, sweetheart, it's late. I need to go in the other room and get some sleep."

"Sleep here." Her voice was barely a whisper, and Cam wasn't sure what to do. They were simply sleeping—nothing wrong with that. He was so exhausted that even walking the ten feet to the next room felt like a Herculean task. Settling farther under the blankets, his decision made, Cam finally allowed himself to relax.

Pulling Lily a bit closer, he ran one hand gently up and down her spine. The urge to venture just a little farther and cup her bottom was almost too much to bear. She was temptation, pure and simple, and Cam was only human. He was allowing his fingers to barely graze below her waist when Lily stirred slightly.

"Cam?"

His hand instantly froze. "Hmm?"

"It's okay."

"What is?"

"You can touch me," she said so quietly that Cam wasn't even sure that he'd heard her correctly. "I've always wanted you to touch me."

Surely he'd misunderstood her. "Lily?" he murmured and waited a heartbeat before realizing she was already asleep.

Chapter 4

THE NEXT MORNING, LILY WOKE UP ALONE. SHE SAT UP A little dazed and confused, and looked around and listened for any sign of Cam. Turning her head, she looked at the bedside clock, saw that it was after ten, and groaned. He had left hours ago and she had missed it. Stretching, she got out of bed and wandered around the suite, noticing that the sofa bed was folded away and was back in its daytime position. Clearly Cam had taken care of it before he left, but she wondered if he'd ever slept in it last night.

She knew he'd joined her on the bed to watch a little TV and vaguely remembered asking him to get under the blankets with her, but she couldn't be sure what happened after that. At one point in the night, she had dreamed of Cam being in bed with her, spooned against her back with an impressive arousal nuzzled against her bottom and one hand cupping her breast. It had to have been a dream because Cam would never have done something like that.

Or would he?

The thought made her giddy. With a little more pep in her step, Lily went to the phone and ordered herself breakfast before jumping in the shower. Today she would do some sightseeing around Times Square. While Cam was deep in conferences, she was going to shop and experience some of the foods he would definitely tell her to stay away from, and then she'd return in time to get ready for tonight's dinner.

Breakfast arrived just after she had finished with her shower, and Lily felt rather decadent as she lounged in the fluffy, spa-like robe the hotel provided. Looking at the view through the window, she wished Cam were there with her. It was so exciting to see all of the activity going on below. The snow had stopped, but everything still had a coating and looked magical. While she knew that Cam had come here for a definite reason, Lily wished she could encourage him to play hooky and go sightseeing with her.

After breakfast, she threw on jeans and a sweater, added a touch of makeup, and put her hair up in a ponytail. She'd do something more glamorous with it later. Grabbing her coat and room key, Lily left the room and went off on her adventure.

———

Cam was mentally and physically exhausted when he returned to the room at five thirty. He had wanted to call and meet Lily for lunch, but he'd been sidetracked by colleagues eager to discuss future projects. All he wanted now was a little peace and quiet and a lot less socializing. God, he hated these conferences. They were too loud, too crowded, and by the end of the day, he always ended up craving solitude.

His mind immediately went to Lily, knowing that he wasn't going to get that solitude with her around either. The only difference was that it wasn't solitude he was craving where she was concerned. Last night had been like some personal brand of torture. He had no right sharing a bed with her or touching her the way he had. Even though Lily had said that she wanted his touch — hell, that she'd always wanted his touch — she was half-asleep when she said it. Could he believe her?

Cam cursed himself mentally as he walked into their suite. Part of him hoped she was furious with him for last night and would yell at him when she caught sight of him. The other part hoped she was prancing around in that silky robe she'd worn yesterday and would greet him wearing only it and a sexy smile.

He had a problem. A very serious problem because things were not going as he'd planned, and Cameron always made sure that his life followed his plans. He and Lily were just supposed to be friends on a trip together. He had never given any thought to what looking like a real couple would entail or how it would affect him. So much for being a genius. If he wasn't careful, Lily was going to realize his feelings for her were more involved than just being friends. And then she'd walk away. Lily always tended to walk away from the men she was dating when things got serious.

And Cam wanted serious.

Or did he just seriously want?

Either way, he noticed then that the suite was eerily quiet. Housekeeping had been through, so the room was spotless, but he had no clue where Lily was. Cam immediately pulled out his phone and dialed her number. He waited and then cursed when the call went directly to voice mail. "Lily? It's Cam. I'm back at the room. It's five thirty-five, and you're not here. Please call me." He hung up and then cursed himself again.

"What if she's pissed about last night and left?" he

asked out loud. But he sighed with relief when he walked over to their closet and saw her belongings all still there. That relief was short-lived when he thought about what could have happened to her as she wandered the streets of New York by herself. Raking a hand through his dark hair, he began to pace. "Where do I even begin to look for her?"

Unsure of what else to do, he called the front desk to ask if she had used any of the hotel amenities today, or if anyone remembered when she left the building. They told him about her ordering breakfast, but after that, no one knew where she'd gone. Cam felt sick. What if something horrible had happened to Lily? It would definitely be his fault. All he'd wanted was a chance to enjoy the holidays without the hassle of his family, but thanks to his selfishness, maybe something had happened to her.

Grabbing his coat from the closet and the room key, he pulled the door open—and ran smack into Lily. "Cam? What the hell?" she said as she nearly fell backward. "Where were you going in such a rush?" He pulled her into the room and then into his arms and simply crushed her to him with relief. "Uh…Cam? What's going on? Did something happen?"

Pulling back, he stared at her beautiful face. Her cheeks were red, her green eyes were wide, and her smile was nervous. God, how he loved her. "You scared the hell out of me, Lily," he finally said, a tremble in his normally strong and stable voice. "I got back to the room and you weren't here, and…and I thought that something… I don't know." Then he noticed all of the packages on the floor around them and chuckled. "You went shopping." It wasn't a question; he was just stating the obvious.

"Boy, did I!" she said excitedly. Bending over, she began to pick up her packages and smiled when Cam helped. Together they brought everything over to the sofa, where they sat and she told him all about her day. "There were so many places to see, Cam! It just seemed endless!"

Cam looked at the seemingly endless pile of packages and then back at Lily. "Seriously? What could you possibly have needed that required this many bags?"

Lily smiled at him wickedly. "Silly, silly man. Never underestimate the shopping powers of a woman." She started going through each bag one by one and showing him what she had purchased while telling him about the store. Thirty minutes later, Cam stopped her. "What? Too much?" she asked.

"No, no… This is…riveting, really. But if we don't stop, we'll be late for dinner. As it is we only have"—he looked at his watch—"about twenty minutes to get ready."

"Well, damn," she sighed and then looked at all of the stuff around them. "Sorry. I didn't mean to lose track of time. Again."

"No worries, Lil," he said, standing and holding out a hand to her. "But we really should get ready."

Lily took his hand and stood. "Unless…"

"Unless what?"

"We don't go to the dinner and play tourist instead," she said quickly, clearly excited at the prospect of having time to explore with him. The look on his face told her they weren't on the same page.

"I promise we'll go out tomorrow night," he said

solemnly. "Tonight, I need to talk with some people about an upcoming project. I'm sorry." Cam saw the disappointment on her face and hated being the one to put it there.

Doing her best to shake it off, Lily pulled her hand from his. "No biggie. Let me go freshen up and change. I promise to be quick." She flounced away, and although her tone was light, Cam knew she was putting on an act for his benefit. When he heard her go into the bathroom, he went to the bedroom to retrieve his things and use the half bath to get ready. A shower would have gone a long way to revitalize him after such an exhausting day, but he'd just have to make do with what he had.

Fifteen minutes later, Lily joined him in the living room, wearing a more conservative dress than before but still with a killer pair of stilettos—black this time to match her dress. Cam stood back and admired her while she gathered up her purchases and took them into the bedroom. The dress came to just above her knees but was still formfitting like the red dress from the night before. The simple black sheath was sleeveless and delicately adorned with black sequins along the hem, and had a sheer back. Her accessories were minimal, and when she came back into the room, he noticed a simple black wrap.

"It helps so much that we don't have to leave the hotel to go to dinner," she said as she draped the wrap around herself. "I get to wear pretty dresses without having to worry about freezing to death." Walking toward Cam, she admired his dark suit and then smiled at his light-blue silk tie. "Nicely done, Cam," she complimented him. "Not quite so somber."

"I'm learning," he teased and then held out his arm to escort her to the elevator.

They rode down to the main floor and joined a group of Cam's colleagues as they walked toward the banquet hall. Outside the entrance, they had all stopped and were chatting when Lily spotted the mistletoe from the night before. Turning toward one of the other women in the group, she said, "I love the holidays. Everything looks so festive and bright. Plus"—she pointed upward and winked—"it gives us an excuse for a little PDA, right?" The other woman nodded, and before Lily knew what was happening, Cam turned her in his arms and kissed her.

Oh, and how he was kissing her.

It took Lily less than a second to happily wrap her arms around him. When Cam's tongue gently grazed her lower lip, Lily more than willingly opened for him and let him deepen the kiss. Never in her wildest dreams had she imagined that Cam could kiss like this. He was all heat and passion, and she let out a small whimper of need before she could stop herself.

Someone cleared their throat behind them, and Cam reluctantly ended the kiss. Pulling back, he looked at Lily's flushed face and hated that they were here in this crowd. All day he had dreamed about kissing her again under the mistletoe. This time he wanted to be the one to initiate the kiss, to see if it would be any better than his fantasies.

And it was.

Without a word, Cam took Lily's hand in his and joined the group heading into the banquet hall for dinner.

It was going to be a long night.

—⁓—

Cam couldn't say why he was doing it, but he was being a jackass. There was no other way to put it. By ten o'clock he had had enough of social chitchat and talk about projects and research and work in general. He was done. Every time he heard Lily laugh at something somebody said, he felt rage building inside him. When she turned to talk to anybody else, he wanted to demand that she talk to him. He was out of control and mad as hell, and he didn't know why.

Actually, he was lying to himself. He knew exactly why.

The kiss.

Looking around the room, Cam decided he was done for the night because he wanted Lily all to himself. They had danced, they had mingled and socialized, but now it was time for them to be alone.

And to hell with the consequences.

He stood suddenly and made their excuses and then held his hand out to Lily. She looked at him questioningly but didn't object. After she said her good nights to everyone, she and Cam walked out of the room. They silently rode the elevator up to their floor, neither saying a word until they were safely back in their suite.

"Are you okay?" Lily finally asked. The room was bathed in only the soft light of one small lamp set in the corner. It felt oddly intimate and she had to wonder why neither of them seemed willing to move from the confines of the entryway.

"No," he said, his voice a low rumble. "I'm not." He didn't elaborate, didn't think he'd be able to find the words, so he did the only thing that he could. He stepped in close and kissed her again. Without the crowd, without the noise and the flurry of activity around them they'd had earlier, he was completely focused on the scent of her perfume and the feel of her body pressed against his as he backed her up against the wall. It was madness, and Cam made sure that he never let himself succumb to madness.

But it couldn't be helped.

He had wanted Lily for so long, and all of the pretending in the world wasn't going to be enough—not after he'd touched her and tasted her. That only made the longing worse. His mouth left hers only long enough to trail kisses along the slender column of her neck, and then he needed to feel her lips under his again. He said a silent prayer of thanks when she wrapped her arms around him and pulled him even closer, her hands seeming as frantic as his to explore and touch.

"Cam?" she whispered when he broke away to stroke his tongue along the delicate shell of her ear. He reached up and placed one strong finger over her kiss-swollen lips. Her own tongue reached out and licked a path along his finger, and she smiled when he groaned with pleasure. "Is this wrong?" she asked. "We never... We've always been..."

His mouth silenced hers. Cam didn't want to think about before or what they'd never dared to do. If he allowed his mind to go in that direction, his overly practical side would take control and he'd never get the chance to experience this incredible sensation of intimacy with Lily again.

Just tonight.

For just this one night, he'd allow himself the pleasure of stepping out of himself and loving her the way he had always wanted to. "Tonight, Lily," he murmured against her lips. "Please. Just give me tonight." His words were tinged with a hint of desperation that was foreign to Cam. He almost didn't recognize himself. His own voice sounded like it was coming from somebody else. When Lily didn't immediately respond, he forced himself to pull back, hating how cold and alone he suddenly felt without her body pressed against his.

Lily's breathing was ragged, and her eyes were glazed and intense as she studied him. "Yes."

The relief he felt at that one little word was so great that Cam nearly sank to his knees. Both of his hands snaked up into her hair and ruined its beautiful, upswept style, but he didn't care. He kissed her with a ferocity that scared him. For once in his life, he was going to give in and be impulsive and allow himself to simply feel. He heard Lily's purse drop to the floor and then felt her wrap shimmy down her arms. "I want to make love to you, Lily Cavanaugh," he said huskily as he leaned his forehead against hers and did his best to regain his breath.

She smiled shyly. "I'd like that very much."

And then, hand in hand, they walked into the bedroom where Cam closed the double doors and turned to the woman who was his every dream come true.

Chapter 5

THE SUN WAS JUST BEGINNING TO RISE WHEN LILY OPENED her eyes and instantly smiled. They had made love. Repeatedly. She felt a little giddy when she thought about it, because she'd always known that Cam was thorough in everything he did, but that thoroughness had a whole new meaning now.

He was pressed against her back, completely wrapped around her, and Lily loved the way he felt. She wanted to bask in the afterglow of it all, but a little voice of doubt crept into her thoughts. One night. That was what he had asked for—just the one night. After such a night, could she really be okay with it never happening again?

Cam's lips on her shoulder told her he was awake. Turning her head slightly, she looked at him and smiled. "Good morning."

Rather than speaking, he continued to trail kisses along her shoulder and then down her spine, all the while, his hands conducting their own exploration.

Interesting, Lily thought. Clearly, the super-genius mind of Cameron Greene did not recall his one-night rule. That was more than fine with her. If she had her way, there would be no rules, no limits. Forever actually worked quite well for her.

Arching her back, she purred with delight as he worked his way back up and rolled her beneath him before diving in for a kiss so hot, so deep, and so wet that she simply forgot how to breathe. Just when she was about to completely wrap herself around him in silent invitation, Cam pulled back and smiled at her.

"Good morning to you too." His hair was mussed and he had stubble on his chin, but he looked good enough to eat. Cam always was the portrait of neatness, never a hair out of place, but she liked this look a heck of a lot more. She smiled as she ran her hand along his cheek and then down to his chest. "See anything you like?" he asked lightly.

Her green eyes met his, and her expression turned serious. "Everything." And then she pulled him down for another searing kiss, forgot all about rules and nights, and gave him a morning he was sure to remember.

<hr />

For the first time since…well, ever, Cam was late for a meeting. He'd felt a moment of pure panic when he first looked at the clock after he and Lily had nearly destroyed one another with their enthusiasm, but then he couldn't find the strength to care. Time had no meaning right now because he had a beautiful woman wrapped around him. Now *that* had meaning.

He just wasn't sure what it was.

Everything was different and yet it wasn't. Cam had expected that they'd make love and be done. Maybe there would be a little awkwardness, but then they'd move on. He'd never expected her to respond to him the way she had or that he'd be so insatiable for her. And she for him! He certainly hadn't expected them to still be so needy for one another this morning, and if he wasn't careful, he'd never want to leave this room today.

Reluctantly, he slowly got up and smiled at her sleepy protest. He kissed her forehead. "Believe me, I'd much rather stay here, but I'm already late."

Lily instantly sat up and looked at the clock. "Oh my gosh! I'm sorry! I'm really sorry, Cam! I didn't mean… I mean, I didn't even think that—"

He silenced her with a kiss. "Stop worrying," he said. "I'm going to grab a quick shower and then I'm leaving, but after this afternoon's session, I'll let you show me all around Times Square."

"Because I'm such a pro after my day yesterday?" she teased.

"Something like that," he said as he walked toward the bathroom and shut the door.

Lily sighed and smiled at the same time. Okay, so Cam had completely forgotten about his rules and about time. That had never happened. Ever. But what did it mean for them? For all Lily knew, this morning was just a small detour or an extension of the night, and now Cam was done. She pouted slightly. Well, she wasn't ready to be done. No, she was about as far from done as a person could get. Pretending wasn't an option for her anymore, and she only had six weeks to convince him that their reality could be so much more than either of them had imagined.

Cam had never been a clock watcher, but today he was. Every meeting seemed endless, and all of his conversations were forced. All he wanted was to be done and to get back upstairs to Lily. The thought of going out on the town with her filled him with anticipation. Images of her

from the night before kept flashing through his mind—
and when he thought about the things they had done this
morning? Well, several times during his meetings, he
found himself shifting uncomfortably in his seat.

This wasn't supposed to happen. While Lily didn't
seem outraged or even shocked by them becoming
intimate, Cam wasn't sure it had been smart. Lily was
a woman who led with her heart; she put everything
she had into everything she did. Cam was a lot more
closed off. He was studious and serious, and while their
friendship had always worked for them, there wasn't a
doubt in his mind that if he pursued a serious romantic
relationship with Lily, he'd end up killing some of the
essence that made her who she was.

What made him love her.

Shaking his head at his own negative thoughts, he
almost wept with gratitude when the afternoon session
finally came to a close and he was free to leave. Doing
his best to stay under the radar, he quickly made his exit
and hit the bank of elevators before anyone noticed his
departure. Tapping his foot and waiting for the doors to
open, Cam looked at his watch and saw it was only two
minutes after five.

A new record.

At the sound of the elevator's arrival, he was glad
there was still no one around as he quickly stepped on
and pushed the button to close the doors. By the time
he arrived at the suite, he had only used up another two
minutes. His fingers fumbled with the key card, and
when he finally got through the door, he was treated to
the sight of Lily walking across the room in nothing but
a towel.

"Cam!" she cried and then looked for the nearest clock. "You're early. Is everything okay?"

He tried to tell himself he had planned on coming back to the room and taking Lily sightseeing, and making love to her wasn't on the agenda. He wasn't going to allow himself to do that again. But one look at her, and all of his good intentions flew right out the window.

He knew the second she caught his train of thought because her smile went from sweet to sexy in the blink of an eye. She walked toward him slowly, and Cam began to wonder how she had become as anxious to be with him as he was to be with her. For years he had pined after her, and she had never given even a hint that she was interested in pursuing a more intimate relationship. But now? Now they were clearly on the same page, and he loved it.

"So?" she said sweetly as she stood nearly toe-to-toe with him. "Are you okay?"

Cam's hand crept slowly up to where her towel was knotted between her breasts and lingered there. His eyes met hers, and the heat he saw there mirrored his own. With a gentle tug, the towel dropped to the floor. "I am now."

—✳—

Snow had begun to fall again as Lily and Cam walked along Seventh Avenue. "Isn't this amazing?" Lily asked excitedly. It had been well after seven when they finally left the hotel, and an hour later, they were strolling hand in hand and trying to decide where to eat. Every few minutes, she would stop Cam so they could either take selfies in front of something she considered fun or ask random strangers to take their picture. She was having a blast. "All of the lights and the activity are invigorating."

Cam wasn't sure he fully agreed. What they'd done earlier in the room had been invigorating. Walking along Seventh Avenue and now Broadway in the cold and the snow was something he could easily live without. He was starving, and as much as he hated to admit it, he'd go along with anything Lily wanted for dinner at this point, even if it came from a street vendor.

"Ooo, we have to go in here," she said as she dragged Cam into the Disney Store.

"Why? Why do we need to stop in here?" The sheer magnitude of the colors, music, and lighting assaulted him as they walked in. "Seriously, Lil. Why?"

"I haven't been to Disney since I was a little girl. I came in here yesterday, and it just made me wish I could hop on a plane to Florida right now."

"It would be a lot warmer, I can tell you that," he grumbled.

"Oh, stop being such a baby. We're having fun."

"If you have to remind me, then no, I'm not."

Lily stopped and made a face at him. "Remember the trip we took to Disney World when we were eight? Remember how much fun we had?"

"Remember how I got sick on the rides?" he replied sarcastically, then hated himself when her expression fell. "Okay, okay... Yes, it was a fun trip. If you don't count the throwing up. So, we're here in this...monstrosity of a store. What are you looking for?"

"Looking for? Cam, you don't come in a place like this to look for something specific. You come in and explore and then surprise yourself when you find something that you absolutely have to have."

Cam didn't need a store to do that. He'd already found something he absolutely had to have.

Lily.

She dragged him around and commented on just about everything they saw. The way her whole face lit up with each new thing she discovered had Cam smiling as well. It was hard to stay serious and stern when she was bursting with excitement. Cam wanted so badly to be able to free himself up enough to find something that made him so happy and carefree. Something that would make him grin from ear to ear when he saw it.

Something like the woman standing in front of him wearing a sparkly tiara and posing like a princess.

Cam took the tiara off her head and led her to the front of the store. When they approached the registers, she blushed as she watched Cam pay for the tiara and then hand her the bag.

"Thank you," she said as she leaned in close and got on her tiptoes to kiss him on the cheek. Once they were back outside, she looked around, trying to decide which direction they should go to find a place to eat. "Okay, what are you in the mood for? Italian? Burgers? Steak?"

He chuckled at the fact that she mentioned burgers, even though she knew his feelings on them, but decided to throw caution to the wind. "You decide," he said lightly. And found that he liked letting go. The smile that lit up Lily's face was worth it.

Even if it meant eating burgers.

"Um... Let's see," she said, looking around again. "There's a diner with singing waitresses we can try."

Looking at Cam, she saw him merely shrug. "Or…we can do the Hard Rock." Another shrug. "You know, it's a lot easier when you just tell me where we're going rather than letting me decide. We'll probably eat a lot quicker, too."

"You were so excited about going out and exploring that I want you to choose the place," he replied. "Tonight is all for you, Lily."

Well, if he had said that sooner, life would have been a whole lot easier. "Okay then," she said with a firm nod of her head. Taking his hand, she turned them around and took off in the direction she wanted with a purposeful stride. It didn't take long for Cam to question what she was doing.

"Uh, Lil? Why are we back at the hotel?"

With a saucy glance over her shoulder, she smiled. "You said tonight was for me, right?" Cam nodded. "Well, then what I want is room service and…you."

Far be it from Cam to argue.

—⁓—

The next night was their last in New York because they had a flight out the following morning. Cam's last session of the conference had ended at noon, so they spent the afternoon doing more sightseeing and finally went out for an Italian meal outside the hotel. As they lay in bed, Cam knew what he had to do. It wasn't what he wanted to do, but in the long run, he was doing what was best for Lily and their friendship.

"I'm really glad you came with me this week," he said softly as he tried not to focus on the way her hand was tracing lazy circles on his chest.

"Mmm…me too," she said. "This was a great idea."

It was hard to focus but Cam trudged forward. "We're supposed to have dinner with everyone tomorrow night, and I know we had planned to pretend to be involved and announce our relationship, but…"

Lily lifted her head from his shoulder, not liking where this was leading. "But what?"

"Well, things took a bit of a turn here, and I think that it would be best if…this stayed here," he said awkwardly.

Lily sat completely upright and looked at him with disbelief. "Excuse me?"

Cam sat up beside her. "Lily, you and I have been friends forever, and I don't want to do anything to risk that. I wouldn't be able to handle it if you weren't a part of my life. Your friendship has gotten me through some pretty rough times, and I treasure what we have."

"I do too, Cam. I don't understand where this is all going." Lily was thoroughly confused. Her gut was telling her that he no longer wanted to sleep with her, but more than that, he didn't even want to have a fake relationship with her.

"The physical turn in our relationship wasn't something I had planned on, and I think lines are getting blurred. We both know it's never good to combine sex with friendship. Eventually things get too awkward and the friendship suffers. I don't want that for us. So I'm thinking that this"—he cleared his throat—"isn't something we should continue once we get home."

She stared at him like he was insane. Not continue this? Was he out of his mind? This was some of the most amazing sex of her life, and things hadn't gotten weird between them at all. Why end it? Which is exactly what she asked him rather snappishly.

"It has been amazing; I'm not denying that. I just value our friendship more. Can you understand that?" His eyes were earnest as he tried to get her to see his point of view.

"And the fake relationship?" she asked coldly. "Is that something we should continue when we get home?" Cam nodded. "Just without the sex," she stated matter-of-factly, and Cam nodded again. Lily considered her options. While this was not the way she had envisioned things going, all was not lost. The rules had changed several times already, and after these past few days, she was certain she could get him to change the rules again.

And she could even make him think it was his idea.

Reclining back on the pillows, Lily pulled the sheet up snugly around her and stared at the ceiling as she continued to ponder. She knew it was a tactic that would drive Cam mad. He was used to people quickly falling in line with what he wanted, and whenever she didn't, it infuriated him.

Good. Let him stew.

Without a word, she kicked off the sheet, walked completely naked into the living room, grabbed a bottle of water from the mini-fridge, and then came back to bed as she drank. Then she resumed her earlier position and stared at the ceiling again. The tension was rolling off Cameron in waves to the point that Lily had to stifle the giggle that was dying to come out. After a solid five minutes, she turned and simply said, "Fine."

Cam's eyes grew wide. "Fine? That's it? All this pressure, and all you have to say is *fine*?"

"What would you have me say, Cam?" she asked innocently. "Should I kick, scream, and carry on? I can't force you to keep having sex with me, so what would you have me do? You want to go back to us just being friends who are pretending to date? Fine, that's what we'll do."

"And you're okay with it?"

"Sure."

He didn't like it. Cam couldn't quite put his finger on what was wrong, but Lily never gave in to anything this easily. "So...we're good?"

Lily nodded. "Of course. Why wouldn't we be? We tried something new, and it didn't work for you. Besides, you're right; being friends is a better option. You'd probably make me crazy after a while with this dating thing. This way, we stop before any real damage is done. Plus, this means that if either of us meets someone we're really interested in, even if it's during the holidays, we're free to date or sleep with them." Lily did her best to sound blasé about the whole thing and the play of emotions on Cam's face was nearly comical.

"No," he said adamantly. "Absolutely not."

Lily quirked an eyebrow at him. "Excuse me?"

"Until the week after New Year's, we are exclusive. No dating—and certainly no sleeping with anybody else!" Cam never raised his voice to Lily and he was surprised he was doing it now, but how dare she even suggest such a ridiculous concept! Sleep with other people while they were pretending to date? Why would she even consider that?

"So you're telling me that I'm not only supposed to play the part of the fake girlfriend but I'm supposed to be celibate too?"

"I didn't think it was such a sacrifice," he replied

snarkily. "I mean, I never knew you to be unable to go for a couple of weeks without being intimate with a man."

Unable to help herself, Lily burst out laughing. "Being intimate with a man? Is that how we're speaking now? It's sex, Cam. *Sex*. And I happen to enjoy it. And since you're just my *friend*," she reminded tartly, "and not my real boyfriend, you have no real say in what I do on my own time."

This was so not going as he had planned. How had he lost control of the situation? Pinching the bridge of his nose, Cam counted to ten and then looked at Lily, who was sitting beside him like the picture of innocence. "Look," he said calmly. "All I'm saying is that we both know a lot of the same people, and how would it look if someone knew you were sleeping with somebody else when you were supposed to be dating me?"

"How do we know it's going to be me sleeping with somebody else? Maybe you'll meet someone you want to sleep with."

He highly doubted that. After these last couple of days, Cam doubted that he'd want to sleep with another woman for a very long time. "I'm not the one who can't go without sex."

"Good to know," she said confidently. "Then you won't mind if this last round of sex we just had was indeed our *last* round of sex."

Cam jaw dropped. "What are you saying?"

"I'm saying that since you think our sleeping together wasn't the smart thing to do, you won't mind sleeping on the sofa bed tonight. We go back to our old relationship starting now."

Like hell. If he was going to sacrifice having Lily to himself from now on, he wasn't going to give up his last night with her. "As a matter of fact, I do mind."

Lily smiled confidently. "You can't have your cake and eat it too, Cam. I'm just following your rules."

With lightning speed Cam turned and pinned Lily beneath him. "I don't want cake," he said huskily, "but I could definitely eat." His mouth claimed hers, and Lily didn't even bother trying to fight it. She instantly wrapped herself around him, and Cam wasn't sure who the winner was in all of this. But as her tongue dueled with his, he realized that, right now, he didn't even care.

Chapter 6

THEY WALKED INTO THE USUAL CONTROLLED CHAOS AT the home of Cam's parents, Richard and Angela Greene. Everyone was talking at once while they were hugging and kissing Cam and Lily hello. After years of experiencing the same scene, Lily was able to have several conversations with different people as she made her way through the group and into the kitchen where she found her own parents and said hello.

Cam was by her side with his hand low on her back, and Lily couldn't help but smile. He might not want to touch her, but she knew that deep down, he couldn't help himself. Was he even aware he'd done nothing but touch her since they'd left the hotel that morning? He'd held her hand, touched her arm, kept his hand on her back... Other than while she was getting ready at her apartment once they got back into town, Cam had always had his hands on her in one way or another.

It was both amusing and arousing.

Cam had stepped away for a moment to tell his father and Lily's dad about the conference when he noticed his mother heading toward Lily.

"So what's new with you, Lily?" Angela Greene asked as she handed Lily a glass of wine.

"Well," she began and then looked over her shoulder at Cam. He nodded, so Lily turned back and faced their parents and siblings. "Cam and I just got back from New York."

"Oh really?" Angela said. "Did you have business in the city too?"

"No," Cam said, coming over to stand beside Lily and put his arm around her. "I invited Lily to come with me. I thought it might be nice for us to get away before the hectic holiday schedule kicks in." The room fell silent as their parents all looked at one another and then back to Cam and Lily.

"I-I don't understand," Angela said, confusion written all over her face.

"Well," Lily said with a shy smile, "Cam and I wanted to have a little time away before we came here and told all of you that"—she looked at Cam again for confirmation—"we're dating!"

The room became a flurry of activity, and it was like walking in all over again. Everyone began talking at once and asking questions. Lily and Cam were so in sync with one another that even though they had never discussed their "story," their accounts were close enough that no one seemed to notice.

"It's just so romantic…"

"We always hoped the two of you…"

"So it was a romantic getaway?"

"How long has this been going on?"

The questions came at them in rapid-fire succession, and they each took turns answering. Lily had to wonder if their announcement was real or fake because they seemed to be pulling it off. They really weren't lying, because in her mind, what she and Cam were doing was one hundred percent real. She just had to convince Cam.

Conversation moved to the dining room as dinner was served. Angela made sure the two of them sat together, and by the time everyone was seated, their mothers seemed to be of one mind. "So this is real? This is serious?"

Cam picked up one of Lily's hands and kissed it. "Yes, it is. I've been in love with Lily for a long time, but I never wanted to risk our friendship."

"So what changed?" Mary Cavanaugh asked, grinning from ear to ear.

Cam looked lovingly at Lily as he spoke the truth for what seemed like the first time tonight. "Some things you just can't fight. We didn't plan this. It just sort of happened, and now that it has, I'm sorry we waited so long." Lily's gaze softened at his words, and it took all of Cam's strength to not lean in and kiss her right now. But he remembered his rules. Although he knew he would have to kiss her in front of other people at times during the upcoming weeks, he had to be strong and only do it when absolutely necessary or he'd make himself crazy.

"The trip was amazing," Lily said while everyone at the table simply sat and grinned at them. She told them all about Times Square and their hotel and the dinners they'd had with Cam's colleagues. "We danced, and the food was amazing, and everything was already decorated for Christmas. It was all so beautiful. There was this spot by the banquet hall that had the most amazing display of mistletoe, and we always made sure we stopped and kissed under it before going in to dinner." The women at the table sighed collectively, and Lily glanced back at Cam while doing her best to look like the adoring girlfriend. "It was all very romantic."

"It sounds like it," Angela said and then looked at

her son with a wink. "Who knew my son could be such a romantic? I'm glad you finally came to your senses, Cameron. We've all known for years that you cared for Lily as more than a friend. I think I can speak for all of us when I say this is going to make the holidays even more special." She looked over at Mary. "Just think of the excitement this is going to cause at all of the parties! I think people were starting to take bets on when the two of them would get together, weren't they?"

Mary nodded. "I believe so." She turned and looked at her daughter and Cam. "Seems like the two of you were the last to know."

Lily knew she shouldn't take that as a dig, but somehow she did. Her whole body tensed, but Cam gave her hand a slight squeeze to let her know that he was there for her. He spoke up. "We don't really care what everyone else was thinking; we needed the time to be right for us. Let them think what they want. What Lily and I feel for each other needed to come out when the time was right. Our trip only confirmed it was the right decision to wait." He kissed her hand again. "She was worth it."

Their fathers finally interrupted and turned the topic of conversation to something they all could participate in. Cam was more than a little relieved for the break. He'd known their mothers were going to be thrilled about their dating, but he hadn't expected them to make such a big deal out of it. Slipping under the radar was no longer an option, and he had a feeling they were going to be thrust into the spotlight more than he had ever dreamed possible.

Once dinner was over and things were cleaned up, Angela and Mary took out their calendars and went through the list of social engagements they were all expected to attend. "And now with Cam and Lily's big news, you know everyone is going to want to see them," she said to the group as a whole. They were all sitting in the living room, and Cam had Lily tucked beside him with his arm around her. It felt natural and very comforting, although at the same time a little bizarre, because everyone kept looking at them and wanting to talk about them.

When Cam had come up with this idea, he'd figured they'd announce they were dating, and everyone would be happy and then move on. He didn't expect them to become the event of the season.

"We're going to decorate here tonight, and then we'll all meet for dinner on Sunday at Mary and Jack's to do all of their decorating. Thanksgiving will be here on Thursday," Angela continued as she checked her list, "and then the Christmas parties will kick into gear!" Everyone began talking at once, and then Mary spoke up.

"We'll be doing the Christmas cookie baking for the exchange at our place on the fifth, followed by the open house for friends and family on the eighth, and," she said, looking to Angela to confirm, "you will be hosting the neighborhood get-together on the tenth, and then you have Richard's company party on the twelfth, right?" Both Richard and Angela nodded. "Then"—she double-checked her list—"we have Jack's company party on the sixteenth." Again, everyone nodded.

"But this year we have a surprise," Richard Greene said, addressing the group. He looked at his daughters, Megan and Lisa, and their husbands, John and Michael, and then to Cam and Lily and Lily's sister, Beth, and her husband, Kevin, before finally focusing on the senior Cavanaughs with a smile. "We're breaking tradition this year for the first time. We've rented a place up in the mountains to spend Christmas week and New Year's!" All of the adult children looked at one another and then their parents, and mass confusion ensued as everyone began asking questions at once.

Jack Cavanaugh stood and tried to quiet everyone down. "Now, we realize some of you here have in-laws you will want to spend part of the holidays with, and we understand. The house is ours for ten days, and you are free to come and go as you please. But we're hoping you'll want to spend a lot of that time up there with us. We have the house from the twenty-third to January first, and it would be wonderful if we could enjoy some quality family time after all these parties," he said with a laugh.

"Well, we know Cam and Lily will be there the whole time because the only in-laws they have are us!" Angela said with obvious delight. "We'll be able to spend time talking about what your plans are, and—not to put too much pressure on you—we can maybe talk about engagements and weddings and all of that good stuff." Mary readily agreed and threw in her own two cents on how she saw them spending time with the couple and helping them plan their future.

Cam felt ill, and Lily wanted to run screaming from the room.

"Um…" Lily interrupted and raised her hand. "I don't think I'll have the whole week off, Dad. Especially after taking this week to go to New York."

"Oh, for crying out loud, Lily," her sister, Beth, said with a hint of irritation. "It's not like you have a real job. I'm sure the coffee shop will run fine without you. Get a grip."

Cam literally felt Lily shrink beside him as she simply nodded and bowed her head. He loved the Cavanaughs; they were a second family to him. But he had listened to them all dismiss Lily for years, and he'd never understood why. Furious with himself for never speaking up before, Cam knew that even as her pretend boyfriend, he needed to do it now.

He turned directly to Beth. "And why exactly isn't it a real job?" Before she could answer, Cam cut her off. "I mean, she goes to the coffee shop. She has a schedule. She works her shift, and she gets paid for the work she does. Tell me, Beth, how is that not a real job?"

"Well…um…" Beth stammered, looking around the room for someone to back her up. Usually her parents would, but they were remaining surprisingly quiet.

"Lily may not go to an office to work, but that doesn't mean what she does is any less important. Instead of giving her life to a company, she tries to find the things that give her pleasure so she can actually enjoy her life." He looked around the room now with condemnation. "We could all learn something from Lily. How many family dinners were missed because of work? How many school events did you skip because of your jobs?" Finally, he turned to Lily.

"You are an inspiration because you are out and experiencing life while the rest of us experience the four walls of our offices. I, for one, am proud of you." Leaning in, he kissed her on her forehead and then leaned back and put his arm around her to pull her close. With one last sweeping look around the room, he asked, "Anyone else have a problem with Lily needing to work a couple of shifts that week?"

Everyone shook their heads in stunned silence. "Good," Cam said with a nod. "I'll probably have to work a couple of days myself, but I'll be sure to line my schedule up with Lily's so we can enjoy our time together with all of you."

Only Lily knew that was really a tactic so they could present a united front and wouldn't have to deal with either set of parents on their own. Once again, he was her knight in shining armor. She leaned over and kissed his cheek and murmured a thank-you to him.

"Well," Richard Greene said as he stood up, "I guess we can work out all of those details later. For now, why don't we break out the decorations and get things going here?" Everyone stood and they all knew the drill because it had been a tradition for years.

When Lily started to walk away, Cam took her hand and held her back. "You okay?" She nodded, still unwilling to speak. He forced her to look at him. "Hey, it's me. Are you sure you're all right? Because if not, I'll make an excuse for us and we can go."

She smiled weakly. "I'm fine. I know I shouldn't let those little comments get to me, but they do. And really, it's not like they enjoy having me around, so I don't see what the big deal is if I miss a couple of days. If anything, you'd think they'd be glad. A little less time they have to spend staring disappointment in the face."

"That's enough," Cam said with more force than he

intended. "I'm not going to stand here and let you keep putting yourself down. I'm done listening to it, Lil. I should have spoken up and put an end to this years ago, and I'm sorry I never did. But from now on, they'll have to deal with me if they open their mouths against you."

Tears filled Lily's eyes, and she didn't even try to wipe them away. "You really are my knight in shining armor. You know that, right?"

Cam actually blushed at her praise. "I don't know about that."

"It's true. No one ever stands up for me except you, and I want you to know I really love—"

"Hey, you two!" Angela popped back into the room and walked toward them with a big smile on her face. "We're about to start."

Cam looked from his mother to Lily and then back again. "Uh, Mom…could you just give us a minute?"

"Okay, but just a minute because we have a ton of decorating to do, and you know it takes all of us to get it done." She gave them a knowing grin and a wink before leaving the room.

"You were saying…" Cam prompted.

Lily could have kicked herself. She had almost blurted out that she loved him in the middle of his parents' living room. What was wrong with her? "I just wanted you to know I appreciate you being such a good friend."

Disappointment flooded him. Cam had been certain Lily was going to say she loved him. True, she could have been about to say she loved him as a friend, but he had a feeling it was more. Was that even a possibility? Could she really feel more for him than friendship, or had their vacation fling simply confused her? Cam hoped that wasn't the case, but he was too afraid to get his hopes up.

"I'll always be here for you, Lil. Always." He kissed her forehead again, and together they joined their families to get the Greenes' house ready for the holidays.

Standing back, everyone admired their handiwork. "Great job," Angela said as she stood beside her husband and beamed at the way the house had been transformed. "I love the way we all come together to get this done. Every year it just comes out better and better." They all nodded in agreement. "But…" she said with a big smile, "there is one final touch and I saved it until the end."

Cam did not have a good feeling about this. There was never anything left until the end. His mother ran holiday decorating like a five-star general, and there was never any room for surprises. When she reached behind her and pulled out a box, he had a feeling that he and Lily were about to be forced into the spotlight.

"Mistletoe," she said as she pulled a sprig out of the square, gold box. "I know it usually gets hung during all of the hoopla, but after Cam and Lily's story of how magical their mistletoe time was in New York, I wanted them to hang it and to see them kiss under it."

His mother was going to be the death of him. Before he could say or do anything, Lily spoke up. "Angela, you know Cam isn't big on PDA. Don't embarrass him, or I'll never get him to do anything spontaneous again." She said it lightly, like his reaction wasn't a big deal, but Lily knew that if their families forced the issue, Cam would back out of the fake relationship out of sheer embarrassment.

Then, much to her surprise, Cam stepped forward, took the mistletoe from his mother, and then winked at Lily. "C'mon," he said, moving across the room to take her by the hand. "You know the drill. The mistletoe goes right in this doorway." The archway was ten feet tall, and normally one of the men stood on a ladder to hang it. Lily let out a screech when Cam lifted her up and balanced her on his shoulder before handing her what she needed to hang it.

"Cam, let me down." She giggled as the whole family formed a crowd behind them.

"Nuh-uh. Not until you hang the mistletoe," he said teasingly, loving the happiness he heard in her voice again.

"I can't believe you are making me do this," she said, but reached up and put the decoration in its proper place. "There. All done."

Cam maneuvered her so she was facing him as he slowly slid her body down the front of his. He was torturing himself and figured in for a penny, in for a pound. "You know what they're waiting for," he whispered with a wicked grin.

Without a word, Lily looped her arms around his neck and pulled him in for the kiss she had been missing all day. This was no kiss between friends; it had the intimacy of lovers, and soon there were hoots and hollers behind them and a whistle or two. She smiled against Cam's lips as she reluctantly pulled away. She hugged him as they faced their audience. "I guess he's getting over his aversion to PDA," she said with a laugh, and everyone joined in.

The remainder of the night was uneventful and when

it was time to say good night with the promise to do it all again on Sunday, Cam walked Lily out to her car. "Do you think they'll think it's weird we didn't drive here together?" he asked, searching for something to say to take his mind off the kiss they'd shared.

Lily shook her head. "We're dating, Cam. That doesn't mean we're joined at the hip. They know we still have our own lives."

"I guess." When they reached Lily's car, he wasn't sure what he was supposed to do. She turned to face him and then looked behind him and chuckled. "What? What's so funny?"

"I don't mean to put any pressure on you, but clearly we're still this evening's entertainment."

"What do you mean?" He started to turn around but Lily stopped him. "What? What's going on?"

She giggled. "They're trying very hard to be discreet, but I can see them all peeping through the curtains to watch us say good night."

"Why? What's the big deal about us walking out to our cars?"

Men were so clueless, Lily thought to herself and sighed. "They aren't used to you being so...affectionate. They're hoping to catch you kissing me again."

"Seriously?" The urge to look over his shoulder was strong but he held back, not wanting anyone to think he was doing this for show. Well, that was exactly why they were doing it, but there was no reason to give their families something to doubt already. Cam had seriously hoped to not have to be this...physical...again with Lily, especially not for an audience of their family, but he had a feeling this was only the beginning.

With his mind made up, he decided he might as well give the people what they wanted. Lily was digging in her purse for her car keys when he stepped in, cupped her face in his hands, bent his head, and kissed as if his life depended on it.

And on some levels, it did.

—⁓—

Lily couldn't sleep. She had been home for hours, and yet her mind wouldn't shut down enough for her to relax. The events of the evening kept playing through her mind. The looks on everyone's faces when they announced their relationship, the way that their moms were so excited, and then the announcement of the trip to the mountains for Christmas and New Year's.

And the kissing.

Oh, the kissing.

She sighed and reached for her tablet and kicked up a game of solitaire. The fake dating had seemed like such harmless fun in the beginning, but now? Now it was torturing her. She thought back to that innocent first conversation and the fun it seemed it would be to touch Cam and flirt. The fake dating had seemed like a good idea. Not so much now. No, now she wanted it to be real. The flirting and kissing for the crowd just made her feel empty, because at the end of the night, she was here alone.

Her cell phone rang, and a glance at the clock showed it was after one in the morning. She reached over, saw Cam's face on the screen, and smiled sadly. "H'lo," she answered, trying to sound sleepy so that he wouldn't know thoughts of him were keeping her awake.

"Hey," he said softly. "Did I wake you?"

"Not really." It wasn't a total lie.

"Are you winning?"

"What?"

"At solitaire? Are you winning?"

She couldn't help but laugh and look around her room. "How do you do that? Seriously, do you have a camera hidden in here somewhere?"

"I just know you, Lil. So…are you?"

"No," she said and relaxed back against the pillows. She loved lying in bed and listening to the sound of Cam's voice. "Actually, I just turned it on. What are you doing still awake?"

"I can't sleep."

His honest confession spurred her own. "Me either." They were both silent for a long time. Lily turned off the game and simply lay in the dark waiting for him to speak. Finally, she broke the silence. "Cam?"

"Hmm?"

"Was it weird for you tonight?"

"What? With the family?"

"Yes."

"I don't know. Was it weird for you?"

"A little," she admitted shyly. "I guess I wasn't expecting such a big reaction from everyone. They're all so excited and already beginning to make plans, and now I feel kind of bad lying to them."

"I know what you mean. I wasn't expecting all of that either." He sighed wearily. "So what do we do?"

The easiest thing to do would be to just end it and force herself to go back to playing the part of his buddy. Although it would be awkward with their families, she'd survive. Hell, most of the time she spent with her family was awkward, so why should this be any different? She was just about to suggest that to Cam when he spoke again.

"I think it will get easier as the weeks go on. Soon the newness will wear off. They'll get distracted by the actual holidays, and we'll be able to push them off a little. Honestly, they can't keep up this level of enthusiasm forever. Once the parties get going there will be so many other people around who are bound to have bigger and more exciting news than you and me."

Lily considered his words. "I guess you're right. How much worse can it be?"

Chapter 7

Famous last words.

Lily was sitting next to Cam as they drove up to Blowing Rock for the first day of their vacation. The last month had been near exhausting, and her nerves were on edge now every time she and Cam were near one another. After they had decided to continue with their farce of a relationship, things had indeed gotten worse.

It started with the decorating party at her parents' house. Just like at the Cavanaughs, a little ceremony was made of the two of them hanging the mistletoe and kissing. They got a round of applause after that one.

Then there was the Christmas cookie baking party. How that ended up the way it did, Lily still didn't know. Normally just the women did it, but somehow all of the men decided to join in. Her mother had made a game out of all of the couples decorating batches of cookies and—surprise, surprise—had found a way to incorporate mistletoe into the project. Every time a cookie was done being decorated, Lily and Cam had to kiss.

Her lips had practically been numb by the end of the night, and who knew Cam had such a talent for cookie decorating?

The open house wasn't any better because everyone who came in was greeted first with a cheery "Happy Holidays!" and then a *Reader's Digest* version of Cam and Lily's newfound romance. And, as predicted, they were positioned under the mistletoe.

She left that party with a migraine.

And so it went with the neighborhood get-together and then each father's company Christmas party. No one seemed to remember the reason for the season, focusing solely on the fact that Cameron Greene and Lily Cavanaugh were finally an item.

In the midst of the family party schedule, both Cam and Lily had social engagements of their own to contend with. Seemingly keeping with tradition, Cam had taken Lily to his company Christmas party—she had met some of his colleagues in New York—and Lily had done the same with her small work party. At least those two events didn't hold the same kind of pressure as the family ones.

Even though Lily knew she wouldn't be home for Christmas, she had wanted a tree and so Cam had gone with her to pick one out. On a rare night off from celebrating—and she used that term loosely—they had shared a pizza and decorated her little tree. She asked Cam if he was going to decorate this year, and he declined. The sensible part of him didn't see the need since he wasn't going to be there on the actual day, and thanks to their loaded social calendar, he wasn't home much at other times to enjoy it.

He had a point, but Lily couldn't imagine coming home during December and not seeing a tree in her living room. It just wasn't right, and it wouldn't seem like Christmas. That was silly, since everywhere they went, everyone was celebrating the holiday. But tucked into her own place at night, Lily found a little peace sitting in front of her own tree and dreaming about a time when she'd get to start traditions of her own that weren't dictated by somebody else's schedule.

Now, as they drove to meet their families, she wasn't sure what to expect. There had been an awkward conversation with their parents one night when they approached the topic of the rental. "When we rented this place, well, we had no idea the two of you were dating. So, there are six bedrooms and we are a party of twelve, but…" Jack Cavanaugh looked to his wife to continue.

"We just figured, Cam, that you'd sleep on one of the sleeper sofas," Angela finished.

"That's fine," Cam said, wondering what the big deal was.

Angela blushed a little. "What we're saying is that we're not going to be…prudes about this. You and Lily can share her room. We don't mind, and we completely understand you'll want some…private time to be alone."

Cam and Lily had looked at one another and did their best to not look horrified. Lily didn't think they'd pulled that off. "Um…do we really need to talk about…this?" she had asked, feeling uncomfortable and queasy at the same time.

"We're just letting you know we respect your relationship," Mary Cavanaugh had added. "We're just so thrilled that the two of you are together. We know ten days is a long time, and we want the two of you to be comfortable enough to want to stay, rather than find some excuse to leave and head home so that you can have some privacy."

It was quite possibly the most awkward conversation of Lily's life—and that included the infamous

birds-and-the-bees talk she had gotten when she was
twelve. "Well...um...thank you," Lily had said on both
her and Cam's behalf. "We appreciate the fact you're
all being so...cool...with all of this. We certainly don't
want anyone being uncomfortable." *Especially us.* "We
were going to be completely fine, no matter what the
sleeping arrangements were. Normally in these big
houses you end up with some twin beds or bunk beds, so
really, you don't need to make any special arrangements
on our account."

"Nonsense," Jack added. "We were all young once
too." He winked at them before standing and getting
himself a drink, and Lily thought she was never going
to want to have sex again after this conversation.

Brought back to the present, Lily noticed their exit
on the freeway and listened to the GPS instructions. "I
don't know if I mentioned this, but I don't have to go
into work until after New Year's," Cam said blandly,
clearly not excited by the prospect at all.

"Oh," she said just as dejectedly. "That's good."

Before she knew what was happening, Cam pulled
into the first parking lot they came to and turned the car
off. "Okay, spill. What's going on?"

Lily looked at him with pure confusion. "Spill what?"

"Clearly you're not happy, and if I can tell, then
they're all going to be able to. So what's going on? Let's
clear the air before we get to the house and have to get
into happy-fun mode."

"That!" she cried, pointing a finger at him. "That
is the problem. I'm sick and tired of happy-fun mode!
It's exhausting! I can't walk around like I'm freaking
ecstatic over everything when I'm not!" She banged her

head back against the seat and sighed with frustration. "This wasn't supposed to be this much work!"

Cam mirrored her position. "I know, I know," he said wearily. "Who knew we would be the biggest news of the season? Why isn't anyone getting married or divorced or having an affair?" That was the normal gossip around the holidays, and it really stunk that there was none this year to take the spotlight off of them.

Lily turned her head and looked at him sadly. "Ten days. We have ten solid days to be the picture of a happy and in-love couple, and you know what? I don't know if I can do it." Tears sprang to her eyes, and this time she did her best to wipe them away.

Reaching over, Cam did his best to pull her into his embrace with a console between them. "I'm sorry. This is all my fault."

Lily pulled back and looked at him with surprise. "Your fault? How is this your fault? If anything, our crazy parents are to blame! If they had just left us alone, we wouldn't have had to concoct this stupid act that has everyone we know throwing mistletoe at us at every turn!" She growled with frustration. "Or, even if we did have to go with this farce, if they had just reacted like normal people and not carried on like 'Oh, thank goodness our two misfit children finally found people to love them' and turned it into a spectator sport, it wouldn't be so bad. But it's exhausting. And that whole private-time conversation? What was that?"

"Oh, I know. I had nightmares for a week after that. I feel like every time we leave a room while we're there, they're all going to be smirking."

"Exactly," she said. "So what do we do?"

"Well, I don't see we have a choice." Cam thought for a minute, and then a wicked glint in his eyes told Lily he had come up with the perfect solution. "What if we turned the tables on them and used all of their enthusiasm against them?"

"Cam, you're starting to scare me. You used to be so mild mannered, but lately you've been walking a little too close to the dark side."

"No, this will be perfect. Our original plan was to break up after New Year's, right?" Lily nodded. "Well, our reason for the breakup is going to be because of all of the pressure *they* put on us. We couldn't handle it. We had no privacy. They pushed too much...blah, blah, blah. You see where I'm going with this?"

Lily gave him an equally wicked smile. "I do, and you know what? I like it. I like it a lot."

"We're going to have to fight a bit in front of them. You know I hate that because in all of our lives, we've never had a fight."

"I know," she said thoughtfully. "What's wrong with us?"

Reaching out, he traced his fingers on the side of her soft cheek. Cam loved just touching her and soon there would be no reason to because they'd go back to being just friends. Well, if he was honest, he'd acknowledge they didn't have an audience now and there wasn't a reason to touch her, but he couldn't seem to help himself. "There's nothing wrong with us," he said softly. "There was just never a reason to fight."

Lily sighed and rested her cheek in his palm and simply enjoyed the feel of the skin-on-skin contact.

"I don't know if I'll be able to do it, Cam," she said honestly. "I'll want to argue with them, not with you."

Cam leaned forward and placed a gentle kiss on her forehead. "Don't worry. We'll work something out."

———

The house was magnificent. There was no other way to describe it. As they drove onto the property, Lily marveled at the scenery. "Dad said the property was big, but it just seems to go on and on and on," she said.

"I think it's over one hundred acres," Cam commented, equally in awe of their surroundings. "There's supposed to be a private lake where we can go fishing, but it's catch and release because it's stocked by the North Carolina Wildlife Resources people." Lily nodded, and Cam remembered that fishing was not something she was interested in.

When the house finally came in to view, Lily gasped. "Oh my goodness! Look at that, Cam. I can't believe that we're staying here for Christmas!" It was designed to look like a log cabin, but to Lily it was like a luxury log cabin on steroids. There were tons of windows and decking that wrapped around the exterior, and no matter where you stood outside, you had a magnificent view. Even if she hadn't gotten the week off work, she would have called in sick because the house was too amazing to leave. And she hadn't even seen the inside yet!

Both sets of parents were waiting on the front porch when Cam and Lily pulled up. With a quick look around, Lily guessed they were the first of the siblings to arrive. "Oh," she sighed in awe as they got out of the car. "I'm just blown away."

When she turned and smiled at him, Cam knew exactly what she meant. While yes, the house and property were amazing, her and her smile and her enthusiasm were what never ceased to blow him away.

"We can get the luggage later," Lily said as she walked over and grabbed his hand. "Let's go pick out our room!" She fairly dragged him up the front steps, and they stopped to hug their parents. "This place is amazing," she gushed to them. "It's so much bigger than I imagined." Bouncing on her toes, her hand still firmly gripping Cam's, she asked, "Can we go in? Can we go in?"

Opening the front door of the house, Lily stopped and gaped. Their families had always been well-off, but nothing that she had ever seen compared to the natural beauty of this home. Log walls and stone fireplaces, exposed beams, and twenty-foot ceilings in spots... It was breathtaking.

"There are three master suites, and since you were the first ones to arrive, you are more than welcome to the third one," Angela said.

Cam and Lily both looked at one another and grinned. As the youngest in each of their families, they always seemed to get the last pick of everything, so with one mind, they turned to their parents and said, "Done!"

Mary Cavanaugh was the one to take them through the house, and by the time they got to their room, they had seen all six bedrooms, four stone fireplaces, a kitchen that was a chef's dream with granite countertops and stainless-steel commercial-grade appliances, and views that were awe-inspiring.

The main living area boasted floor-to-ceiling

windows with vistas of three mountain ranges and had one of the biggest flat-screen televisions Lily had ever seen. On the lower level there was a family media room and a game room that rivaled an arcade. Outside there was a large private Jacuzzi spa, a fire pit overlooking the mountain sunsets, a badminton court, and a backyard big enough to host any sport they might want to play.

By the time they were alone in their suite, Lily felt like she had walked a mile. Cam shut the door and smiled at the fact that all of their luggage was already there. He mentally reminded himself to thank whichever father had done it because he was exhausted from the drive and then the tour. Both he and Lily collapsed on the bed side by side.

Lily giggled and Cam turned to look at her. "What's so funny?"

"You know our sisters are going to be majorly upset that we snagged the last master suite, right?" Cam couldn't help but nod and laugh. "And I mean, they totally should be, because look at this place! King-size bed, private bathroom with a Jacuzzi tub, and what is that? Like a fifty-inch TV mounted on the wall. Never mind going home. I may not leave this room all week."

Cam found he was completely on board with that idea, especially if it meant they could spend some of their time here like they had in New York. And then he got worried. He knew their parents had implied it and everyone had joked about it, but the reality was that for ten days he and Lily were sharing this room, and it was positioned far enough away from everyone to afford them more privacy than they would probably need.

The problem was that he wanted to take advantage of

that privacy and forget his rules and reasons for making those rules, and have what they'd had on their last trip. He would never, ever suggest that to Lily because he knew she was struggling with keeping up appearances, but he couldn't help but wonder what was going to happen when just the two of them were under the blankets later that night.

It took a moment for him to realize she was staring at him, and he quirked a brow at her. "What?"

"Nothing. You just got really quiet over there. Don't you think this room is amazing?"

Cam nodded. "It certainly is. We are definitely going to be the envy of our sisters."

"We can't cave, Cam," Lily said seriously as she sat up and looked at him. "We can't let them bully us into giving up this room. You know they're going to try, so we have to mark our territory now."

Cam had his own ideas on how they could do that, but he waited to see what Lily was going to suggest.

"We have to unpack right now, put all of our stuff away, and totally settle in." She scrambled from the bed and began unpacking her toiletries in the bathroom. "It is like a spa in here," she called out to him.

Laughing once again at her enthusiasm, Cam forced himself to rise from the bed and join her. There was nothing any of their sisters could do or say that would make him leave this room. He had ten days left with Lily, and they were going to spend it in this luxurious room that was making her happy.

By the time he joined her in the bathroom, Lily had pretty much commandeered the entire vanity area. Cam carefully placed his meager belongings in one corner and neatly arranged them before examining the space more closely. It was spa quality with tiled floors, a jetted tub, granite countertops, and a shower that could easily fit two people.

An image came to mind that was so vivid he almost blushed.

By now, Lily had moved on to the closet and was hanging her clothes. "It's a shame we're only here for ten days because this closet looks a bit ridiculous with just our few measly belongings in here. We'd have to stay a month or so to fully utilize it."

Cam followed suit and hung up his stuff and then placed the rest of his belongings in the dresser in the main bedroom. Even though he and Lily had shared a hotel room, this seemed more intimate. They had pretty much lived out of their suitcases in New York, but now they were sharing a dresser and a bathroom—and definitely a bed. There wasn't even a sleeper sofa so he could offer to be a gentleman. They were in this room, pretending to be a couple, for ten days.

Heaven help him.

He was placing their suitcases in the large walk-in closet when he heard a weird sound coming from the bedroom. Walking out, he saw Lily jumping on the bed. He stopped dead in his tracks. "What are you doing?"

She looked down and stopped, a guilty smile on her face. "The final step to staking our claim. I'm messing up the bed so they'll think we've already done all kinds of things on it and no one will want to take the room from us!"

All she had to do was ask, and he would have gladly done all kinds of things with her on the bed. He quirked a brow at her. "Are you done?"

Carefully, she sat in the middle of the bed. "Spoilsport."

Cam joined her and gently pushed her so that she was flat on her back. Then, for no reason except that he couldn't seem to help himself, he kissed her. Lily instantly wrapped her arms around him and pulled him close, and Cam felt himself sigh with relief. It was wonderful to do this because they wanted to and not because someone had positioned them under some blasted mistletoe or they had an audience. He was kissing Lily because he wanted to, and she seemed more than willing to do the same. He didn't want to read too much into it, so he simply let himself enjoy the moment.

When he finally raised his head and looked at the peaceful expression on her face, he smiled. "Hey."

"Hey," she said. "You know, I kind of like doing that when it's not so forced."

"I was just thinking the same thing." Cam saw her features relax even more, and when she reached up to touch his face, he turned and kissed her palm. "Lily, I—"

They were interrupted by a knock on the door. "Hey, you two!" Angela said. "The others are starting to arrive, and we've got food out in the kitchen. Are you coming down?"

Boy was he.

Lily stared up at him with wide, green eyes, unsure of what they should do or say. When Cam didn't say anything, Lily shouted, "We'll be down in a few minutes!" and waited until she heard Angela walk away. Then she waited to see if Cam was going to finish his earlier thought. When he rolled off of her, she figured the moment was gone but held on to the hope that maybe he was feeling all of the things she was. Maybe

MISTLETOE BETWEEN FRIENDS

he wasn't as unaffected by their pretend relationship as he was letting on.

And maybe, just maybe, by the end of the ten days, there would be no more pretending.

"But that's not fair," Beth was saying snappishly as she looked accusingly at Lily and then back to her parents with a pout. "Why do they get the master suite? Shouldn't it be done in age order?"

Lily rolled her eyes but held her ground. "Aren't we a little bit old for that? I mean, honestly, what's the big deal?"

"If it's no big deal, then take another room. I'm the oldest and I should get the master." Beth looked imploringly at her parents. "It's only fair."

Cam had heard enough and was just about to open his mouth when Jack Cavanaugh did something Cam had never witnessed before. "Stop being such a pain in the ass, Beth. I mean, really. Aren't you a little old to throw temper tantrums?" When his oldest child nearly gaped in horror at him, Jack shrugged. "Too bad there isn't a room with bunk beds. It seems to me you would have done well in there."

Beth stood in pure, infuriated glory and stared at her mother for help. Mary simply picked up her glass of wine and followed her husband out to the deck. Then Beth turned to Cam and Lily. "I bet you're feeling pretty smug right now, aren't you?"

Lily walked by and picked up her own glass of wine and then handed one to Cam. "I don't need to feel smug, Beth. The house is huge, and each room is magnificent. I don't see why you're making such a big deal out of this."

"Then like I said, take another room."

Cam pulled Lily in close and kissed the top of her head. "That's not really an option. You see, we've already unpacked and settled in and…used the bed." He gave Beth a wink and then led Lily from the room before either of them could burst into hysterical laughter at the horrified look on Beth's face.

"Cameron Greene," Lily said as she pulled him into a tiny alcove on the deck. "I do believe I have corrupted you."

He gave his best evil laugh, and when he heard someone approaching, he pressed his body against Lily's, pinning her against the wall and kissing her. Cam heard her soft whimper as he touched his tongue to hers and sank into the kiss. If he could have, he'd have taken them right back up to their room and said to hell with all of this family bonding. So far, they weren't off to a great start with that. He heard a disgusted snort behind him and slowly lifted his head to see Beth glaring at them. "For crying out loud, if the two of you are going to carry on like that, at least have the decency to use the room you stole from me."

This time there was no hiding the hysterical laughter as they joined hands and went to join everyone out on the deck.

⁓

Cam had put it off as long as he possibly could.

It was time to go to bed.

The day had gotten way better after their little

confrontation with Beth. Once Cam's sisters arrived and neither of them even commented on not having a master suite, Beth calmed considerably. They'd all worked together to do some makeshift decorating with supplies both the Greenes and the Cavanaughs had brought with them, and the men had gone out and purchased a live tree.

All in all, it was a festive afternoon and evening. Dinner was lively, and thankfully Beth had been the only one to draw any attention to Cam and Lily, so they had been able to enjoy themselves for the first time in weeks.

Looking over to where Lily was sitting beside the fire pit with her parents, Cam was hesitant to go over and interrupt them. They seemed to be deep in conversation, and from where he was standing, Lily definitely looked relaxed. That was out of the ordinary for whenever Lily talked one-on-one with her parents. Cam looked at his watch and saw it was nearly midnight. His whole family had gone up to bed. Should he interrupt their discussion to say good night or just go up to their room?

Good manners prevailed, and he walked over and quietly excused his interruption. "I'm going to head up," he said to Lily. The Cavanaughs looked around and noticed everyone else had turned in.

"Are we the last ones up?" Lily asked, and Cam nodded.

"I didn't mean to interrupt. I just wanted to say good night to you," he said to Mary and Jack, "and to tell you I'll see you upstairs," he told Lily. He kept his tone light and hoped her parents were still able to see him as Cam, the boy they'd always known, rather than Cameron, the man who was sleeping with their daughter. Without checking to see their expressions, Cam leaned down and kissed the top of Lily's head and turned to walk away.

"Wait," she said as she stood and stretched. "I'll see you both in the morning." Lily turned and kissed both of her parents good night and then walked over to catch up with Cam. Her gait was a bit lazy, and she hadn't realized how tired she was until she got up from her comfortable position by the fire. Taking Cam's hand in hers, she walked into the house with him and up to their room.

As soon as her hand slid into his, Cam was certain he knew what a ticking time bomb sounded like.

Chapter 8

CAM QUIETLY CLOSED THE DOOR TO THEIR ROOM, LEANED against it, and watched as Lily walked around, settling in. She took off her earrings and placed them on the dresser, then opened a drawer and pulled out what he guessed were her pajamas. With a sleepy smile, Lily went into the bathroom and closed the door, and Cam finally let himself breathe.

"This is ridiculous," he muttered as he did his best to settle in. Kicking off his shoes and putting them near his side of the bed, Cam sat and wondered what he was supposed to do. In the grand scheme of things, this situation was nothing new. They had shared a bed in New York for four nights, so he knew they could do it.

They'd even managed to sleep that first night.

The problem with the current situation was that Cam didn't want to sleep. He and Lily were supposed to be laying the groundwork for their breakup, and making love was not going to be help make them believable. "This is why I hang out in a lab all day," he said quietly, rising to get his own pajamas from the dresser. "I should have just made the move overseas, and none of this would be happening."

"Are you back to moving overseas?" Lily asked around a big yawn as she stepped out of the bathroom. As in New York, she had on a pair of red flannel boxers—this time with snowflakes on them—and a green cami.

"Very festive," he said, motioning to her attire.

"Thanks. It came with a Santa hat, but that just seemed like overkill." Lily trudged over to her side of the bed and began the task of moving the mountain of decorative pillows off it and pulling the blankets back so she could crawl in.

Cam took that as his cue to take his turn getting ready for bed. With any luck, Lily would be asleep by the time he came out, and all of his worries would have been for nothing. He worked slowly and went through every nighttime hygiene chore he had ever been taught. Confident he had wasted enough time, he shut off the light and quietly opened the door to the bedroom.

And there sat Lily with her tablet, playing solitaire.

"Seriously," he said with a chuckle as he walked toward the bed, "you have a problem."

Lily looked up from the screen and smiled at his green flannel pajama pants and white T-shirt. "Are you sure you don't want to add a hat and gloves to that getup?" she teased.

"We're in the mountains, Lil," he said blandly as he climbed into the bed. "We have no idea how well the heat works in this house."

She shot him a look of utter disbelief. "Really? That's what you're going with? Poor heating in the luxury house?" With a tsking sound, she went back to her electronic card game. After a moment, she spoke. "I'm a little disappointed in you, Cameron."

"Me? Why?"

Lowering her tablet to her lap, Lily turned her head to look at him. "We've known each other our entire lives, and you're tiptoeing around here like I'm a land mine or something. It's painfully obvious you're uncomfortable with this whole situation, and I don't understand why."

How could he tell her he wasn't as much uncomfortable as he was turned on? Was there a delicate way to say he wanted to lose himself in her arms and her body that wouldn't come off sounding crude?

"For crying out loud, Cam," she sighed. "I can hear you thinking from here." Lily twisted around to place her tablet on her nightstand and turned off the bedside light, leaving the room dimly lit by the lone lamp on Cam's side of the bed. "Fine. Don't tell me what's going on." She flopped down and turned on her side, her back to him. "I'll see you in the morning."

Staring at the ceiling, Cam tried to think of something to say to break the tension, but he had a feeling that no matter what he said right now, it would only serve to anger Lily. With a sigh of defeat, he reached over and turned off his own bedside lamp and then simply lay there in the dark, wide awake and still staring at the ceiling.

He could hear her breathing and could smell the soap she'd used to wash her face before she came to bed. Even though it shouldn't have been sexy, it was. Cam inhaled deeply and closed his eyes, savoring the scent. He let out his breath slowly and was surprised when Lily rolled over toward him.

"Want to watch a movie?" she asked quietly. "We have that ginormous TV at our disposal. I'm sure we could find something." As she spoke, she managed to curl up beside him, and Cam lifted his arm so her head could rest on his shoulder and her hand could touch his chest.

"I thought you were tired," he said softly, his hand playing with her long, silky hair.

Lily shrugged. "You know I'm a night owl. I always want to go to sleep, but sometimes…" She sighed. "Sometimes it's hard to just unwind and relax."

"And a movie will help you with that?"

She was taking a huge risk. Thoughts of their earlier time in this room came back to her. She may very well regret what she was going to do, but for now, Lily didn't have the strength to care. "No," she said huskily as her hand wound up Cam's neck and into his hair to pull him toward her. "But this would." And then she kissed him.

In a heartbeat, Cam had Lily beneath him and cursed his excessive attire. If he had just worn boxers like he usually did, he'd be feeling Lily's silky skin as she wrapped her legs around him and her soft hands as they raked up and down his back. They had all night, and yet right now he was desperate for the feel of her. His mouth left hers briefly to rain kisses along her cheek and her jaw, and then along her throat until he reached the swell of her breasts right above the lacy edge of the cami she wore.

"Are you mad at me?" Lily asked as she writhed beneath him.

"Mad?" he asked between kisses. "Why would you even ask that?"

"Your rules," she said breathlessly. "I'm making you break your rules. I know how you hate that."

"To hell with the rules," Cam growled as he worked his way back up to her lips. He felt her smile against his own. "I need to break the rules more often."

"I don't know," she said as she pulled Cam's shirt

over his head. "I think I've become a very bad influence on you."

As soon as his shirt was off, he returned the favor and rid Lily of hers. "I don't look at it that way at all," he said as he reverently ran a hand over her breasts and heard her sigh of pleasure. "You're finally freeing me to live."

And that was the end of that.

Christmas Eve dawned like something on a Christmas card. Snow was falling, and the house smelled of freshly baked cakes, cookies, and pies as Christmas carols played on the sound system. Lily skipped down the stairs—in her Santa hat—with a grin from ear to ear. When she entered the kitchen, she found her mother and Angela hard at work on the preparations for the evening meal.

Clapping her hands together, Lily asked, "Okay, what can I do to help?" Both women looked up and gave her knowing smiles. "What? What's with the creepy smiles?"

"Look at you," her mother said. "You've got a spring in your step and a smile and glow on your face. Cam is good for you."

"Eeww, Mom, please…"

Angela nodded. "And you're perfect for him. I always knew that. When I see him being affectionate with you, it just makes my heart smile. Cameron's always been a bit…standoffish, and yet with you, he just seems… lighter. Happier. It's just so obvious he loves you." She came around the counter and hugged Lily. "I am so happy for the two of you. You've given us the best Christmas present ever."

Lily felt majorly uncomfortable. She hated lying to her parents and the Greenes, but if she had her way, this wouldn't be a lie for much longer. She and Cam had made love all through the night. And despite how he had talked about rules and them not doing that again, the scout in him had come prepared.

She loved that about him.

A blush crept across her cheeks, and both women laughed and hugged her again. "It's good to see you so happy too, Lily," her mother said. "Maybe with Cam's guidance, you'll finally be able to settle down and find a career."

And there it was. Lily knew last night had been too good to be true. She'd had such a wonderful time just sitting with her parents and talking about current events and topics that interested her without them making snarky comments on how she lived her life, but clearly Mary Cavanaugh could only keep her opinion to herself for so long.

"I don't think Lily needs any such guidance," Cam said as he walked into the kitchen. He walked straight to Lily and kissed her, leaving no doubt in her mind that he wanted more of what they had shared last night. When he finally stepped back, he smiled as his mother handed him a cup of coffee with a sappy grin on her face. "Good morning to you too, Mom," he said and kissed her cheek.

He took a sip of the hot beverage before returning his attention to Mary. "You know, Mary, not everyone has to define themselves by a nine-to-five job. I love that Lily is out there exploring the things she enjoys. When she finds the one she wants to stick with, maybe she'll make a career out of it. In the meantime, you should be proud she has so many talents."

"Well, I realize she has always been creative, but she's easily distracted and I think that's why—"

"Maybe it's not that she gets distracted, but that she doesn't get encouragement or support from the people around her to make her want to stay with any one job or position. Every time somebody shoots down or dismisses what she does, maybe Lily takes that as her cue to move on to something else in order to please you. Have you ever considered that?" His words weren't harsh, but they were truthful. Cam had always felt that part of Lily's inability to choose a career was because her parents always disapproved of what she did.

In his heart, Cam knew Lily wasn't a typical career woman. She would never be happy sitting in an office or a cubicle. She was too carefree for that. When he pictured Lily, he saw her working with kids or with animals, doing something that allowed her to nurture and be creative.

Lately he pictured her being the mother of his children, but he wasn't going to say that in front of their mothers because they had been on their best behavior and not gone overboard talking about planning for weddings and grandchildren. No need to encourage the crazy ideas already in their heads.

Mary put down the spoon she was using to whip up another batch of cookie dough and walked around the counter to hug Cam. Taking his face in his hands, she forced him to look her in the eye. "I always knew you were the one for Lily, Cameron. When you remind me of how often I forget how gifted my daughter is, it just reinforces the fact I was right about you. I'll never have to worry about Lily as long as she has you." She kissed him on the cheek. "Thank you."

Then she turned to Lily. "I know saying I'm sorry doesn't make up for all of the times I've belittled the things you do," she began as tears welled up in her eyes. "But I want you to know that not a day goes by that I'm not proud of you. You're a beautiful, independent woman. Believe it or not, I envy your ability to try new and different things. I'm sorry if I ever made you feel inferior. I'm so sorry." She wrapped Lily in her arms as the two of them cried.

Angela looked over at her son as her own tears began to fall. Cam rolled his eyes as he put his mug on the granite countertop and pulled his mother into his embrace. "You're quite a fine young man, Cameron," Angela said as she held her only son tight. "I am so proud of you, and I love seeing this new side of you. I knew Lily would be the one to bring it out in you, if the two of you only gave one another a chance."

He didn't know how to respond to that, so he simply held on to his mother until she was ready to let him go. "How about some breakfast?" Angela finally asked when she stepped away from Cam and wiped at her eyes. "I could whip up some pancakes if you're interested."

Picking up his mug, Cam smiled at her. "You know they're my favorite." Turning, he saw that Mary and Lily had moved to sit at the large kitchen table, and he continued to smile. He had done some good here. Even if he was forced to go back to just being Lily's friend, Cam knew that during their short time as fake boyfriend and girlfriend and real lovers, he'd helped Lily and her mother repair a broken relationship.

Just as Lily was repairing a part of him that hadn't been whole for far too long.

———～～～———

They ate dinner in the massive dining room, which could easily have housed another two dozen people. They talked endlessly about previous Christmases and their hopes for the New Year. Cam was puzzled by how much the focus on his relationship with Lily had lessened. It was almost as if their parents had some insight on what he and Lily had talked about and were purposely pulling back so they wouldn't have anything to argue about.

Everyone helped with the cleanup, and then Richard called them all into the family room to hand out a small part of the pile of presents under the tree. As was tradition, each child (and he used the term lightly) got to open one present on Christmas Eve. They could each decide if they wanted to give any presents that evening as well. Richard reminded them all to make sure something was left under the tree for everyone to open on Christmas morning.

In keeping with tradition, Lily and Beth both received new Christmas pajamas. "Seriously, Mom," Beth said. "Aren't we getting a little old for this?" Her tone was light, but it had been an ongoing argument for years. "How do you know I even wear pajamas?" she teased and watched as both of her parents blushed.

Lily joined in the laughter with her sister. It was the first time in recent memory that the two of them had seemed to be on the same page about anything. While

Beth's pajamas had been of a tailored, two-piece design, Lily's were far more risqué. "Mom!" she said with embarrassment as she pulled the slinky, green silk from its wrapping. There were hoots and hollers all around, and she saw Cam grinning from ear to ear.

"What?" he said. "You don't think I'm going to complain and tell her to stop, do you?"

"That's my boy." Mary beamed at him. "Consider it a gift for the both of you."

Cam shifted in his seat, more than a little uncomfortable with that thought, but he smiled and thanked Mary anyway. Lily quickly put the garment back in the box, put on the lid, and inquired who was opening the next gift.

The Greenes didn't quite have the same tradition, but each of their children received their practical gifts on Christmas Eve. Cam was expecting a new shaving kit or a robe or something of that nature, so he nearly choked when he saw green silk that looked suspiciously like it matched what Lily had just received. "Um…" he began and looked up to see everyone grinning at him.

"Whatcha got there?" Lily said teasingly as she nudged his shoulder with hers. "It's not fun when the shoe is on the other foot, now is it?" Cam mumbled his thanks and quickly put the lid on the box and placed it on top of Lily's as he glared at her.

"What?" she asked innocently. "You don't think I'm going to tell her to stop, do you?" The entire room erupted with laughter as a blush crept up Cam's face. Leaning over, Lily kissed him on the cheek and whispered for his ears only, "I can't wait for the fashion show when we get upstairs."

Before he had a chance to respond, more gifts were exchanged and then everyone headed back into the dining room for dessert. Once they were all around the table, Cam's father stood and addressed them. "I want you to know how much it means to me that you were all willing to come and spend Christmas here with us. I know there are in-laws who are missing you right now, but when the opportunity came to rent this house, I just couldn't pass it up. So I thank each of you for indulging me."

Taking a moment to compose his thoughts, Richard looked at his wife and smiled. "We have so much to be thankful for. You kids are such a blessing to me and your mother. We're so proud of each of you, and it does my heart good to see you all doing so well." He turned to the Cavanaughs. "Jack, Mary," he began, "you've always been more like family to us than friends, and Angela and I are so thankful you wanted to spend Christmas with us like this. We've been friends for a long time, and your friendship is the greatest gift we could ever ask for."

With a final nod, he turned toward Cam and Lily. "We realize we all went a little overboard when you first announced you were dating, and you both were obviously uncomfortable with all of the attention. We're trying to tone it down, but it was the greatest surprise when you announced you were a couple. We don't want to put any pressure on you because you're still in the early stages of your relationship, but nothing would give us more pleasure than seeing the two of you build a life together. You've always been the best of friends, and that is the single greatest component to a successful marriage. So we promise to do our best to stand back a little and give you space to explore your relationship—but just know," he said with a laugh as he looked to his wife and his friends, "that we would not be opposed to some grandchildren." Holding up his wineglass, he toasted the group and sat down.

Dessert was being passed around, but Lily had lost her appetite. No one seemed to notice she was pushing her pie around her plate and not really participating in any conversation. Grandchildren? Heck, she was just wrapping her head around not being in a fake relationship with real sex—and everyone was already thinking about grandchildren? That signified marriage and futures and…forever. A sigh escaped before she could stop it.

"Are you okay?" Cam whispered as he leaned toward her, his voice laced with concern.

"Yeah, sure," she lied, unable to meet his knowing gaze.

Cam wanted to pursue the topic, but sitting around the dining room table with ten other people was not the place. He rejoined the conversation, which was about whether they were going to hike or ski over the next week. Cam wasn't athletic in any way, shape, or form, so if it was up to him, he'd opt for hiking. Less chance of embarrassing himself that way.

He wasn't immune to the fact that Lily had gone quiet after his father's toast, but he wasn't sure what he was supposed to do about it. They'd known from the get-go that their folks were going to start planning their future, and if he was allowed to be honest, there was nothing Cam wanted more than to plan a family with Lily. He glanced at her and saw she was still playing with the pie on her plate and figured that was a sign she wasn't on the same page. Clearly, the thought of having kids with him wasn't appealing.

Now he fell silent.

Conversation was flowing, and without looking at Lily again, Cam excused himself from the table and left the room. He didn't expect anyone to follow, and he wasn't disappointed. There was something he had to do and it seemed like now was as good a time as any.

———

Where the heck did Cam go?

Lily watched as he left the room and had to wonder where he was going. True, it could just be a simple trip to the bathroom, but she was still irritated that he left her alone with the grandchildren-hungry family.

Okay, so maybe that was an overexaggeration; no one had picked up where Richard left off, so maybe they weren't as baby-crazy as Lily had been telling herself. Maybe she was the one who was feeling a little baby-crazy. And speaking of babies, why weren't their sisters being harassed about procreating? Why was the comment about grandchildren directed solely at her and Cam? Seriously, each of Cam's sisters had been married for more than three years, and Beth had been married for two. Where were the grandchildren requests to them?

"You're frowning, Lily," her mother said from across the table. "Are you all right?"

Lily looked up and saw everyone looking at her. "What? Oh, yeah, I'm fine. Just a little tired. Mountain air and all that."

"Hmm..." Mary said and winked at her daughter

before addressing the table. "I know we have a mountain of desserts here, but I also brought all of the makings for s'mores! Who wants to join me out by the fire pit?"

You would have thought none of them had eaten in days given the level of enthusiasm that request was met with. Before Lily knew it, they were all sitting around the fire pit roasting marshmallows.

Except Cam.

Lily kept looking over her shoulder for him, and she had finally put together her first gooey concoction when he reappeared. "Everything okay, Cameron?" his mother asked from across the fire.

Cam nodded, took a seat behind Lily on the lounge chair she had pushed over, and pulled her back against his chest. He loved the way she instantly relaxed against him, and then he smiled when she offered him her first s'more. Reaching out, Cam wrapped one large hand around Lily's wrist as she fed him the first bite. His eyes never left hers. As the sweet chocolate melted on his tongue, he nudged her to take a bite. Hesitantly, she did.

They held one another's gazes as they each finished their taste of the s'more, and then Cam noticed the chocolate at the corner of Lily's mouth. Lowering her hand, he did his best to turn her toward him while he leaned in, touched his tongue to that sweet spot, and slowly licked the chocolate away. He heard her soft whimper right before claiming her mouth with his.

Audience be damned. Lily Cavanaugh was like an addiction Cam couldn't get enough of. He might never get enough of her, and that suited him just fine. For once, no one seemed to be paying them any attention, so he took his time teasing her lips with his tongue before she opened for him. Cam deepened the kiss, wrapping a hand around the nape of her neck and into her hair to hold her to him. He never wanted to let her go.

A popping sound from the fire startled them both, and they reluctantly ended the kiss. They shared the remaining few bites of their treat before Lily leaned forward to make another one. Deciding to rein in the passion that was becoming so easy to ignite, Lily handed Cam a s'more to enjoy on his own. "Spoilsport," he murmured against her ear, and she shivered with delight.

They sat around the fire until well after midnight, when everyone began to rise and say their good nights. "Since we're all adults," Jack said with a smile as he stood, "there's no need for us to be up too early. Let's plan on brunch at eleven, and then we'll open the rest of our presents. How does that sound?"

Everyone was in agreement, and soon Lily and Cam were approaching the door to their room. "Where did you go earlier?" Lily asked as Cam stopped and blocked her entry.

Cam shrugged. "I just had some last-minute Christmas wrapping to do."

Lily rolled her eyes. "You are such a guy," she said with a laugh. "I could have helped you when I was wrapping all of my stuff." Without another word, Cam opened the door to their room and Lily gasped with surprise. She turned to him with wide-eyed wonder. "You did all of this?" He nodded.

The room was set up as their own Christmas wonderland. As Lily walked around, Cam lit some of the candles he had strategically placed around the room. Twinkly lights were also scattered around the room, a small live tree sat on top of a makeshift stand in front of the large picture window, and beneath it was a pile of presents. Cam flipped a switch, and the tree lit up with what seemed like hundreds of white lights. He watched as Lily stepped closer and looked at the decorations on the tree before turning to look at him. "How did you do all of this?"

"I have to admit I wasn't sure I was going to be able to do it, but I packed some ornaments in my luggage. Then when I went into town with everyone to get the big tree for the family room, I saw this little guy and knew we had to have him. I know you're a sucker for a Charlie Brown tree."

Tears glistened in her green eyes. "This is just amazing. I am simply blown away that you put so much thought into this." Closing the distance between them, Lily leaned in and kissed him softly, then stepped back and eyed the presents under the tree. "So..." she began, looking from the gifts to Cam and then back again. "Who are all the presents for?" Now she was back to being the Lily he had always known, the woman who would forever be a kid on Christmas. She was practically bouncing on her toes with excitement.

"Oh, there might be something for you under the tree. But I have to ask something—and it's on Santa's behalf."

Her eyes went even wider as her smile spread. "On Santa's behalf? That sounds pretty serious."

Cam nodded. "Oh, it is." Now it was his turn to step closer. "Have you been naughty...or have you been nice?" His tone was very seductive. Lily wanted to strip them both down and forget about the presents, but the lure of the twinkly lights and the tree was just too much. "Well? Which is it, Lil?"

"I think I have been...nicely naughty." Her grin turned wicked as she got up on her toes and kissed him again. She smiled against his lips. "Was that the right answer?"

She shrieked when Cam lifted her up and playfully tossed her onto the bed. "I'd say that just about sums it up," he teased as he laid down beside her. Reaching out, he played with her hair and then stroked her cheek. "Merry Christmas, Lily," he said softly.

"Merry Christmas, Cameron." They lay there studying one another for a long time. Lily rested her head in the palm of Cam's hand. "I have to admit, I have your presents hidden under the bed."

He smiled lovingly at her. There was no way he would ever grow tired of looking at her. Thinking back, Cam realized he knew Lily's face better than his own. For years he had watched her, watched over her, and being here like this with her just felt...right. His mind flashed back to the look on her face earlier in the evening when his father had mentioned grandchildren. Cam had to wonder if Lily truly felt what he did, or was she doing as she always did and just living in the moment?

Right now, he didn't care. She was his, and he was going to enjoy whatever she wanted to give him. "Well, I have an idea," he finally said. "How about I draw us a bath in that massive tub while you put your presents under the tree."

"Ooo, a bubble bath?" Lily said as she waggled her eyebrows.

Cam ducked his head and shook it with a laugh. "I

may get my man card revoked, but yes, a bubble bath. Then we can slip into the matching green silk robes that I still can't believe we received, and then we can open presents. What do you say?"

Scooting up onto her knees, Lily leaned forward and kissed Cam soundly. "I like the way you think!" She bounced off the bed and began gathering her bounty from under the bed while Cam started the water in the tub and moved some of the candles into the bathroom for softer lighting.

Lily came up behind him a few minutes later. "You've been holding out on me, Cameron."

Looking behind him, he arched a brow at her. "How's that?"

"All this time you've come off as being kind of stuffy and straitlaced, and yet underneath it all, you are quite the romantic."

He kissed her nose and turned so he could take her in his arms. "Well, I had to keep some mystery in our relationship," he said lightly. "I can't have you knowing all of my secrets."

Lily's expression turned serious. "But I want to know them. These past weeks have shown me that as well as we know each other, we still have so much to learn. And to be honest? I'm really enjoying it."

"Me too, Lil," he said solemnly. "Me too."

~~~

Soaking in the large, jetted tub almost overflowing with bubbles, Cam found Lily's laughter contagious. "Maybe we added too much bubble bath."

"You think?" he asked, but rather than being annoyed

by the mess, he was feeling light and playful. They were blowing bubbles off the top when Cam finally realized they needed to shut off the jets to get the bubble factor to calm down.

"You're no fun," Lily said with a pout as she leaned back against his chest and sighed. "Good thing we're sleeping in tomorrow because I am not the least bit tired after all this."

"The bath was supposed to be relaxing," he reminded her.

"Well, that was before we had to deal with the tower of bubbles."

He smiled as he rested his head against hers. "Hey, Lil?" he asked softly, tentatively. "Can I ask you something?"

"Anything."

"Tonight at the table, after my dad made that toast, you got really quiet. What were you thinking about?"

Lily squirmed slightly before settling into his embrace again. "This is just such a weird position. I mean, what are we doing, Cam? This was supposed to be about dodging bad blind dates, and now we're...we're lovers and our parents are asking us about grandchildren." She sighed. "I'm not used to anyone taking anything I do so seriously, and I can't believe that they chose this to get on board with."

"People take you seriously," he corrected. "It's just hard keeping up with you sometimes."

"How do they know I'm not going to lose interest in you like I do with everything else? How do they know I'm not just going to walk away and leave you brokenhearted?"

Cam was worried about the same thing. Lily could just be passing the time with him and, after New Year's, be content to go back to the way things were. For all he knew, she was just making the best of a bad situation. His body tensed at the thought.

"Now you've gotten quiet," she said, twisting around to look at his face. "What are you thinking right now?"

His gaze was serious as he met hers. "Are you?"

"Am I what?"

"Going to lose interest in me and just walk away at the end of the month?"

"Isn't that what you wanted?" she asked hesitantly, not sure if she was ready for the answer.

Cam wasn't ready for this. He wasn't ready for them to talk about the end when the present was so gloriously fine. Without a word, he turned her around so she was straddling his lap. Water flowed over the edge of the tub, and Lily gasped at the intimate contact. "I want you," he said roughly, right before his mouth descended to devour hers. Water continued to slosh over the edge of the tub, but neither seemed to care.

———

"I'm not going to lie to you—I feel utterly ridiculous. What were they thinking?"

Lily couldn't help but giggle. The hunter-green silk boxers Cam was walking around in were completely out of character for him, and with every step he took, she could see and feel his discomfort. "I think you look cute," she tried to say with a straight face but failed.

"Keep laughing, and you'll have to wait until tomorrow to open your presents."

"It is tomorrow," she reminded him.

"Well, then after brunch. How do you like that?" Hands on his hips, he faced Lily, who was sitting on the bed in the super-short, green silk slip nightie she had gotten. The color matched her eyes perfectly, and with her hair beautifully mussed up, she made a very erotic picture. If it were up to him, he'd forgo opening presents and spend his time unwrapping Lily from her silky garments.

"Okay, okay…no need to get all cranky," she was saying, holding up her hands in surrender. "You know I don't want to wait until after brunch. I'll go crazy before then." Scooting off the bed, Lily walked over to their tiny tree, picked up a stack of presents, and carried them back to the bed. She watched as Cam arched a brow at the pile.

"We're opening all of our gifts tonight? You don't want to do that with the family tomorrow?"

She shook her head. "I like that it's just the two of us. Do you mind?" There was no sarcasm, only concern.

In response, Cam gathered the rest of the gifts from under the tree and brought them to the bed. Once he was comfortable, or as comfortable as he was going to get in the ridiculous boxers, he handed Lily his first gift.

Her eyes lit up at the generic-sized box. "What is it? What is it? What is it?" she said as she tore at the paper. Lifting the lid and moving the tissue paper aside, she stared at the contents and smiled. "*One Hundred Careers for Creative People Looking to Change the World*," she read aloud and then looked up at him and smiled. "I cannot even believe someone actually wrote a book about this."

"It just screamed Lily to me," he said, relieved when she laughed with him. "I figured I'd start with something light first."

Lily's eyebrows shot up in surprise. "First? That sounds promising." She looked at the pile in front of him, which had several more boxes, and her mind raced at what could possibly be in the rest. "Okay, my turn." Looking through her stack, she chose a box and handed it to him.

Cam opened the box and smiled. "Ah, how did I miss getting one of these for myself?" he asked as he held the T-shirt up in front of him.

"See? It's an 'I heart New York' shirt, but the heart is in the shape of Mickey Mouse! How cool is that?" She was bouncing on the bed with excitement. "Do you like it?"

"Absolutely. Thank you." Leaning forward, he kissed her on the cheek and then picked another box from his pile and handed it to her. He laughed at how fast she tore through the wrapping. "You know, it took me a really long time to wrap this stuff. Maybe you can slow down and admire my handiwork for more than a tenth of a second."

"What fun would that be?" she asked as she took the top off the box and gasped. "Oh, Cam," she said with a dreamy sigh. Inside the box was a snow globe she had admired when they were in New York. It was a miniature of Times Square. "I love it." Her eyes shone bright with tears. "Every time I look at it, I'm going to remember our time there." Before she gave in and cried, Lily reached for the next box and handed it to Cam.

He smiled as he opened a hardcover copy of the

latest bestseller by his favorite author. "Thank you for not mocking my refusal to switch over completely to an e-reader. As much as I see their appeal, there is still nothing like holding a book in your hands."

When Cam handed Lily her tablet rather than another box, her brows furrowed. "What's up?"

"Turn it on," he prompted and then sat back while she did and waited for her response.

"Oh. My. Gosh." She looked up at him with a big grin. "Is this the super-deluxe solitaire app I'm seeing?"

He nodded. "That's right," he said proudly. "I figured if I can't get you into a twelve-step program for your obsession, I might as well feed it." He saw her getting ready to boot it up and placed a hand over the screen. "Seriously? You're going to play solitaire when there are still presents to unwrap?"

Grumbling about too many rules, Lily placed the tablet back on her nightstand and handed Cam his next gift. He smiled when he opened the new iPod. He was forever dropping his, and he thanked her for remembering he needed another.

Taking the next present from Cam's hand, Lily made a big production of shaking it and admiring his skill as a gift wrapper before slowly opening the paper—only tearing where there was tape so nothing got ripped. After five minutes of theatrics, Cam gave her the go-ahead to tear into it. There was an envelope inside the box, and Lily looked at him quizzically. "What in the world…" she began before opening the envelope. She gasped with giddy surprise when she saw it was five days of park passes to Disney World. "Oh my God, Cam!" she squealed and launched herself into his arms, toppling him over and almost off the bed. "When are we going? When are we going?"

Trying to right them on the bed, Cam sat up with Lily in his arms and laughed at her impatience. "They don't expire for a year, so you can go anytime you want."

Lily's head tilted to the side. "You're going with me, right?"

He hadn't wanted to make that assumption because for all he knew, by the time she wanted to go, she might be dating somebody else. "We'll see," he said lightly and then looked around her for his next gift.

"Well, now I feel silly because I wasn't nearly as extravagant as you," she said, reaching for the last box. It was large and flat, and she felt a little embarrassed as she handed it to him.

"Hey," he said softly, tucking a finger under her chin so she'd have to face him. "What's the matter?"

"You got me a Disney vacation, and well...I didn't think... I should have..."

Cam moved his finger from her chin to cover her lips, silencing her. "It wasn't a competition, Lily. I love everything you got for me...and whatever is in this giant box? I'm going to love it too." Silently she sat back and watched as he unwrapped it and then held her breath as he studied it.

"It took me a little while to get it right," she said quickly, "but once I figured out the software, I really had fun with it."

He was speechless. In his hands was a large, framed collage of pictures of the two of them from their trip to New York. Lily had done them all in black and white because she knew he preferred that to color photos.

Looking at the dozen or so pictures, Cam barely recognized himself. Gone was the geeky scientist who spent his days deciphering the secrets of the universe. In his place was a man who stood smiling from ear to ear, looking more relaxed than he ever had in his life.

Looking up at her, Cam saw her uncertainty, her hesitation. His throat was clogged with emotion. "It's the most perfect gift I've ever received," he said hoarsely. "You outdid yourself, Lily." He studied the photos again and then ran his hand along the frame before looking up at her. "Did you make the frame too?"

She nodded. "There was a Groupon deal for a woodworking class. I decided to try it."

He smiled as his heart swelled with love for her. Of course there was a class. "You do beautiful woodwork." Standing up, Cam took the framed picture to their dresser and placed it in front of the mirror so they could see it from the bed. "It's perfect."

He turned back to the bed and collected all of the boxes and placed them back around their tree. Then he picked up all of the discarded wrapping paper and crammed it into the bathroom trash can before turning off all the lights in the room except for the twinkly ones. Walking back over to the tree, Cam reached behind it and pulled out one last gift, a small, rectangular box. His heart raced as he sat beside Lily and handed it to her.

She wasn't sure what to expect. Every year, they got each other several gifts, but this year there was more meaning behind them. In years past, they had done gag gifts and practical gifts, but these were more from the heart. Her hands shook as she unwrapped the small velvet box.

Nestled inside was a simple gold chain with two charms—a gold moon and a diamond star. Carefully lifting it from the box, she wordlessly handed it to Cam before turning and lifting her hair so he could put it on her. Once it was in place, Lily turned back to face him and then touched the delicate charms. "It's absolutely beautiful," she said reverently.

"Remember all the nights when we'd sit out in the yard and look up at the sky?" he asked, and she nodded. "You would listen to me talk aimlessly about constellations and the names of the planets, but you were always fascinated with finding the brightest star after questioning the size of the moon. Do you remember that?" Again, Lily nodded. "When I saw this necklace, it reminded me of all of those nights. I wanted you to have this so you would remember them too."

"I've never forgotten," she whispered. "Thank you." She continued to touch it and memorize the feel of it while Cam reached forward and cupped her face in his hands. Lily didn't question the move; she welcomed it.

Someday, she thought, *we'll make love under the brightest star, and then…maybe then…he'll love me.*

Chapter 9

Tomorrow was New Year's Eve.

They were supposed to be planning their breakup.

Neither Cam nor Lily had broached the subject all week. Instead, they'd spent their days and nights living like lovers, much to the delight of their families. Lily had spent the morning out shopping with her mother and Angela. When they returned to the house, she went out in search of Cam.

"He went on a hike," her father said. "He seemed pretty somber when he left. Did the two of you have a fight?"

Lily shook her head. No, if anything they had been getting along better than ever—and that was really saying something because they had always gotten along. "How long ago did he leave?"

"About an hour ago. I'm sure he'll be back soon. It's pretty cold out there today."

He didn't need to tell her that. Unease settled in the pit of her stomach, and before she could doubt herself, Lily pulled her gloves out of her pocket and walked out on the back deck to see if she could spot Cam. For ten minutes she walked from one end of the large deck to the other, trying her best to find the proverbial needle in a haystack. Just when she was about to go back in the house, she spotted a splash of blue among the greens. Zipping her coat up higher and taking a fortifying breath,

Lily headed down the deck steps and in the direction of where she had spotted Cam.

The cold air burned her lungs as she walked out into the lush greenery in hopes of being able to navigate it and find him. She wasn't feeling overly optimistic and was losing her bearings when she heard Cam say her name. Turning, she smiled with relief. "Hey, you. Dad said you went out hiking. I thought I'd try to find you."

"Well, you did," he said flatly.

"Cam? Is something wrong?" His tone worried her. Things had been going so well, and she'd thought they were both happy. She had no idea what had brought on this change of attitude. "Did something happen?"

"I got a call from work today," he began, not look- ing directly at her. "I need to be back in the office on the second, and then they've scheduled me to do a lecture circuit in Canada and then in Europe. It's a three-month gig."

"Oh." Lily wasn't sure what she was supposed to say. The thought of not seeing Cam for three months was like a kick in the gut. They had never spent much time apart, not when Cam had gone to college, and he'd never taken such a long business trip. "Wow. That's a really long time."

He nodded. "A colleague got the assignment, but she just had an emergency appendectomy and won't be able to travel. I was next on their list."

"Don't you want to go?"

No, he didn't. Career-wise, it was the trip of a lifetime and would help him, but personally? It was the last thing he wanted to do. Being away for that long didn't bode well. Cam knew that if he went, his friend Lily would be right here waiting for him when he got back. But Lily, his pretend girlfriend and real lover? She would probably move on without him, and he hated that. Hated the fact that he had doubts and that they hadn't taken the time to talk about their future. They had been so focused on living one day at a time to get through the holidays that they'd never taken the time to stop pretending.

"Cam?" she prompted, doing her best to get a read on him.

"It's a great opportunity," he said simply, emotionlessly.

"Then you should do it," she said with equal emotion.

Cam's head snapped toward hers. "What about us?" he finally asked, needing the answer more than he needed his next breath.

Lily had always known how important Cam's career was to him. Ever since he was a little boy, Cam had been fascinated with the workings of the universe, and she had admired his determination. Deep in her heart, she wanted him to stay. She wanted to be selfish and tell him he could let this opportunity go because there would be other ones. But by the dark and serious look on his face, she didn't think he would agree.

Maybe that was why he was out here in the frigid cold, wandering aimlessly in the woods. Maybe he was trying to find a way for them to end their make-believe relationship so he would be free to follow his dream and achieve the level of success in his field he had always wanted.

Taking a breath she didn't feel she had, Lily stood a little taller, willed herself not to cry, and kept her voice steady. "We had planned to break up right after New Year's," she said, forcing a confident edge to her voice. "So really, this plays perfectly into the grand scheme of

things. We won't have to stage some fake fight. You'll
leave for your trip, and then we can just phase out. You
know, long-distance relationships and all that."

Cam's whole body went rigid. He was furious. Had
he been truly alone in his feelings all this time? Did he
not know Lily at all? How could she have made love to
him with such emotion and carefree abandon and then
stand here and talk about ending their relationship as if
it were meaningless? Was he that big of a fool, or had
he only been seeing what he wanted to see? Was he so
naive about relationships and the opposite sex that he
hadn't realized this relationship was all one-sided?

"I suppose," he said through clenched teeth.

Lily looked away and shifted uncomfortably, not
knowing what else to do or say because she didn't think
she could hold back the tears much longer. "Well then,
that settles it. Are you planning on staying for the festivities, or do you need to leave sooner to go home and
get everything in order before you have to fly out?"

Cam hadn't allowed himself to think that far ahead
because, in his mind, he'd thought he would tell Lily,
and she would ask him not to go, that she'd say she
didn't want them to be apart. He shook his head with
disgust. This was why he didn't do relationships. Clearly
he had no clue about the opposite sex—even when it
came to his best friend.

"I guess there's no point in hanging around. I have to
close up my town house, stop the mail service, organize
my notes, and all that." He looked around at the scenery,
the sky, his shoes—anything to keep him from looking
at Lily. "No time like the present, I suppose." And with
that, he strode off.

Lily watched him go and stood perfectly still until she could no longer hear his footsteps crunching on the frozen ground. It was only then that she crumpled to the ground and cried for all she was worth. Her heart was breaking, and it hurt more than she'd ever thought possible.

How did this happen? How had she gone and fallen in love with her best friend? This wasn't supposed to be the way it went! Tears fell hard and fast until she couldn't see her hand in front of her face. Cam had gone away before, but never for long periods of time, and she'd never hurt like this, never ached as if a part of her were missing.

She wasn't sure she'd be able to survive it. Lily knew she was going to have to go back into the house at some point and return to an empty room, then look at the sad expressions on her family's faces. She was going to have to sleep alone in their bed and then drive home with her parents, back to her lonely life.

Without Cam.

Why hadn't she stopped him? Why couldn't she, for once, be selfish and go after what she wanted? It wasn't fair that she always stepped back and let the things that made her happy slip through her fingers. Over the years, she had left jobs she loved and lost touch with friends she enjoyed because of someone else's disapproval.

This time it was all on her. Cam wasn't leaving because of anyone else's issues, only hers. She wasn't confident or brave enough to tell him how she really felt. Lily was certain Cam must have been able to tell how she felt during their time together over the past six weeks. But in the end, at the ultimate moment of truth, he couldn't see it and Lily couldn't say it.

Some pair they made.

For all of their talk about how in tune they were with one another, at a pivotal point in their relationship, they had no idea what the other was even thinking or feeling. What did that say for them and their friendship?

She was freezing and her teeth were chattering, but Lily wasn't ready to go back into the house. She needed to wait a little longer to make certain Cam was packed and gone. He was very efficient when something needed to be done, and she had no doubt he'd gone straight to their room to collect his belongings. He'd want to be on the road before it got too late, to be back at his home before dark.

Her ears perked up when she heard footsteps approaching. Was it Cam? Was he coming back to tell her he wasn't leaving? That he didn't want to leave her for three long months because he loved her? "Lily?"

It was her sister.

Could she not catch a break today?

"Over here," she murmured and turned to see Beth making her way through the trees. Lily didn't move from her spot on the ground and was surprised when her sister—her forever neat and tidy sister—sat on the cold ground beside her.

"So Cam said he's leaving," Beth said, staring forward. Lily simply nodded. "He said he got this great opportunity to travel to Europe and Canada and whatnot, and it's supposed to be some big feather in his cap."

"That's what he said," Lily confirmed, hating having to have this discussion with anyone.

"So what are you going to do about it?" Beth asked as she finally faced her sister.

Lily shrugged. "It's something he's worked his whole

life for. He'll leave, he'll travel, and I guess we'll see what happens after three months."

Beth snorted with disgust. "Wow, I cannot believe you just said that."

"What? Why?"

"The two of you are crazy about one another, and you're willing to just let him leave and get all wishy-washy about the future? What is wrong with you?" Beth demanded.

It was no use pretending anymore. What good had it done her? "Look, the truth is that Cam and I were never really dating. We made the whole thing up."

Beth laughed out loud, and Lily's head snapped toward her. "What the hell's so funny?"

"You know, I was a little suspicious of the whole thing when you first announced your relationship. I mean, after all of these years, why now? But then I watched the two of you these past weeks, and you know what I think?"

"No," Lily said with a weary sigh, wishing her sister would just get up and go away.

"I saw two people who were genuinely in love."

Lily shook her head. "You're wrong. It was all an act."

"Please," Beth snorted. "I've seen your acting, and that, little sister, was no act. Not on your part and not on his. You're lying to yourself if you believe otherwise."

Lily looked at her with sadness and confusion. "Aren't you listening? We did this to get Mom and Angela off our backs. We were tired of the endless stream of blind dates, so we thought we could have at least one peaceful holiday season if we pretended to be involved."

"Were you just pretending?" Beth asked gently with a tone that was very unlike her usual self.

Shaking her head, Lily began to cry. "I don't know what happened. It wasn't supposed to be real, and yet... after that first kiss? It was like everything I had been searching for my whole life was finally right there in front of me." She did her best to compose herself, wiping furiously at the tears streaming down her cold face. "But at the end of the day, Cam is this supersmart guy who has this amazing career that means more to him than anything. How could I possibly ask him to stay?"

"How could you possibly let him leave?" Beth took Lily's hand in hers and tugged to get her sister to look her way. "Most people aren't lucky enough to fall in love with their best friends. Normally you fall in love and then learn to be friends. You and Cam? You've always been perfect for one another. We all thought so. Watching the two of you together? It was like watching...a love story. Look, we've known the Greenes all of our lives, so I've known Cam as long as you have. He's always looked at you with longing, Lil, but lately? He watches you with love. You can't just let that go."

"He didn't want to stay, Beth," Lily said sadly. "Maybe he's a better actor than I am because when all was said and done, he was able to just walk away."

Cam had packed with his usual efficiency, even as he kept one eye on the door. He kept expecting to see Lily come barreling through it to stop him, but she didn't. When he had no other choice, he loaded his belongings in his car and said his good-byes to everyone and drove away.

For the first twenty miles, he was numb. For the next sixty miles, he was indecisive about whether or not he had done the right thing. Indecision turned to sadness, and sadness gave way to anger. "Dammit!" he cursed, slamming his hand on the steering wheel. Why hadn't he fought more? Why didn't he demand that Lily tell him what she was feeling? He'd known her his whole life, so he knew that when Lily was faced with a difficult situation, she tended to retreat and say what she thought other people wanted her to say. How could he have forgotten that?

Thinking about the upcoming trip, Cam felt annoyance rather than excitement. He was damn good at what he did, and he had made a name for himself in his field. This was a great opportunity, but it wasn't a once-in-a-lifetime opportunity, no matter how much his bosses tried to tell him that. And even if it was, what would it really do for him? He would have a higher title; he'd have the accolades and the fame, but when he returned home, what would he have?

Nothing.

Just like six weeks ago, he'd still have nothing. His work was thrilling and fulfilling, of that he was certain. But it wasn't everything. It didn't give him joy, it didn't make him smile, and it certainly didn't fill him with a sense of lightheartedness or make him laugh.

Only Lily did that.

And he had walked away.

For as successful as Cameron was, his career was fairly safe. He was studying the universe and there were infinite possibilities and new things to find, but he was part of a very small community where even if people didn't agree with his theories or his findings, the masses still did.

Taking a risk with Lily was something completely different.

What if he drove back to the mountains and professed his love to her and she told him it hadn't been real? That what they had shared had been nothing more than a pleasant diversion and that was it? What if she laughed in his face, and he lost the best friend he had ever had?

Could he risk it?

Should he risk it?

Back at his house, he looked around. Everything was neat and tidy. The only personal items were the things Lily had given him, not just for Christmas but over the years. Cam had already placed the collage from their trip over his fireplace. Standing in the middle of his living room, he looked at the images and his chest ached. Over on his coffee table was a photo of the two of them from their high school graduation.

Turning around, Cam realized that every photograph in his home was of the two of them or of his family. Lily was everywhere, surrounding him because he needed her to feel safe, to feel secure in his lonely home and to feel loved.

What had he done? Had his plan—his stupid plan that had seemed so simple when he thought it up—ruined everything? By avoiding a few unwanted dates, had he lost everything important to him and vital to his very existence?

Cam's first instinct was to get in the car and go back.

Go back and beg Lily's forgiveness, profess his love, and even if she didn't love him back, ask for just one more night to hold her in his arms. He'd have to learn to be okay with having her in his life as just a friend and watching as she went on and found the man she would settle down with, have children with. He'd do his best to be happy for her.

He was tired. He was used to spending hours pondering the workings of the cosmos, and yet the exhaustion he felt after doing that was nothing compared to what he was feeling now. His sense of duty told him he had a team of scientists expecting him to do the right thing.

And Cam always did the right thing.

It was what was expected of him, and what he was good at.

Sometimes doing the right thing and living up to everyone else's expectations wasn't all it was cracked up to be.

Chapter 10

"Lily, sweetheart, come inside," Mary called from the doorway. "It's freezing out here."

It was New Year's Eve, 11:00 p.m., and Lily stood out on the far end of the deck and stared up at the sky. It was a cloudy night and there were no stars to be found, but she was determined. "I'll be in soon, Mom," she said distractedly. "Don't worry."

Mary Cavanaugh stepped out onto the deck and walked over to her daughter. She came to stand beside her, leaned against the rail, and looked up at the night sky with her. "It looks like snow again."

Lily nodded. "Smells like it too. I love that."

Sighing, Mary placed an arm around Lily and pulled her close. "I'm so sorry," she said quietly. "I know how upset you are about Cam leaving, and although I still have hope the three months apart won't mean the end of your relationship, I hate that it happened now, over the holidays and when everything was so new for you."

Surprisingly, Beth had kept Lily's secret. She didn't tell anyone that Cam and Lily's relationship had been a sham. Part of Lily was thankful, but another part of her simply wished Beth had been her usual self and blabbed the news to everyone so they would be angry with her rather than looking at her with sympathy and pity.

She hated the pity.

Lily knew how to deal with a bratty sister. She didn't

know how to deal with a sister who was kind. It was a novelty, and somewhere in the back of her mind, she was waiting for the time when Beth would use that secret information for her own personal gain and to make Lily look stupid.

It felt wrong even thinking it.

During those precious thirty minutes when they had sat on the cold ground and actually talked, Beth had shared how her own marriage was less than perfect. She told Lily that she had actually been jealous of her and Cam because she and her husband had never had the kind of affection they had. Hearing that had filled Lily with both pleasure and pain. There had been affection between her and Cam, and it had been real. It wasn't the stuff of friendship; it had been the kind of affection shared between two people who were soul mates.

Cam and Lily had often joked about how they believed they were soul mates but in the context of being friends. She realized now that really wasn't the case. Looking back, she knew she had always been in love with Cameron Greene, scientist, computer geek, and all-around good guy—and she had let him walk away.

"You really should come inside by the fire," her mother said, breaking the silence.

Lily turned to her mother and placed a gentle kiss on her cheek. "Soon."

Once Lily heard the door close, she breathed a sigh of relief. She didn't want to cry in front of her mother. Again. She had done enough of that yesterday and today. Most of the current day had been spent wallowing in bed—until her mother had physically dragged her out of the bed and forced her to take a shower and come downstairs for something to eat. Lily had to admit she had been starving but it had taken too much energy to physically move.

She missed Cam.

She'd hated having to sleep alone last night and dreaded going to sleep tonight.

Maybe after the ball dropped at midnight and they spent the next hour drinking and laughing and having fun, Lily would sneak down to the media room to watch a movie and sleep in one of the plush leather recliners. No one would have to know, and it would save her from another night of torture. The sheets still smelled of Cam's soap and cologne, and that big bed was just too much for one lonely person.

Nodding with approval at her own plan, Lily resumed her search of the night sky. Why couldn't she find one measly star? It was one of her favorite things to do every New Year's Eve. She'd step outside right before midnight, find the biggest and brightest start to wish upon, and then go back to whatever party she happened to be at and wish on it again at midnight before she kissed whomever she happened to be at the party with.

Funny how she'd never wished to be with the person she was actually at the party with. They were all very nice guys who just… Well, they weren't Cam.

Another sad sigh escaped her as the clouds seemed to move restlessly in the sky. "Just keep moving," she said with an urgent whisper. "Just clear out for a little bit so I can find my star."

The door opened behind her, and Lily silently prayed that another family member wasn't coming out to offer her sympathetic advice.

"You have your star," a deep voice said from behind her.

No. It couldn't be. Lily was too afraid to turn around. Maybe her mind was playing tricks on her. Ignoring the voice, she leaned out farther over the railing, craning her neck to get a better view of the night sky.

And then a pair of strong arms wrapped around her from behind.

Okay, that was a little harder to ignore. "You have the brightest star around your neck, over your heart, for whenever you want to make a wish," he whispered against her ear and felt her shiver slightly before she relaxed against him.

Without missing a beat, Lily spoke. "I can't break tradition," she said simply. "I always stand outside and find a star to wish on. Help me find one."

Wrapping her more securely in his arms, Cam felt like he had truly come home. He looked up as the clouds seemed to part, and there, barely visible to the naked eye, was one lone star. "Look up there," he said softly and pointed to the break in the clouds. "It may not be the biggest one, but it's there just for you, Lily." He inhaled the sweet scent that was solely hers and said, "Make a wish."

Lily closed her eyes tightly and did just that. Satisfied with her wish, she turned in Cameron's arms and looked up at a face as weary as her own. "You came back."

He nodded. "I did."

"You got all of your things organized that fast?"

This time he shook his head. "There was nothing to organize."

Lily's brows furrowed at his words. "Why? Are

you just going to use the notes from your New York presentation?"

He shook his head again. "No, I'm not recycling my notes."

Now she was even more confused. "Then what are you going to do? Did your boss make up a presentation for you? Can he even do that? I mean, doesn't it work better if you create the presentation for yourself so you know what you're—"

He cut off her words with the kiss he'd needed and craved ever since he left. Cupping her face in his cold hands, Cam pressed his body fully against hers and did his best to pour everything he had, everything he felt, into the kiss.

At first, Lily was too stunned to respond. Cam was here! He came back, and he was out here under the night sky kissing her. As soon as her brain shut off, she wrapped her arms around him and returned his kiss with the same urgency she felt from him. Soon she no longer felt chilled. The coolness of the winter night was no match for the body heat they were generating.

Finally, Cam lifted his head and rested his forehead against Lily's and took the first real breath he'd had in days. She was here, in his arms, and no matter what happened next, he had this moment with her under the stars.

Well, star.

"Stop talking," he said as he caught his breath.

"But…"

Cam placed a finger over her lips to silence her. "I have something I need to say, and if you keep talking, I'll never say it." He took a small step back and smiled at the wide-eyed confusion on her face. "I'm not going on the lecture circuit."

"What? Why?"

He rolled his eyes. "You're talking again." Lily promptly closed her mouth and pretended to zip it so he could continue. "I made it all the way home before I realized I didn't want to do it. I didn't want to be away from home for three months." He stepped back to her. "I didn't want to be away from you for that long." His heart felt full to overflowing when he watched her sigh with obvious relief. "This whole thing between us started out as a joke, as a way for us to pull one over on our parents to keep them from making our holiday miserable. But the joke was on us because it's real."

Cam's gaze deepened as he looked into Lily's upturned face. "It stopped being fake for me the first time you kissed me. I've wanted you for so long, and once you took that step, even though I know it was for show, it just made me realize I didn't want to pretend. I want you for real, Lily Cavanaugh. I want what we've had these past six weeks to be real."

"Cam—"

"I'm not finished," he said, cutting her off gently. "I know I'm not the type of man you usually date. I'm boring and straitlaced. And we're best friends…but I don't want to go back to just being friends. I'll do it, if that's what you want, but I want more, Lily. I want to be your boyfriend, your lover, and if you'll have me, your husband."

"Cam—"

"Still talking," he said and put his finger back over her lips to silence her, because if he didn't finish what he had to say, he might never get the chance to do it again. "I went back to my house, and it was quiet and empty. Yet everywhere I looked, you were there. The only items that personalize my home involve you. If it wasn't for you, Lily, I wouldn't have a life. You make me live. You make me step out of my comfort zone and try new things. You make me stop taking myself so damn seriously, and I don't want to be that man anymore. Please don't make me be that man anymore." Cam rested his forehead against hers and let out a breath. There. He had said it all. The ball was now firmly in her court. He waited for her to respond.

And waited.

And waited.

Finally, he realized his finger was still resting on her lips and she was looking up at him with amusement. He quickly pulled his finger away and rested both of his hands on her waist. "Sorry."

"Am I allowed to speak now?" she asked, tapping her foot in mock irritation. Cam nodded. "One of the greatest things about our friendship was that we always told one another everything. It was the thing I treasured most. Whenever I had a problem or something was bothering me, I always knew I could talk to you." For a moment she just stopped and studied Cam's face. He looked so serious and she knew he was patiently waiting for her to speak her piece, and she gave a small smile at that.

"But then I fell in love," she said with a shrug. "And I really wanted to talk to my best friend about it, but I couldn't because the man I fell in love with and my best friend were one and the same. I didn't know how to tell you what I was feeling because I thought I'd scare you away. As much as I know you've always been there for me, I also know that you, just like everyone else, think I have a short attention span. That simply isn't the case here, Cameron Greene. You see, I don't see myself ever tiring of being with you. And not just as a friend, but as your girlfriend, your lover, and yes…even your wife."

Cam felt as if his knees were going to give out because his relief was so great at hearing his words coming back to him. Lifting Lily into his arms, he held her tight. "I'm so sorry I left," he said, his breath warm against her neck. "And I know exactly what you mean because I fell in love with you, but was afraid to talk to you about it because I didn't want to risk hearing you didn't feel the same." He placed her back on her feet. "No one has ever loved me and accepted me for who I am like you have, and I realized when I was all alone last night that I don't want anyone else. It's you, Lily. It's you and only you I want. I love you."

Not waiting another minute, Cam kissed her. Lily's arms immediately wound around his neck as her fingers raked through his hair, anchoring him to her. They stayed like that, drinking from one another, for a long time until a strange noise slowly brought them out of their haze. Cam lifted his head. "What is that?"

Lily pulled back and looked around and then burst out laughing. "What?" Cam asked. "What's so funny?"

Taking him by the shoulders, she spun him around so he was facing the house. There, lined up against the wall of windows were their families, watching them and applauding. Lily rested her head on Cam's back until she could compose herself.

"We'll never have any privacy, will we?" Cam asked with a chuckle.

"With this group? Never."

Cam took a step to the side and then put his arm around Lily so that they could both face their families with a smile and a wave. "I guess we should go inside."

Lily nodded. "Absolutely. My work is done out here."

Frowning, Cam looked at her. "Work? What work were you doing out here?"

She rolled her eyes. "Sheesh, Cam. You've forgotten already?" When he still looked at her with confusion, Lily shrugged and pulled him toward the house. He'd figure it out eventually, but as far as Lily was concerned, she'd done a great job of finding a star to wish on tonight.

And that wish had already come true.

Epilogue

Nine Months Later…

"I FEEL RIDICULOUS."

"You look fine."

"Easy for you to say. I don't see you wearing anything like this."

"Even if I were, I wouldn't feel ridiculous in it."

Cam sighed. It didn't matter how long he and Lily had known each other, which was basically since before either of them could talk. She'd always had a way of talking circles around him and making him crazy. "How long do I have to do this?"

Lily looked up at her new husband and grinned from ear to ear…at his ears! Actually, they were mouse ears, compliments of a mouse named Mickey. Lily had asked that they spend at least part of their honeymoon at Disney World, and she had chosen a groom's top hat with mouse ears for Cam. She was letting him sweat it out for a bit before she pulled out her white sequined mouse ears with the veil to match. After all these years, it was still fun to make Cam squirm.

"Lighten up. We're on our honeymoon. We're having fun, remember? You're even supposed to smile and laugh once in a while," she teased.

"Well, maybe I'd smile and laugh if we could just go back to bed and spend the day as I suggested earlier."

Lily blushed at the memory of what Cam had suggested. It was rather decadent, and she promised that when they arrived at the second stop of their honeymoon—New York City—she'd let him have his way. For now, however, she was going to act like a little kid and run around the theme park and have fun.

"I have waited years to come back here, and not even sexy promises will make me miss my chance to skip down Main Street."

"I'm not skipping, Lil. I love you, but there is no way I'm doing that. Isn't the hat enough?"

Giggling, Lily reached into her suitcase, pulled out her mouse ears, and put them on before striking a pose and grinning at Cam. "How about now? We can match, and then we can skip!"

He shook his head, sending his own ears flying across the room. "You'll have to do better than that to get me to skip." He saw that familiar look on her face, the one that told him she had gotten an idea, and held up a hand to cut her off before she could even say what it was. "Don't even bother. There is nothing in the world you can come up with that will make me skip anywhere, especially while wearing the ears, so forget it."

She turned to pouting. "Well, I was going to say we could come back here to the room after lunch and do the second thing you suggested," she said seductively with a wicked smile to match her words. "Twice."

All of Cam's blood seemed to head south at the image she put in his head. With a growl of frustration, he stalked over and picked up his mouse-eared top hat before grabbing his wife's hand and dragging her out the door, her laughter trailing behind him.

"What's the hurry?" she asked as she giddily tried to keep up with him.

"We've got some skipping to do."

Six Hundred Miles Away...

"It was a beautiful wedding, wasn't it?" Angela asked her best friend as she poured them each a glass of wine.

"It certainly was," Mary said, savoring her first sip. "Cameron looked so nervous but so handsome. I can't wait to get some of the pictures back from the photographer."

Angela nodded as she came and sat across from Mary at the small table on her deck overlooking the pool. "By the time the kids get back, we should have some proofs. I never thought it was going to happen, you know."

Mary looked at her and smiled. "I was running out of misfits to fix Lily up with!" She laughed at her own clever doings. "I think Biff was the last straw!"

"Biff." Angela chuckled and shook her head. "That name is just a cruel thing to do to a child." Settling down, she turned toward her friend. "And you want to know the best part?" Angela asked, waiting for Mary's attention. "Biff is now engaged to Kitten!"

"No! How in the world did that happen?"

Angela had to stop laughing before she could continue. "Well, you know how we all run in the same circles. After Cam's date with her ended so perfectly and then Biff took Lily home practically before the date began...I thought that I'd play matchmaker. I ran into them both at Richard's company Christmas party and introduced them to each other."

Mary held up her hand for her friend to high-five her. "I pray the two of them have mercy on their future children and give them normal names!" She laughed at the thought and then sobered as her thoughts returned to their own children. "I had my doubts we'd ever get the results we were looking for. It wasn't easy to keep fixing Lily up with men I knew she would hate."

"I felt the same about Cam, like I was being a bad mother." Angela took another sip of her wine. "They just needed a little nudge."

Nodding, Mary agreed. "They are going to make beautiful grandchildren."

"Which is what we wanted all along." They raised their glasses to one another before sitting back and enjoying the scenery in companionable silence.

The

SNOWFLAKE INN

Prologue

RILEY WALSH WAS A FREE MAN.

Only it wasn't by choice.

"So what are you going to do with yourself now?"

Riley stood staring out the window of his command-ing officer's office, lost in contemplation. Turning, he faced the man who had become like family to him over the past twelve years. "I'm heading home to see my mother. After that, I'm not sure."

"How's her recovery coming along?"

Riley shrugged. "I guess it's going okay."

His CO quirked a brow at him. "Okay? Don't you know for sure? When was the last time you talked to her?"

Riley shrugged again and began to pace the sterile office space. "Before I got injured."

The lieutenant colonel stood and came to halt in front of Riley. "Is there a problem?"

Riley knew that tone of voice. Over the years, it had made him tremble in fear at times. There was no fear this time. "No problem. I just didn't want her to worry. If I'd called while I was in the hospital, she would have instantly known something was wrong. I didn't want to add that kind of worry while she was dealing with her own recovery."

Relaxing his stance a bit, his CO placed a hand on Riley's shoulder. "You did an outstanding job for your country, Riley. I know this isn't the way you wanted your career in the marines to end. Go home, spend some time with your family, and finish recovering. You've got your whole life ahead of you."

"To do what?" Riley asked with more than a hint of bitterness.

For the first time in his military career, he saw a hint of a smile on his CO's face. "Whatever you want."

If only that were true. Riley knew what was waiting for him at home, and he didn't like it one bit. Truth be known, if he hadn't gotten injured, he would have made the marines his entire life and only gone home when absolutely necessary.

That sounded cold even in his own head, but it was the truth. His whole life, he'd been told how the family business would one day be his. Riley shuddered at the thought. There was no way he was taking over the family business. Not in this lifetime. Maybe now that his mother was dealing with her recovery, she'd see that running the place was too much for her. Of course, he'd have to make it abundantly clear that although his time in the service was up, he wasn't coming home to take over the reins.

After all, how could anyone expect Riley Walsh, a dedicated marine injured in the line of duty, to run a bed-and-breakfast? Especially one called the Snowflake Inn.

Chapter 1

"WHOSE IDEA WAS IT TO MOVE TO THE MOUNTAINS?" Grace Brodie mumbled to herself as she pulled her wool scarf a little tighter around her neck. "I left the possibility of sun and sand…for this?" As if Mother Nature herself had heard her, a biting wind kicked up. "Perfect."

Actually, it had been her own idea to make the move, and on most days, she loved it. Today, however, was not one of those days. It was cold, it was gray, and Cute Angry Guy was walking behind her again. Grace chuckled to herself. She was sure he had an actual name, but she hadn't had an opportunity to find out. When she had first noticed him around town a couple of days ago, she had named him Cute Serious Guy. The next day he had become Cute Brooding Guy, but today, he was looking pretty fierce, so she went with Cute Angry Guy.

Every morning, Grace came into town, did a jog around the park, ran her errands, and grabbed a coffee at Starbucks before heading to work. The park was the first place she had noticed him. There was something oddly familiar about him, but for the life of her, she couldn't put her finger on it. He was well over six feet tall and clearly worked out, because as he jogged around the same path she did, he didn't seem to get winded.

She usually felt like stopping to vomit three times.

Every day.

Sure, she could feel nervous about the fact that this

guy had suddenly appeared out of nowhere and seemed to be following her around, but she had a feeling he was harmless. But she was rattled a bit when he showed up at Starbucks. The first thought to pop into her head was that he was clearly attracted to her and had followed her to get coffee in hope of striking up a conversation.

But he stayed ten feet away from her at all times. The closer she moved toward him, the farther he moved away. It was a little odd.

And disappointing.

Now, as she finished the last quarter mile of her jog, Grace couldn't help but wonder what his story was. Did he live here? Have family here? Did she somehow know him and had just forgotten?

Hell no. If Cute Angry Guy had ever been in her life before, Grace was certain she would have remembered him. Clearly. In great detail. And he would have starred in every fantasy she ever thought up.

She was feeling the burn and could clearly see the light at the end of the tunnel—or in this case, the clearing in the trees that meant the parking lot was close— when it happened. Her knee buckled. A cry of dismay escaped before she could help it, and next thing she knew, she was on the ground.

"Dammit," she cried, pulling her knee to her chest as she rocked. "Why now?" Tears threatened to fall, and all she could think about was the walk to the car and how painful it was going to be. As much as her physical therapist had told her recovery would take time, Grace felt like her body had betrayed her.

"Are you all right?" a deep male voice said from behind her.

Uh-oh... Cute Angry Guy is here, and he's talking to me! Looking up...and up...and up, her eyes finally met his. *Holy cow*.

"Miss?"

Oh, right. He asked you a question. "What? Oh, sorry... Um... Yes, I'm fine," she stammered and tried to stand. But her darn knee wasn't quite on board with the rest of her, and she went down again. She muttered a curse and felt a blush creep up her cheeks in embarrassment.

He quirked a brow as he looked at her. "You don't look like you're fine," he said seriously and crouched beside her. "Did you hurt your knee?"

Grace nodded. "About six months ago in a skiing accident. I was in rehab and physical therapy for months. I just decided to try to go back to my jogging routine—at a slower pace, of course—and I thought I was doing okay. Until about five minutes ago."

Cute Angry Guy nodded. "You probably just pushed yourself a little too hard."

She shook her head. "In therapy, I can run twice as long without any issues."

"That's on a treadmill. This is an uneven jogging path. It's completely different."

Now she glared at him. "Thanks for pointing out the obvious," she snapped. If she had better luck, she'd be able to jump to her feet and walk away with a sassy sway to her hips.

Clearly, she had no luck. On her third attempt at standing, Cute Angry Guy wrapped a strong arm around her back and helped her to her feet. "Thank you," she said quietly and did her best to disengage from his embrace. But he didn't let her go. Looking up, Grace found herself trapped by the bluest eyes she had ever seen. Her breath seemed to catch, and she couldn't speak, couldn't breathe. The only thing saving her from complete and total embarrassment was the fact that he seemed just as mesmerized by her as she was by him.

"Can you walk?" he finally asked, his voice sounding rough to her ears. Nodding weakly, unwilling to break their eye contact, she tried once again to move away, but his arm seemed to tighten around her. "I'll walk you to your car."

He clearly wasn't big on conversation. At the moment, that suited Grace just fine because she was having a hard time remembering how to form words. Cute Angry Guy was big and a feast for all of her senses, but she had to be careful to remember that he was a stranger. She knew nothing about him, and as much as she wanted to ask him at least a dozen questions, there was something to be said for companionable silence.

And walking really close together.

Deciding to just enjoy the moment, Grace pressed herself more firmly against his warm, solid frame and began to walk slowly with him toward her car. With the way they had been seeing each other all around town for the past couple of days, she figured he'd know which car was hers without her saying anything.

Sure enough, he did.

When they reached her little white sedan, they stopped and Grace pulled her keys out of her jacket pocket. It was then that she realized what a complete mess she must look like: black leggings, white jacket, and a green wool scarf to match her green socks…ugh. And then there was the hair.

She was so *not* going to think about the hair.

Normally after her jog, Grace would take a few minutes in the car to relax and apply some lip gloss and fix her hair before going anyplace else. That was why she hadn't been worried about approaching him the other day in Starbucks. But now that he'd seen her in this—well, in all her ill-fated glory—she was certain her current appearance had killed any attraction (real or imagined).

Quickly and painfully.

Awesome.

"So, um…thanks for the help," she said, feeling awkward. She fidgeted with her hair, doing her best to tame it, and cursed herself for refusing to wear a hat. At least a hat could have camouflaged the flyaway mess.

His lips twitched with an almost-smile as he watched her fidget around. "Are you going to be okay to drive?"

Grace ran her hand through her hair and cursed when it got stuck. With a wince, she pulled it out and forced herself to play with her keys and try to remain calm. "Yes," she said, wishing that the parking lot would just open up beneath her and take her away. "I'll be fine. I'll go home and do the whole ice-and-heat thing, take some ibuprofen, and call it a day."

"You should probably call your therapist and let him take a look at it."

She shook her head. "I don't have one here."

"Then you should set up an appointment for when you get home."

Grace gave him an odd look. "Get home? I am home. I live here."

Now it was Cute Angry Guy's turn to give her an odd look. "You live here?"

She nodded. "I just moved here about six weeks ago. I thought I was done with therapy, so I haven't bothered to look up a therapist. But I guess I'll have to now." She shrugged and turned to unlock her car. Once the door was open, she turned and forced a smile on her face. "Anyway," she said and did her best to relax, "thank you for the help."

"My pleasure." His voice was deep and a little rough, and Grace almost wanted to purr. Hearing the word *pleasure* come from that mouth—which was pretty spectacular too—had her heart rate going into overdrive.

"Well, I guess I'll see you around," she said brightly and sat in the car, wincing slightly as she bent her leg.

"Don't wait to find a therapist. Call the one you know and see if you can get a referral."

"Thanks, I will." She was just about to ask his name, but he turned and walked away. And the rear view was as enticing as the front one. Grace almost had to fan herself. Her first instinct was to call out to him, but really, it was probably better not to. If he had been following her these past couple of days, wouldn't he have asked for her name or phone number? The fact that he hadn't just proved Grace was imagining things. Bad hair and wardrobe aside, the man couldn't seem to get away from her fast enough.

With a depressed sigh, Grace pulled the car door shut and decided to cut her losses and go. The drive through the small downtown area didn't take long, and when she saw Starbucks coming up, she decided she could deal with the pain for a little bit longer. A white-chocolate peppermint mocha would go a long way in helping her deal with it, of that she was certain.

It didn't take long to park, and then she was surrounded by people she was coming to know. She smiled and made small talk while she waited her turn in line at the coffee shop. When one person was left in front of her, Grace felt an odd tingle go down her spine. Turning her head, she had to suppress a grin. There in the doorway stood Cute Angry Guy, and if her eyes weren't deceiving her, he was doing his best to suppress his own smile.

She wished he'd stop trying to hide it. With a face like that, he had to have a smile that was positively breathtaking. Certain she'd never really know, Grace turned her attention back to the counter, placed her order, and made her way to the register to pay. She was mentally congratulating herself on the fact that she hadn't turned around again. Self-control—she'd known she had it in her somewhere.

"Thank you," Grace said with a smile as she took the hot beverage from the young barista. Turning slowly in the crowd, she made her way carefully to the door, still doing her best not to look around and see if Cute Angry *Smirking* Guy was still there. *I guess I'll never know.* She sighed inwardly and headed back out to her car.

If her knee hadn't been in so much pain, Grace was certain she'd have a little pep in her step. Being rescued by a sexy stranger was certainly a great way to start her day. A quick glance at her watch showed she needed to get moving or she'd be late for work. And with so much on the line, the last thing she wanted to do was mess that up.

Although she doubted anyone would blame her if they had seen the sexy reason for her delay.

Chapter 2

SHE LIVED HERE? HOW COULD SHE POSSIBLY LIVE HERE? Riley's mind was spinning. For three days now, he had been trying to make himself go home to the B and B to see his mother, but when he checked, only one car was parked there. *Her* car. He'd figured she was just a guest and would be gone by now. If she wasn't a guest and she lived in the area, what did that mean? Maybe she was just working part time at the B and B during his mom's recovery. Or maybe she was a friend who was staying there to help out.

Slamming his head against the headrest in his car as he sat in front of Starbucks, Riley had to face the hard truth. He was going to have to face his mother, and chances were there was going to be an audience.

Dammit.

The thought of going to see his mother and not only telling her he was out of the marines, but also that he wasn't planning on sticking around and helping her with the business wasn't going to go over well. First, he would have to relive the hell he'd gone through in combat and how it had landed him back in civilian life. She'd most likely be devastated that he hadn't told her about his injuries sooner. Biting back a curse, Riley knew she had every reason to be angry. What kind of son doesn't let his mother know he almost died?

The same kind of son who plans on letting her family business go to a stranger.

Not his finest hour.

He scrubbed a hand over his face. This was so not the way he'd imagined his homecoming. Choosing to go to a hotel outside of town for a few days to mentally prepare suddenly seemed like the coward's way of doing things. It had seemed like a good idea at the time, but now he knew he'd just been delaying the inevitable.

Out of the corner of his eye, he saw the little white sedan pull away. Without knowing her name or anything of significance about her, Riley knew somehow that the woman was going to be a factor in how things went down with his mother. Growling with frustration, he started his own car and decided he was done mentally preparing himself.

Or hiding, whatever.

He was going back to the hotel to pack his meager belongings, and then he'd do what needed to be done. He was a U.S. Marine, damn it. He had faced the enemy in combat. He'd killed when necessary and walked into dangerous situations where he had no idea who he'd be facing more times than he cared to remember.

And yet the thought of facing his mother was scarier.

Still, Riley knew waiting wasn't going to change anything, and he believed in owning up to his fears and overcoming them. She was his mother; she'd raised him. Surely, she wasn't going to be surprised when he told her about his plans. On some level, she had to have seen this coming.

He *hoped* she'd seen this coming.

With everything packed up, he headed to the front desk, checked out, and walked back to his car.

Here we go…

———

Grace closed the heavy front door behind her and promptly sagged against it, thankful to finally be home.

"Is that you, Grace?" a voice called out.

"Yes…" And before she could utter another word, her good friend Corrine was rushing toward her.

"You're back sooner than I expected. Is everything okay?" One look at Grace, and Corrine had her answer. "Oh no…your leg?" Grace nodded. "I knew you were going to overdo it. Come on, let's get you on the couch."

"Corrine, I'll be fine. I just need…a minute."

"Please…how many times have I said the exact same thing to you?"

Grace frowned. "Dozens?"

"And how many times did you listen?"

"None."

With a look of victory, Corrine helped Grace cross the main entryway and led her to the sofa in the massive living room. Once she was settled, Corrine looked at her friend and waited.

Grace knew that look and swiftly rolled her eyes in defeat. "Okay, so I overdid it. I'll survive."

"Grace, you know what the therapist said. You have to take these things slowly."

"How much slower can I possibly take it, Corrine? It's been months! Months!" She threw up her hands in disgust. "I'm tired of walking on a treadmill. I'm tired of not being outside and enjoying the fresh air."

"Oh, don't be so dramatic," Corrine admonished. "No one is locking you away, Grace. You can *walk* outside, just don't jog every day. Eventually, you'll build yourself back up."

"It wasn't supposed to take this long," Grace said softly, emotion welling up inside her. "People break their legs all the time, and within six weeks, they're back to normal."

"You broke your leg in four places, Grace. You're lucky to be walking at all."

That was something she had heard what seemed like a hundred times while in the hospital and in therapy. It wasn't that she wasn't thankful that she was, indeed, walking, but Grace wanted to be back to her old self. Right now, she doubted that would ever happen.

"Look," Corrine began, "you came here to start over, for a new life. This recovery is part of it. I don't want to see you hurting yourself because you think you have something to prove."

"I don't think that," Grace protested, but when her eyes met Corrine's, she knew she was lying. "Okay, so I'm trying to prove to myself that I can be like I was before the accident. That's not a crime."

"No, it's not. But wouldn't you rather do this the right way so that you *can* get back to your old self, rather than overdoing it and ruining those chances?"

Grace hated when her friend was right. Well, that wasn't completely true. She valued Corrine's honesty and friendship. She just hated when it meant she herself was wrong.

The two had met while Corrine was recovering from hip replacement surgery and staying at the rehabilitation center where Grace had not only spent her own recovery but was also working as a chef. The two had bonded because Grace saw a lot of herself in the older woman. Actually, they had gravitated toward one another, and a friendship had been born.

Having lost both of her parents ten years earlier, Grace found in Corrine the mother figure she had been missing. And Corrine? Well, she only had one child—who was in the military and rarely came home—so Grace figured she was filling a hole in Corrine's life as well. For whatever reason, they had become fast friends, and when Corrine was released from rehab and ready to go, she had asked Grace to come and help out with her bed-and-breakfast in the mountains of North Carolina.

Over their many conversations about their lives, Grace had told Corrine about her previous life as a chef at an exclusive hotel in New York City. Unfortunately, when she returned from the extensive rehabilitation after her skiing accident, she found her position had been filled, and she was out of a job. Not one to sit still for long, Grace had taken a position in the kitchen at the facility where she had recovered. "Came for the therapy, stayed for the job," she always said.

"Is this really what you want to do with your life?" Corrine had asked one afternoon.

Grace shook her head. "No, this is definitely not where I imagined myself."

"So? What's keeping you here?"

"Essentially, I have no place to go. I don't have a job to go back to. My roommate put my bigger stuff in storage, sent me my personal items, and found someone who could actually live there and pay the rent. So really, until I find someplace to go, this is it for me."

"If you could have your dream job, what would it be?"

A slow smile crept across Grace's face. "My dream? Well, if I delved deep into the fantasy, I'd have to say I want to run a place of my own."

"A restaurant?"

Grace shrugged. "I'm not so sure about that. I found the pace at the hotel to be a lot more hectic than I was comfortable with. I think I want something smaller, more intimate. A place where I can create different menus every day. Maybe a café or bistro—you know, a place where I'm not catering to the masses but can actually take the time to leave the kitchen and meet my customers."

A smile of pure joy crossed Corrine's face. "Grace, I do believe fate has brought us together."

"Really? Why?"

Corrine looked around as if she wanted to make sure no one was listening before leaning in close to Grace. "Back home, I own a bed-and-breakfast."

"You do? Why haven't you mentioned it before?"

Now it was Corrine's turn to shrug. "People are funny. Most of the time when I mention it, I get asked if they can stay for free. I pick and choose who I share my information with."

"That's terrible! I would never expect to get a free night just because we're friends. I'm sorry people do that to you."

"You get used to it. But my point is," she began as she reached out and placed a hand on top of Grace's, "I'm getting too old to run the place on my own, and I think you would be a perfect fit."

Grace looked at her in confusion. "I don't understand."

"It's not only my hip and the recovery that are slow-ing me down," Corrine said. "My husband has been gone a long time, and the B and B belonged to my parents, so I've been there my entire life. I love what I do—I've been doing it since my midtwenties—and I can't imagine doing anything else, but..." She sighed. "It's a lot for one person to do."

"How big is your place?"

Corrine's entire face transformed as she spoke about it. "Oh, Grace, it's such a lovely place. It's very rustic. We're in the mountains of North Carolina, and I have about twenty acres."

"Wow! That's huge! How do you maintain it all?"

"I have a groundskeeper, Ben. He and I grew up together, and after my husband died, Ben approached me about helping out. At first I told him no, that I'd hire a landscaping company to do it, but he wore me down. He told me that they'd rip me off and charge me more than the job was worth. And he was right. They did."

"That's terrible."

Corrine nodded. "Ben always loved working out-doors. He ran a construction company for years, but he said he much preferred working with the land rather than building. So he comes around and makes sure our walk-ing paths are clear and the main house and the few cot-tages we have are always in good shape." She blushed slightly. "I have to admit, it's nice to have a man around the house sometimes."

"Why, Corrine," Grace teased lightly. "Do you have a crush on Ben?"

"Don't be silly—I'm too old to have a crush."

"You're never too old to have a crush." Grace

thought it was sweet. Even from the little bit Corrine had shared, Grace had a feeling that, if given the opportunity, Corrine wouldn't mind having Ben in her life for more than his grounds-keeping skills. But Grace would keep that to herself for now.

"The main house is about three thousand square feet, with four guest rooms, and then I have three guest cottages that are each around eight hundred square feet."

"Do you do all of the cooking and cleaning yourself?"

Corrine nodded. "It wasn't so bad when I was younger or when Jack was alive and Riley was home, but since it's only me... Well, I believe all of that contributed to the osteoarthritis and this hip replacement."

"Why don't you hire someone to at least do the cleaning portion?"

"I could, but it's hard to admit I can't take care of it on my own anymore. It's been my entire life. The thought of strangers working here isn't easy to come to grips with."

"What about your son?"

"I'm hoping that once he's done with the military he'll come home, get married, and take it over." Her eyes welled with tears. "He's never made it a secret that it's not what he wants to do with his life, but there's still a small part of me that prays he'll change his mind. If I can't deal with strangers coming in to clean, how will I handle selling my beloved home to strangers to run? To live there?"

Grace squeezed her friend's hand. "I can't even imagine, but I'm still not sure how I fit into all of this."

"Grace, you have become a very dear friend to me. I know we only met a few weeks ago, but...you're like the daughter I never had." Corrine's voice clogged with emotion. "Jack and I always thought we'd have more children, but that wasn't in the cards. I love Riley and I miss him so much, but this was never his dream. I think pushing him about it made him enlist in the marines as soon as he graduated from high school."

"I'm sure that's not true," Grace began but Corrine cut her off.

"I don't try to kid myself. I pushed a lot, started making plans for him to take over, and the next thing I knew, he was leaving for Parris Island." She stopped and composed herself. "I don't know when he's coming home, or if he ever will. We don't talk much. I know mainly because he's been in Afghanistan, but there's always the possibility…"

"Corrine," Grace said softly, "don't think like that. He'll come back. I'm sure of it." She actually wasn't, but she needed to say something to comfort her friend. "You never know. He might come home after years of combat and decide running a bed-and-breakfast is exactly what he wants to do."

Corrine looked at her doubtfully. "From your lips to God's ears." The two women smiled at one another. "The thing is, Grace, I really do need the help, and I believe you are the perfect person. You are a hard worker and a fabulous cook, and really, I've been doing this for so long that it might be a good thing to have a fresh set of eyes to see what I can to do put a little life back in the place."

Grace's heart beat frantically. It was everything she could ever dream of. A bed-and-breakfast had been on her list of possibilities for her future, but she never thought she'd be able to have one. The thought of running her own kitchen and catering to a small clientele was practically making her giddy. While she knew the place wouldn't technically be hers, Grace was certain she and Corrine would work together beautifully.

She looked up and met Corrine's hopeful gaze. "You're on."

That had been eight weeks ago, and when Grace had showed up at the Snowflake Inn six weeks ago, it had been love at first sight. The house looked like something off of a winter postcard, and the thought of decorating it for Christmas—heck, the thought of having a *home* for Christmas—was more than Grace had dared to let herself dream of.

Now, sitting on the sofa while Corrine went to get her some ice for her knee, Grace really felt a sense of belonging. The Snowflake Inn was like no place she had ever seen before. It enveloped you, soothed you. It was as if the structure itself really loved you. In her twenty-eight years of life, Grace had never lived anywhere that felt quite so right. She had lived in beautiful homes with her parents, but to her, they were showplaces that always felt cold and unwelcoming. But this? This was a home.

Grace jumped when Corrine placed the ice on her knee. She had been so lost in her thoughts that she hadn't heard Corrine come back into the room. "Thank you," she said with a sigh as she relaxed back on the cushions. "I'm sorry to be such a bother."

The older woman merely made a tsking sound. "Nonsense. I know that I do more than I should here some days. But luckily, I catch myself before I do too much harm."

"I hope I learn to catch myself," Grace said with a chuckle. "So what's on the agenda today?"

Corrine sat beside her. "Well, we don't have guests coming until Friday, so that gives us three days to finish sprucing up the place." Since Grace's arrival, they had spent most of their days refreshing the inn. There had been guests every weekend, but during the week, the two of them had painted and made minor renovations with the help of Ben and some local college students. "There's not too much left to do. The cabins are the last ones on the list, and we don't have anyone booked for them until next month."

"Perfect," Grace said. "I hope my knee doesn't slow us down."

"Don't worry about that. You know Ben and the crew can handle the heavy stuff. I want you to make sure the kitchen is the way you want it. Make a list of anything else you need, and I'll go shopping for it."

"Corrine..." Grace began.

"Stop. I consider you to be my partner in this now." That discussion had taken place recently. Corrine knew the chances of her son coming home and taking over were between slim and none, but she still wasn't ready to sell the place or to take on a formal partner, even though Grace had made the offer and had the money ready to make good on it. Instead, they had agreed that Grace would lend Corrine the money to do the renovations, but it would be paid back. They were informal partners, and who knew? Maybe someday they would make the necessary changes to become formal business partners.

"I'm more than ready to do that, Corrine. You know that."

"I do, and I'm sorry if I'm making you feel like I don't appreciate the offer."

"I know you have your reasons, and I'm not planning on going anywhere."

Corrine smiled. "I'm so thankful for you, Grace. You not only helped to breathe new life into the inn, but you've encouraged me to be an active participant in my own life again."

"You were always an active participant, my friend. You just forgot to go out and have fun once in a while."

"Well, whatever the reason, I want you to know I appreciate you." They sat back in companionable silence and then heard a knock at the door. Corrine stood. "I'll get that." She made her way to the door and then stopped dead in her tracks. Clearly she was seeing things. It wasn't possible.

Grace turned and noticed Corrine's still form in the entryway. "Corrine? Are you okay?" She tried to stand and grimaced at the pain in her leg.

"It's not possible," Corrine whispered, a hand lying across her heart.

"Corrine? You're scaring me. Who is it?"

She turned toward Grace, her complexion pale. "It's Jack."

Chapter 3

GRACE STOOD IN SILENT CONFUSION FOR A MOMENT. "Jack? Corrine, sweetheart, you have to be confused." Before she could say another word, she saw her friend walk toward the door. Grace slowly made her way to the entryway to see who was there.

Corrine opened the door and gasped. "Riley?" she whispered. "Is it really you?"

"Hi, Mom," a deep voice replied. Grace couldn't see him because the front door was obstructing her view, but he sounded vaguely familiar.

"I can't believe you're really here. How long are you home for?"

Riley didn't answer. He didn't want to be locked into any kind of commitment at this point. Instead of answering, he stepped inside and wrapped his mother in his embrace and then stilled when he felt her sobbing. "Mom..." he began.

Corrine lifted her head. "When I saw you through the glass panel, I thought you were your father. I can't believe how much you look like him. It seemed more plausible to me that he'd be here than that you were actually home. Why didn't you call and tell me you were coming home?"

He smiled at her. "I wanted to surprise you." It wasn't a total lie. With the surprise tactic, Riley was able to put off the list of never-ending questions he was sure he was about to get. He released her long enough to reach for his duffel bag. "Can I come in?"

"Oh my goodness," she gasped and then laughed. "Of course! I can't believe I let you stand out there in the cold for so long!" She bustled out of the way as Riley stepped into the entryway and then closed the door behind him. "Welcome home!" She hugged him again because she simply couldn't help herself. "Come in, come in. Are you hungry? Thirsty? What can I get you?"

Riley chuckled. "I'm fine, Mom. Relax. Let's just sit down."

And that's when he saw her. The redhead, the woman from the park. The woman who Riley knew was going to be here at the inn, and yet seeing her still sent a jolt of surprise through him. He nodded his head in her direction and saw her blush.

The closer he got, the harder Grace's heart beat. She was on the verge of hyperventilating when he stopped in front of her. "How's your knee?" he asked softly, and she almost melted into a puddle at this feet.

"Better," she said shyly. He nodded and walked into the living room where he placed his duffel bag in a corner before sitting in the nearest chair. Not knowing what else to do, Grace joined him in waiting for Corrine, who had gone to get refreshments even though no one wanted any.

Sitting on the sofa, Grace took a moment to compose herself. "So," she began nervously, "you're Riley."

He nodded. "And you are?"

"Grace. Grace Brodie."

Riley couldn't take his eyes off of her. The name fit her, and it seemed odd that after only watching her for a few days, he felt more at ease with her than he had ever felt with anyone else. "So, do you...work here?"

Grace smiled. "I do. I started working for your mom about six weeks ago. She's the reason I moved here."

Riley was about to respond when his mother came back into the room carrying a tray of cookies and, if he wasn't mistaken, her famous hot chocolate. Damn, he had forgotten how much he used to love that.

"I met Grace during my rehab for my hip. She's been a real lifesaver for me," Corrine said as she handed each of them a steaming mug of cocoa. Placing a tray of cookies on the table between them all, she sat on the sofa beside Grace and beamed at her son. "I can't believe you're here. I know I keep saying it, but it still hasn't hit me yet."

"I know I should have called," he began, realizing that his surprise arrival probably had his mother feeling more anxious than if she'd had the time to prepare for him.

"It doesn't matter. All that matters is you're home." Grace watched her friend drink in the sight of her son. "How long are you home for? When do you have to report back?"

It's now or never... "Actually," he began hesitantly, "I don't have to report back."

Corrine stared at him blankly. "I don't understand... Are you... Does this mean...?"

Riley gave a small smile. "It means that I'm no longer employed by Uncle Sam. I'm back to being a civilian again."

His mother jumped to her feet as she clamped a hand over her heart. "Oh, Riley," she cried, "I never thought this day would come!" She looked at her son and then at Grace, who had tears welling in her own eyes. Corrine turned back to Riley. "I didn't realize you were due. I thought you had a few more years, and even then I thought you'd reenlist."

He shifted in his seat. "Well, about two months ago I was over in Afghanistan and…"

Corrine dropped back onto the sofa. "You were hurt," she whispered.

He nodded. "Roadside bomb. I was far enough back that I wasn't in the immediate blast zone, but"—he swallowed hard—"we lost a lot of men that day."

"What happened to you?" Corrine asked cautiously.

"I was thrown pretty far, had debris land on me. Broke my shoulder, several ribs, and…well, was shot several times."

"Shot?" she asked in horror. "But…you said there was a bomb…"

Riley shrugged. "I guess they wanted to make sure that no one was missed," he said. "I could have stayed in the marines, but I would never be deployed again. It was just time for me to go."

"Oh, Riley… Why didn't you call? Why didn't anyone let me know?"

"You were dealing with your own surgery, and although my injuries were bad, they weren't life-threatening," he lied. "I didn't want to upset you. I knew that you were nervous about what you were going through and worried about the inn and how you were going to handle it all while you were recovering. I didn't want to add to that."

"I still should have known," Corrine said adamantly.

"I can see that now," he admitted. "And I'm sorry."

Corrine inhaled deeply and let her breath out slowly. "None of that matters," she said, putting a smile back on her face. "You're home now, and everything is going to be okay."

Riley was afraid to comment on that. He knew that in terms of his recovery, yes, everything was going to be okay. But beyond that? He wasn't sure he was ready to look that far ahead. "How are you feeling, Mom?"

"Oh, I'm fine. Moving a little slower than I'm used to. Grace and I were just discussing that before you knocked. Between the two of us, we've gotten so much done around here to prepare for the holidays, but even then, we've had to have Ben and some local college kids here to help out."

"Well, I'm more than willing to help out while I'm here."

Corrine didn't miss the implications of the statement. "You're not planning on staying, are you?" she asked sadly.

"We'll talk about that later," Riley said. "When we're alone." He looked directly at Grace.

Corrine didn't miss that, either. "Grace is well aware of everything concerning the inn, Riley. She wants to become a partner, but I haven't agreed yet. I was hoping you and I could still… Well, that you'd be open to discussing it."

"Mom, we've had this discussion a hundred times. And now, with your surgery and recovery, isn't this all too much for you? Don't you think it's time to think about yourself? Aren't you tired of working all the time? Wouldn't you like to have a life of your own?"

She stiffened at his words. "I have a life of my own, Riley. I have friends, and I'm involved in just about everything that goes on in this community. There's nothing wrong with my life!" Her tone rose with every word.

Doing her best to blend into the background, Grace started to get up from the sofa. Corrine turned and looked at her. "I think I'll head into the kitchen—" Grace began, but Corrine cut her off.

"Don't feel like you have to leave," she said quietly. Then she turned back to her son. "You've been gone a long time, Riley. You have no idea what my life is like here now. This isn't something we're going to decide right now. Why don't we just let it lie for now and spend some time reconnecting with one another? Okay?"

Riley nodded, but he knew the end result would be the same. He was going to leave, and his mother was going to be disappointed.

—☙—

Grace had gone through the kitchen with a fine-tooth comb and had her wish list ready. The kitchen was fine on its own, but doing the things she wanted to do and creating the meals she dreamed of creating would require a little something.

Leaving Corrine and Riley in the living room had been a bit awkward, but she knew it was for the best. Mother and son had a lot of time to make up for, and she certainly didn't want to be the third wheel hindering their reunion.

With the kitchen project under control, Grace left her list on the counter and went to the basement, where her apartment was. At first Corrine had wanted Grace to take one of the cottages, but they were still in need of renovating, so she had opted for the basement. Truth be known, the basement could use quite the rehab itself, but it gave Grace the opportunity to have some privacy and yet be accessible to guests at a moment's notice.

Her knee wasn't feeling nearly as bad as it had that morning, but that was mainly because after she had gone to the kitchen, she'd put a heating pad on it, downed some ibuprofen, and worked from a stool most of the time. What she really wanted was to soak in the hot tub, but that would have to wait until later. Right now, all she wanted was to grab a hot shower and then make lunch for everyone.

The shower didn't take long, but it had the desired effect. Although she wasn't willing to admit it to herself, she spent a little extra time fixing herself up. Using all the tools at her disposal, Grace straightened her hair until it looked like something out of a hair-care commercial. Then she did her best to use just enough makeup to make her look attractive while still going for the natural look.

It was exhausting.

Climbing the stairs, she began to hear raised voices.

Not a good sign.

"I don't see where you get to have a say in this, Riley," Corrine said sharply.

"You're just delaying the inevitable, Mom. It doesn't matter what this woman is doing here; you cannot keep this place forever."

"If you have no interest in taking over the business, then it really shouldn't concern you how I run it." Corrine stopped, and her voice calmed. "I really did not want to spend your first day home arguing, Riley. Why can't we just let this go for now? Why must you keep harping on it?"

"Because I don't like to think of you working so damn hard! I hate that you feel the need to keep fighting an uphill battle when it's not necessary. You can sell this place and live comfortably for the rest of your life."

"That's where you're wrong. I don't see this as an uphill battle. I love this place. I've always loved this place, and no matter what you think, you'll never convince me to think otherwise. Grace is my friend, and she's been invaluable to me. The guests love her, the people in town love her, and as far as I'm concerned, as long as there is breath in my body and she is willing to help me, I'm staying right here."

Uh-oh, Grace thought. *There's a surefire strategy to get the man to hate me.*

"We'll talk about this later," Riley finally said, and Grace could hear the frustration in his voice.

Tiptoeing along the hall, she made her way into the kitchen and immediately began to prepare lunch for everyone. It was almost time for Ben to come in, and it would be nice to have another buffer. If it were up to her, she'd give Mr. Riley Walsh a piece of her mind. How dare he tell Corrine to sell the place! Didn't he realize how much his mother loved the inn? How could he be so heartless?

Looks aren't everything, she thought as she realized that no matter how attractive Riley was physically, it didn't seem to make him a nice person. That was too bad because he had been really nice to her earlier. She sighed. *What a waste.*

Before long, she heard Ben's footsteps on the outside deck right before he came in through the kitchen door. "There's my angel!" he said cheerfully as he walked across the room like he did every day and hugged her. For as much as Corrine had become a mother figure to her, Ben had easily slid into the father-figure slot. "How's my girl today?"

She told him about the mishap with her knee but left out who'd come to her rescue and the fact that they had an extra guest in the house. She wanted to leave that for Corrine to tell him. "How is cottage number one coming along?"

Ben shrugged out of his flannel jacket and ran a hand through his silver hair. His blue eyes seemed to twinkle with amusement. "As much as I fuss about not ever enjoying the construction business, I have to admit I still get a kick out of doing some carpentry work."

"Anything exciting that needs to be done?"

He shrugged and reached for an apple Grace had placed in the large basket she kept on the corner of her butcher-block island. "Some rotting on the roof, some stones loose on the chimney, but I'm thinking of adding some bookshelves to the cottages on either side of the fireplace. What do you think? Think Corrine will like that?"

It was a question he asked her often. With every idea he came up with, Ben would always ask Grace if she thought Corrine would like it. That made her laugh, because he'd clearly known Corrine much longer than she had, and yet he wanted nothing more than to please her.

"I think it's a lovely idea, and I'm sure she will too," Grace said with a smile.

"So what's on the menu today?"

"Today we are trying a loaded potato soup, ham-and-Swiss paninis, and a field greens salad with a honey-mustard vinaigrette. How does that sound?"

"Like I just gained twelve pounds," he said with a laugh. The sound of a door slamming had Ben turning first toward the sound and then back to Grace. "Do we have a guest?"

Grace was just about to answer when Corrine walked in. "Everything okay?" Grace asked hesitantly.

Rather than answering, Corrine sat on the nearest stool, placed her face in her hands, and seemed to try to catch her breath. Ben was immediately at her side. "Corrine? What's going on?" When she didn't answer, he looked to Grace again. "Grace?"

She hated being in the middle of this. "Riley came home," she finally said and watched the look of shock on Ben's face.

"I can't believe it," he said softly. "Corrine, why didn't you mention he was coming home?"

Corrine raised her face and looked at him. "He wanted to surprise me," she said sadly.

Ben looked back and forth between the two women, confusion written all over his face. "Where is he?"

"He left," Corrine said flatly.

Grace dropped the spoon she had been using to stir the soup. "Already? Why?"

"He just wouldn't drop the topic of me selling the inn. No matter how much I tried to say we could talk about it later and that I wanted to just talk about him and hear about his life, he was hell-bent on settling things once and for all where this place is concerned."

"Why does he want you to sell?" Ben asked. "I mean, I know he doesn't want it, but why should that mean you have to sell it?"

"Probably to clear his own conscience," Grace muttered and then instantly regretted her words when both Ben and Corrine looked up at her in horror. "Sorry."

Corrine sighed. "Nothing for you to apologize for. You're one hundred percent right. If the inn was gone, he wouldn't have to think about it. He'd be able to go about his life and not worry about avoiding this place."

"I still don't see why he's carrying on," Ben said. "If you told him it's okay for him to not want the place, then why keep fighting about it?"

"Like Grace said, to clear his conscience. I told him that I'm okay with him not taking over, but that's not enough. He hates this place, and he doesn't want to have to feel guilty about not running it if he comes here."

"Well, that's just crazy," Ben said and went to set the table for lunch.

"Maybe Riley is right," Corrine said sadly. "Maybe if I really want to have a relationship with him, I need to let go of this place. I probably should have done that after Jack died. I didn't realize how much Riley hated it, and it's doing nothing but putting a bigger and bigger rift between us. We've already lost so much time. Do I really want to lose more?"

"Corrine, you're talking crazy. Riley is a grown man. He is going to have to deal with the fact that this is your home, and you'll sell it or leave it when you're ready. You didn't like the fact that he joined the marines, but that didn't make him quit, did it?" Grace pointed out.

"No, it didn't."

"So why should you have to give up your life to make him feel better?"

Corrine looked up at Grace and smiled sadly. "Because that's what you do when you're a mother. You make sacrifices."

Ben silently kept working on getting their lunch plated while the two women continued to talk.

"Look," Grace said. "I know I'm not a mother, so I don't have the same perspective as you, but I don't believe you should have to make sacrifices for a grown man. If Riley were a child and he was this miserable, and owning this inn was detrimental to his well-being, then yes, maybe you should sell it. But that's not the case. He's here for a visit, and then he's going to leave to do whatever he wants with his life. Where does that leave you? Why does he get to have his way when he's not going to stick around?"

"Lunch is ready," Ben said as he helped Corrine from the stool and led her to the table. "Grace has a point, Corri. If Riley is planning on leaving in a week or two, why do you have to uproot your life? Is he asking you to move with him wherever he goes?"

"No."

"Then he seems to be making some pretty unreasonable demands."

"What he is, is a spoiled brat," Grace said, and this time she wasn't the least bit sorry. No one corrected her, which made her feel a little better.

"So where did he go?" Ben finally asked.

"Just for a walk, I think," Corrine said as she sat down. "He didn't take his bag, and his truck is still out front, so I guess he's just taking a breather."

Grace almost excused herself to go and find the man, but she thought better of it. In her current frame of mind, she wanted to tell Riley off, but that wouldn't help anyone. She hated to see her friend hurting like this, but if she was honest with herself, she would admit she also hated that Riley was threatening her chance to have the job and home she'd always wanted.

There was no way Grace could afford to buy the Snowflake Inn right now. She had money put aside for a business, but not nearly enough for one of this magnitude. The money that she had inherited when her parents died was well invested, and Grace knew there was enough for her to buy a small business. But twenty acres of prime real estate? Not likely. And if she had to take a guess, she could imagine that if Riley forced Corrine to sell, he'd want her to sell for top dollar.

She hated him already.

It didn't matter that this was all just conjecture. Grace had a gut instinct that this man was going to be the reason she lost her dream.

"Grace? Are you all right?" Ben asked.

"Huh? What?" she asked. "I'm fine. Why?"

"You look pretty fierce over there."

"I'm sorry. I'm just thinking about this whole situation, and it doesn't seem fair that we've done all this work for nothing." The look of devastation on Corrine's face almost made Grace regret her words, but she wasn't going to take them back. It was the truth. They had made plans for this place—plans for the holidays—and in a matter of hours, Riley Walsh had marched home and ruined them all.

"It's not a done deal yet," Ben said. "Right, Corri?"

Corrine forced a smile. "No, it's not over yet." She didn't have much conviction behind the words.

"Okay, no more of this depressing talk," Ben said. "Grace, this soup is amazing! It's perfect for a cold winter day."

She beamed at the praise. "Thank you. I was hoping you'd like it. You're my ultimate food critic."

"Me? Why?" he laughed.

"Because I know Corrine is a fabulous cook, and you've been eating with her for years. So if you like what I'm making, then I know I'm doing a good job."

"Oh, you're sweet," Corrine said. "I think I got bored with cooking years ago. I stopped getting creative and stuck with the basics. It's wonderful to think about having such a creative force in the kitchen. I think guests are really going to enjoy that."

"That's what I'm hoping for."

They spoke about menus and Ben's ideas for the cottages and kept the conversation light. However, the sound of the front door opening and closing seemed to kill the mood.

Riley walked into the kitchen and stopped short at the sight of the three of them around the table. Corrine jumped up to make him a plate. "Are you hungry? Grace prepared some wonderful soup and sandwiches—"

"No thanks," he said a little gruffly. "I stopped in town on my way here and ate."

If Grace didn't already have negative feelings toward him, she would have now. How dare he eat in town when she had prepared a damn masterpiece for them! Ben must have sensed her thoughts because he reached out and placed his hand over hers. She glanced at him and tried to smile, but she couldn't help glaring at Riley over the insult he had no idea he had issued.

Corrine seemed a little deflated but came back to her seat to finish her meal. Ben looked back and forth between the two women and tried to make the extremely awkward moment a little less...awkward.

"So, Riley," Ben said as he stood and walked over to shake Riley's hand, "it's good to see you. Come and sit with us while we finish our lunch and get me caught up on where you've been."

While Riley wasn't keen on talking about his last months in the service, he had plenty of other stories he could tell, and his service life seemed like the only topic safe to discuss. He noticed Grace wouldn't even look at him, and his mother seemed a little nervous. Great, less than a day home, and he'd already managed to disappoint everyone.

Taking a seat, he focused on Ben and told him about his travels and the hell of war. Because they were in mixed company who happened to be eating, he chose to leave out the more gruesome details and instead focused on his day-to-day life.

"I'm sure you're glad to not have to go back to that," Ben finally said when Riley was done.

"I would have gone back, but after this last tour, it wasn't ever going to happen. I didn't want to be a desk-job kind of guy."

"So what are your plans?" Ben asked hesitantly.

Riley shifted uncomfortably in his seat and felt all three of them suddenly staring at him. He cleared his throat. "Um...well, I have a couple of friends in Virginia I was hoping to go see, and another couple living in

Florida who I plan to visit too. After that, I'll be honest with you, I'm not sure." He looked directly at Ben. "Do you still have the construction business?"

Ben shook his head. "No, I sold that about four years ago. That's a younger man's game. Like I told your mother, I much prefer working with the land. I should have had a landscaping company." He shook his head again. "Hindsight and all that."

"Well, you're doing that now," Riley said with a small smile. "The grounds look great."

"Thanks. I appreciate that." He smiled back at the younger Walsh. "I still do some carpentry around here, minor repairs and that sort of thing."

"Everything really looks great, Ben. Honestly. I know I haven't even scratched the surface on what's here, but it looks better than I remembered."

"Ben works very hard," Corrine said, her voice laced with pride. "I don't think I could have managed without him." She looked at Ben and saw the effect her words had on him. "I mean…"

Ben placed his hand over hers. "Thank you. You've let me live out the career path I should have taken, so really, we're helping each other out." They gazed at one another until Grace cleared her voice.

"Well, I don't know about you, but we've been sitting here way longer than we should have, and I know there are things to do." She lifted her plate and turned to Corrine. "I made the list we talked about. It's on the counter. If you'd like, we can take a ride into town and shop."

"Actually," Ben interrupted, "I need to hit the home improvement store for some supplies. If it's okay with you, Grace, I'll take Corrine and get what you need."

"Oh," she said, feeling a little displaced. The last thing she wanted to do was be stuck here with Riley. Grace had a feeling that, if left to her own devices, she was going to get into a heated exchange of words with him and make the situation even worse. But one look at Ben and Corinne, and she couldn't possibly object. "That's fine. I've got plenty to do here."

She had nothing.

"Well, the least we can do is help with the cleanup before we go," Corrine said, but Grace stopped her.

"No need. I've got this. You guys are doing me a favor by getting all of the kitchen stuff for me."

"If you're sure…"

Grace nodded. "Positive. You two go and shop. I've got a fabulous dinner planned, so just make sure you're back in time."

"You know I can't wait," Ben said with a smile as he placed a hand on Corinne's back and escorted her from the room, leaving Grace and Riley alone.

Grace didn't even pretend to be cordial. She went about clearing away the dishes and setting them in the dishwasher before putting the leftover food in the refrigerator. Riley sat in his seat and watched her every move. She wanted to scream for him to leave, but instead she used every ounce of her self-control to keep doing what she was doing and pretend he wasn't there.

"It's killing you that I'm still here, isn't it?" he finally said, and she nearly jumped out of her own skin.

"Sheesh, you scared me," she said, willing her rapidly beating heart to calm down. "Actually, I had forgotten you were even here. Which leads me to ask—*why* are you still here?"

"Where should I go?"

There was a loaded question if she'd ever heard one. She must have smirked because she heard Riley laugh. "Something funny?" she asked.

"You," he said simply. "Your face is an open book. There's no way you could possibly play poker."

"My face is not an open book," she snapped. "You don't know what you're talking about."

"Oh really? You're going to stand here and tell me you weren't just thinking of a colorful retort to my question of where I should go? That you weren't dying to tell me exactly *where* you thought I should go?"

There was no way to hide her guilty blush. Dammit. "Fine," she said defensively. "You're right. I was thinking of several options for where you should go, but I decided to keep them to myself. Things are awkward enough around here today without me adding to them."

"Give it your best shot, Red," he said, leaning back in his chair and crossing his arms over his chest.

"Excuse me?"

"Go ahead and tell me what's on your mind. I prefer it when people are honest. I don't like to play games. If you have something to say to me, then say it."

"It's not necessary, Riley," Grace said as she turned around. And screamed. "Seriously?" she cried. "How did you move so fast?" He was right behind her, and she had to press her back against the refrigerator door to keep an inch of space between them.

"Military trick. Can't let the enemy know when you're approaching."

"I'm not the enemy here," Grace said, hating the slight tremor in her voice.

"Neither am I," he said with ease and then laughed at the look on Grace's face. He placed a finger under her chin to force her to keep looking up at him. "Open book," he teased. "Now, are you sure you don't have something to say?"

For just a moment, Grace had forgotten she was supposed to be mad at him. For just an instant, when she turned around and saw how close he was, she wanted to press closer to him like she had been this morning in the park. But once he opened his mouth, all of the reasons she hated him came flooding back.

With more bravado than she actually felt, Grace shoved his hand away from her face and did her best to stand a little taller. But since Riley was over six feet tall and she barely reached five foot five, she'd have to stand on a damn chair to make a difference.

"Fine, you want to know what I'm thinking?"

"Sweetheart, I already *know* what you're thinking. I just want to see if you have the guts to say it out loud."

His arrogance simply added to her anger. "I think you're a terrible son." Riley arched a brow at her words. "That's right," she said, the tremble still there. "A. Terrible. Son. You have no idea what your mother has been going through. All the time she was in that rehab facility, she not only had to battle for her recovery, but she also battled depression."

"What?" he asked with disbelief. "What the hell are you talking about?"

Grace found the strength to shove past him so that she could move around the room. "Every day, that place was flooded with family members coming to visit, and every day, she sat by herself."

"Why? Where was Ben?"

"He was here making sure that the inn was being taken care of. It damn near killed her to close this place for eight weeks. She was scared she'd lose clients and that the season would be ruined. Luckily, the community rallied around her, and they've all been doing free advertising for her since she's been home." She paused a moment and took a drink of water before continuing.

"Her progress was slow because her heart wasn't in it, and not once, *not once*," she added for dramatic effect, "did her son bother to call to check on her recovery."

"I was in the damn hospital myself!" he shouted. "How the hell was I supposed to call her while I was unconscious?"

"Don't be obtuse, Riley," she snapped back. "She didn't know you were in the hospital, but maybe if she had, it would have given her a reason to get stronger faster. She would have had something to work toward."

"That's the most ridiculous thing I've ever heard. Thank God you're a cook and not a psychologist."

"No, the most ridiculous thing I ever heard was you telling your mother she needed to sell her childhood home, her livelihood, so you could walk away with a clear conscience."

"I never said that!"

"You didn't have to!" she yelled back. "News flash, Ace: your mother already knows you don't want anything to do with this place. She may not have made peace with it, but she knows it, and since you've been back, you've made sure you hammered the point home. No one's asking you to stay, hotshot. But why should she have to give up what she loves to do and the only home she's ever known when you're not asking her to come with you?"

"I never said—"

"Oh, shut up," Grace said with disgust and walked out of the kitchen. Riley was right behind her and grabbed her by the arm. She immediately pulled out of his grip. "Don't you dare touch me," she spat out. "You show up here with no warning and try to turn your mother's world upside down for your own selfish reasons." She looked at him with contempt. "Uncle Sam would be so proud."

Riley didn't let her take even one step away from him before he grabbed her, spun her around, and had her pinned against the wall. Grace's breathing was ragged and so was his. He felt rage at her words, and not because she was wrong, but because she was right. As he took in her ivory complexion, he noticed that her green eyes were wide as she looked up at him. "I've had just about enough of the insults and name-calling," he growled.

"You were the one who said you wanted honest," she reminded him, her chest heaving against his.

He nodded. "I'm used to arguing with men who just say what's on their mind and move on. You made it personal."

"This is personal to me," Grace said firmly. "Corinne is my friend, and this is now my home. Your arrival here has not only upset someone who means the world to me, but you're also threatening where I live. So you see? Personal."

"You've only been here six weeks, Grace. It's not like you've put down roots here. Go home to your parents, your family. It's not like you're homeless." The

look of utter devastation on her face told him he had
just said something horribly wrong. She shoved at his
chest to get away, and Riley saw the tears welling up
in her eyes. He cursed himself, but he didn't move. He
whispered her name and smiled as she shoved at him
again while cursing him.

Not sure of what else to do, he wrapped her in his
arms. Two things instantly occurred to him: one, she
felt really, really good there, and two, she'd stopped
struggling. He whispered her name again along with
an apology.

"Why did you have to come back now?" she said, her
voice muffled against his chest.

"Tell me what I said to upset you."

Grace looked up at him with disbelief. "Everything
you've said since you arrived has upset me."

Riley shook his head. "Just now. Tell me what I
said just now that upset you." He wiped the tears on
her cheeks away with his thumbs while he waited for
an answer.

"I lost my parents ten years ago in a boating accident.
I had just graduated from high school. We didn't have
a large family, and there really wasn't anyone there for
me. I literally lost everything. I took my inheritance
and the money from their life insurance, and I vowed
to make something of myself. I went to college and
culinary school and eventually found myself working in
New York." Taking a cleansing breath, she continued.
"I had worked and studied so hard for so long that when
I finally had the chance to get away for a couple of days
with some friends to go skiing, I jumped at the chance.
And then I lost everything again."

"What happened?"

"It had been a long time since I'd gone skiing. I was overconfident in my abilities. I was on an expert run when I basically should have been on the bunny hill. I fell. Badly. I broke my leg in four places. By the time I got through surgery and rehab, I no longer had a job or a home." She shrugged and tried to break free of his embrace, but he held on to her. "I took a job as a cook at the rehab facility because it came with free room and board."

Riley cursed himself. So basically he had hit every sore spot. She was an orphan and homeless without this job. Dammit. He was about to apologize when Grace started talking again.

"I sympathized with your mom when I met her because just a few months prior, that had been me. I felt like I was the only one there with no one coming to visit me. I'm sure it wasn't the case, but it sure felt like it. We gravitated toward each other and found we had a lot in common." She looked up at him, her green eyes shining with unshed tears. "She's willing to sell this place to give you peace, but what does that leave her?"

If a gun were pointed at his head, Riley couldn't have answered that question. Not only because he honestly didn't know what to say, but because the woman looking up at him was so damn beautiful that she simply stole his breath. He knew the instant Grace stopped thinking about their conversation and noticed he had moved just a hint closer. Her eyes widened slightly, and she lightly licked her lips, and he nearly groaned out loud.

Riley knew Grace was beautiful. Hell, it was one of the reasons he kept following her. She intrigued him, and he couldn't seem to help himself. But now, with her standing here in his arms? Everything about her called to him. So he did the only thing he could do.

He kissed her.

Chapter 4

THE MOMENT RILEY'S LIPS TOUCHED HERS, GRACE WAS a goner. For all of their harsh words from moments ago, she couldn't have recalled one of them to save her life. His lips were firm but gentle on hers, and as his hands skimmed up from her waist to the swell of her breasts, she thought she had died and gone to heaven. When those large hands came up and gently caressed her face and then lingered there, she all but purred.

The gentle teasing of lips and the silky glide of fingers were well and good, but she was a woman with some pent-up frustration—it had been a *really* long time since her last boyfriend—and gentle and teasing was not what she wanted, certainly not from a man who looked and felt like Riley Walsh.

Taking the initiative, Grace nipped at his bottom lip, and when his mouth opened ever so slightly, she licked at where she had just bitten and then touched her tongue to his. She was feeling rather proud of herself— and rather aroused—when Riley took the reins. Gone were the gentle kisses of a minute ago, and in their place was an all-consuming kiss that was more sexual than anything Grace had ever experienced before. While he made love to her mouth, his hands began to wander and caress and squeeze, and all she wanted to do was to wrap her legs around him and hold on for dear life.

She let out a cry of dismay when Riley's lips left

hers. But she was instantly soothed when she felt him press more firmly against her as his wicked mouth lingered on her cheek before finding the rapid pulse in her neck and running his tongue over it. Reaching up, Riley moved her glorious mane of hair aside so he could taste more of her. He heard her purr of delight, and it was the most erotic sound he'd ever heard.

This was simply madness. He didn't know this woman, which wasn't something that had ever bothered him before. But for some reason, he didn't want to treat Grace like any other woman he had ever known. Beside the fact that she worked for his mother and he would be forced to see her for as long as he was staying there, he didn't think sex up against the wall within the first six hours of meeting her was something she deserved.

Reluctantly, he pulled back, forced his mouth from her soft skin, and growled with frustration. He straightened and looked at her. Grace's lips were swollen and her eyes were closed and her breathing was harsh. Before he could question his motives, he went back in for another kiss and felt nothing but pleasure when she instantly opened her mouth to his, her tongue dueling with his until he thought he'd lose his mind. Grace's hand raked through his short hair, and he felt her growl of frustration at having nothing to hold on to.

Reaching down, he lifted her, and her gasp of surprise made him smile. Instantly, she wrapped her legs around him, and that seemed to make up for his buzz cut. Riley slanted his mouth over hers again and again, unable to get enough. Grace's fingers dug into his shoulders, her body pulsing against his as he ground his arousal against the very core of her.

"Riley," she whispered as she pulled her mouth from his to catch her breath. He leaned his forehead against hers and waited to see if she'd say anything else. The only sound was their breathing, and Riley wasn't sure if it was a blessing or a curse.

His hands gently kneaded her bottom as he got his breathing under control, and Grace didn't seem in any rush to be back on her feet. He saw her swallow before she looked up and let her gaze meet his. "That was... intense," she finally said.

He smiled. A genuine smile. "That's an understatement," he countered.

"I don't normally...do...this sort of thing." A blush crept up her cheeks at her admission, but she continued to hold his steady gaze.

"You don't normally kiss like someone who enjoys being kissed?" he teased.

She chuckled. "No, I don't normally maul the guests."

"Well, to be fair, I'm not really a guest," he said, trying to lighten the mood but still unwilling to let her go.

Grace looked at where their bodies were molded together and groaned. "This shouldn't have happened. It's not a very good idea."

Unable to help himself, he placed a gentle kiss on her cheek. "Tell me why."

At that moment, she really had no idea why, so she decided to just rest her cheek against his until her brain started functioning again. "You're trying to ruin Corinne's life," she finally said and then regretted her words when Riley lowered her to her feet.

He took a step back. "I'm not trying to ruin her life, Grace," he said quietly, patiently. "I've watched her work herself harder than she needs to. I would love to know that someone is taking care of her, that she's not cleaning up after people all day, every day. When is it going to be her turn?"

Grace looked up at him sadly. "You really don't know your mother at all," she said simply. "She takes pride in what she does, and she loves interacting with her guests. This house means the world to her. She's never looked at this place as a job, Riley. It's who she is."

She was right; he didn't really know his mother. In all his years growing up here, he'd seen this place as a prison, but that was his own perspective. No family vacations, no privacy, always having to be on his best behavior for the sake of the guests. It was hell. He'd never bothered to look at it from his mother's position though. While he always heard the way Corinne talked about the inn, he'd never really *listened*.

"I can't help the way I feel, Grace," he finally said. "I always hoped that Mom would meet someone, get married, and have him take care of her since I wasn't here. That's never going to happen if she never leaves this place."

Grace let out a small laugh. "You really need to stick around for a couple of days and then remember you said that."

"What? Why?"

She waved him off and found the strength to step away from him. "It's not my place to say. Just…stick around for a few days, and don't think about the inn. Don't think about responsibilities. Just…observe."

"I have no idea what you're talking about, Grace," he said with a hint of frustration.

"Trust me, Riley. Spend some time with your mom when the subject of inn ownership doesn't come up. I think you'll be surprised at what you learn." And with that, Grace did manage the exit she had hoped for earlier in the day. With a sassy swing to her hips, she walked away from Riley Walsh.

And missed the smile he couldn't hide.

Ben and Corrine got back from shopping minutes before Grace was ready to put dinner on the table. She had been more than a little worried that she and Riley were going to be the only ones there, and she wasn't ready for more one-on-one time with him.

Once she had walked away from him and made her way to her apartment, Grace had to wonder what in the world had gotten into her. She'd never thrown herself at a man the way she had with Riley, and of all of the men to do that with, why him? He was the enemy! He was Cute Angry Guy! He was the reason she was going to lose her bed-and-breakfast dream. Why did he have to be such a damn good kisser? All Grace knew was that she had to make sure they weren't alone together—ever—while he was here visiting Corrine. She simply didn't trust herself.

When it was time to start dinner, Grace had tiptoed up the stairs and held her breath while she waited and listened for any indications that Riley was in the house. Once she was certain he wasn't, she'd gone to the kitchen and started to cook.

Tonight's meal was going to be braised beef short ribs with four-cheese mashed potatoes, baby carrots, and zucchini cornbread on the side. Grace loved putting together a dinner menu that was different from what diners could find in just about any other restaurant without going over the top.

"Something smells delicious," Ben said as he walked into the kitchen with a big smile on his face. He placed the packages he was carrying on the floor away from Grace's work area. "I hope that whatever it is that smells so good is tonight's dinner."

Grace walked over and hugged him. "You are so good for my ego, Ben," she teased. "And yes, that is tonight's dinner, so I'm glad the two of you are back because it is just about ready."

"Perfect timing," Corrine said as she walked into the room with more packages. "I think I bought out the entire cookware department, but I was able to find everything on your list."

Grace did a little happy dance, and although she couldn't wait to play with all of her new toys, she had a dinner to put out. "I thought we'd eat in the dining room tonight," she said and led both Corrine and Ben to where she had set a beautiful table for four.

"Is Riley around?" Corrine asked, looking and sounding hopeful.

"I...um...I haven't seen him since you left. I just assumed he'd be joining us for dinner. And since it's his first one back home, I thought we'd make it special by eating in here."

"Well, aren't you sweet," Corrine said as she came over and hugged her. "Thank you. I know he didn't make the best first impression, but I think he's going to need a little time to get used to civilian life again."

Grace didn't want to argue, so she simply smiled and

asked Ben to pour the wine while she filled the plates. Corrine went in search of her son, and as soon as she left the room, Ben followed Grace. "How was he after we left?" Making a noncommittal sound, Grace focused on serving the meal. "Grace?"

She put the serving spoon down and braced both of her hands on the butcher block. "He was just as arrogant as he was before you left. I confronted him on his behavior, and he didn't seem inclined to change his mind. I tried to just keep my mouth shut, Ben, I really did, but he just sat there taunting me until I snapped."

And then I wrapped my legs around him and kissed him until I practically passed out. No need to go there right now. Or ever.

"I'm sorry, Grace. I hate that you're in the middle of this."

"So are you," she reminded him and went back to filling their plates.

Ben shrugged. "I think you and I both know where I am in all of this, Grace. I don't need this job. When I sold my business, I invested wisely, and I'm living very comfortably. The only reason I'm here is for Corrine."

Grace shot him a sly smile over her shoulder. "I knew it!" she said with a sense of giddiness.

"The only one who doesn't seem to know is Corrine."

Unfortunately, Grace knew Ben was right. "You know she loves you in her own way, right?"

He nodded. "I do. But sometimes I just want to shake her and force her to see me as a man. I love being her friend, and I love that she knows she can rely on me and depend on me, but it's frustrating as hell to sit here and have her be blind to the rest of it."

"Then maybe it's time to take off the kid gloves," Grace suggested.

"I don't want to scare her off, Grace. I don't know what I'd do if I lost her."

She smiled sympathetically at him. "You'll never lose her, Ben. Maybe now Riley is out of the service, she'll be able to relax a little bit. If we can just get him to let go of this idea of selling the inn, maybe she'll have some peace and finally see what's right in front of her."

"I hope you're right. Sometimes I just wish..." He stopped when he heard footsteps.

"Can you believe Riley was going back into town for dinner? He didn't think we were going to eat together. Honestly, what were you thinking?" Corrine asked Riley as he came into the room behind her.

"He'd miss out on one spectacular meal, I'll tell you that," Ben said as he walked over and patted Riley on the back. "Your mother's a great cook, but Gracie? She's in a league of her own." He walked back to the dining room to pour their wine, and Corrine followed with two plates. Before Grace could get her apron off and take the other two plates, Ben came back and grabbed them—effectively leaving her and Riley alone in the kitchen.

"Is there a reason you seem hell-bent on not eating my cooking?" she asked as she crossed her arms over her chest and tapped her foot in irritation.

"Nothing personal, Grace," Riley said. "I was just trying to maintain the peace around here."

She rolled her eyes. "You're not going to observe anything if you keep running out of here every ten minutes. Spend some time with your mother, keep your mouth shut about the inn, and just...watch!"

He stepped in close to her and liked the fact she didn't back away. "You know, I've spent a dozen years being forced to take orders. I didn't like it then, and I don't like it now."

"Then stop being so difficult," she said simply and then stepped around him and walked toward the dining room.

And once again Riley smiled at the sassy sway of her hips.

Well, she'd told him to observe…

———————

As much as Riley hated to admit it, dinner was exactly as Ben had described it. Spectacular. If this was the type of food they were going to serve guests, it would only be a matter of time before the place was filled with reservations and waiting lists. Why did Grace Brodie have to show up here now? How was he going to convince his mother to sell this place if it was suddenly more successful than it had ever been?

Maybe the better question was why was he pushing so hard for her to sell it. Clearly she had come to grips—sort of—with the fact he was never going to take over. So if he was off the hook for taking over the business, what was his gripe? Looking at his mother, he saw her smiling as she listened to Ben talk about a recent mishap with some mulch. She looked younger than her fifty-five years, and Riley had a feeling Ben had a lot to do with that.

Then he looked over at Ben. His smile seemed to match Corrine's. It was as if they were the only ones in the room. Was that what Grace had been referring to?

Slyly, he glanced in Grace's direction. She caught his gaze and smirked as if to say, *See? Are you seeing this?* Were his mother and Ben an item? Were they dating? Would they get married?

His head began to swim with all of the possibilities, but he knew better than to just blurt out the question. He'd have to wait until later and talk to his mother alone. Or maybe he should talk to Grace first so he didn't put his foot in his mouth and upset his mother again—something he was getting pretty damn good at around here.

The sound of laughter broke him out of his reverie, and it wasn't long before dinner was done and plates were being cleared. "I made an apple pie for dessert if anyone's interested," Grace said as she scooped up her place setting.

"Gracie, you're going to make me too fat to work," Ben said with a laugh.

"Not possible," she said as she glided past him into the kitchen. "You do hard labor all day around here. You work it all off, so I think your girlish figure is safe."

"Girlish!" he bellowed. "Now that's a first!" He walked over, wrapped Grace in a bear hug, and lifted her off her feet until she cried uncle.

"All I'm saying is that you have nothing to worry about," she laughed as he put her back on her feet. Corrine bustled around them, laughing along with them as she loaded the dishwasher.

Riley stood in the doorway and frowned. This was his family home, the place where he had grown up, and yet right now he was the outsider, the stranger. He didn't like that at all. There was an easy camaraderie among the three of them, and he had no idea what his place was here anymore. Maybe you couldn't go home again, as the saying went. Maybe he'd been stupid to believe he could walk away from his years in the service and blend back into a normal life. Maybe he was too damaged for that.

"How about you, Riley?" Corrine asked. "Do you have room for dessert?"

He shook his head. "Thanks, but no. I haven't eaten such a big meal in a long time. Thank you, Grace. Everything was delicious."

She blushed at his compliment and was about to thank him, but Riley had left the room. Corrine excused herself and went after him.

"Riley? Are you all right?"

He smiled at his mother. She hadn't aged much since he'd been gone, and right now, standing in the hallway with her, he felt like a kid again. "I'm fine, Mom. It's not easy getting used to civilian life. My body clock hasn't adjusted yet, and I think I'm just a little worn-out."

"Oh, okay," she said, relief flooding her. "It was so nice having you at the table tonight. I know you want to visit your friends and you're not planning to stay here long, but I just… Well… I hope you aren't going to leave right away. It's almost Thanksgiving, and then Christmas is right around the corner. I really would love it if you were here for the holidays with me. It's been so long since I've had that opportunity." Her voice cracked with emotion she couldn't hide.

Riley knew he wouldn't deny her this one request. He'd probably leave for a few days to see his friends in Virginia, but he'd make sure he was here for the holidays with his mother. She was right. It had been a long time, and maybe that wouldn't be a bad way to ease into his new life.

"I promise to be here for the holidays, Mom," he said softly and watched as the tears she was trying to hold back fell. He walked toward her and kissed her on the cheek. "Good night, Mom," he said as he hugged her and held on for just a little longer than he had in a long time.

"Welcome home, Riley," she finally said, her voice thick with emotion.

Chapter 5

For the next five days, Riley did exactly as Grace had suggested and simply observed the way things were around the inn. Unfortunately, he often found himself observing Grace and nothing else. No matter where she was or what she was doing, Riley couldn't seem to help himself. There had been no repeat of their steamy kiss, which made him completely miserable. It had been a long time since he had been with a woman, and although that was reason enough for him to be watching Grace, he was smart enough to know it wasn't the only reason.

He liked her; he was attracted to her. Grace Brodie was a beautiful woman, and the way she had kissed him? Well, she had been starring in his nightly fantasies since. The problem was that she was impossible to get alone. During the day, they were all working together on refreshing the cabins. When she left to make lunch, his mother went with her. They all ate like a damn family for every meal, and on the weekends, their guests kept her busy.

Now, here he was skulking around like a pouting teenager, and he didn't know what to do about it. He was leaving for Virginia in the morning to visit his buddies, and although he would only be gone for four days, Riley wanted to clear the air before he left.

Every night, he spent time alone talking to his

mother, and while she never admitted she was in love with Ben, Riley got the impression she was. Maybe she didn't even know it. The more Riley observed the two of them, the more he saw that Ben was clearly in love with Corrine. Wouldn't that make selling the inn seem more reasonable? Ben didn't need the income, and between the two of them, they could retire comfortably and have a good life together. Was he really the only one who saw this?

He needed to talk to Grace. Maybe if he told her how he was seeing things now and how much selling the inn would *benefit* both his mother and Ben, she'd finally see things his way.

She had disappeared after dinner, and Riley didn't want to seem obvious in his search for her. He found his mother in the living room with a book. "Hey, sweet-heart," she said with a smile as he walked into the room. "How are you doing tonight?"

Sitting beside her on the sofa, he returned her smile. "Tired, as usual. I'm telling you, Ben should have been in the military, because he runs a tight ship around here."

"Tell me about it," Corrine chuckled.

"I've done some hard drills that didn't leave me feeling this worn-out at the end of the day."

"It's a different kind of work," she said serenely. "There's something to be said about turning a house into a home. It's not just physical work; it's emotional too." She looked up at Riley and winked. "And exhausting."

"Amen to that," he agreed. "I think it's even harder on you and Grace," he said carefully.

Corrine looked at him and frowned. "Really? Why?"

"Well, you're both helping with the renovations, plus

doing all of the cooking and the cleaning… I mean, here you are relaxing with a book. I bet Grace is in her room already asleep."

A laugh escaped before Corinne could stop it. "Grace? Are you kidding me?"

"What? What's so funny?"

"Grace practically needs to be shot with a tranquilizer dart to unwind and go to sleep. If anything, she's probably out in the hot tub relaxing and listening to her iPod or something. Once she does that, she'll go to her room and do yoga or something, and then maybe, just maybe, she'll read for a couple of hours before going to sleep."

"Doesn't she get up at six and start cooking?" he asked.

"Every day like clockwork."

"How is that possible?"

Corinne reached over and took her son's hand in hers. "Grace hasn't had an easy life. Though maybe that's not the right way to put it. Growing up, she had a wonderful family life. When her parents died, she had a tough time of it. She was supposed to be on that trip with them. They went on that boat every summer, and that year, because she was getting ready for college, she stayed home. It haunted her for a long time. She told me that she has nightmares about them drowning and how she should have been with them. I think the poor thing is just afraid to go to sleep."

Riley had no words. That was a lot more information about Grace than he was prepared for. The more he learned about her, the more he felt guilty about the inn and wanting it gone. He had to force himself to change his way of thinking. Nope, he wasn't going to feel guilty. Grace wasn't his responsibility; his mother was.

Kissing his mother on the cheek, Riley stood and wished her a good night before walking back to the kitchen. He meant to simply grab a bottle of water, but he looked outside and saw the lighted path.

He sighed. The lighted path led to the hot tub. It would be wrong to go there. He didn't want to disturb Grace, especially after what he had just learned. If she needed all those things to help her sleep, the last thing she needed was him nagging her about the inn while she was unwinding.

But, he reasoned, he was leaving tomorrow and didn't want to wait. And there was the added perk of seeing Grace in a bathing suit. Sure, he was doing his best to keep his distance—or she was. Either way, they hadn't gotten within five feet of each other since sharing that kiss, and he just wanted to satisfy his curiosity.

All those days in the park, she'd jogged wearing a bulky jacket. Around the house, she usually wore a big sweater or an oversized sweatshirt. He'd felt her curves through the layers of clothes, and he just needed to know if she was as curvy as she felt. What better way to find out than seeing her in a bathing suit? *Well*, he thought with a mental kick, *there are plenty of other ways to find out, especially if you stop tiptoeing around her and do what you want to do*.

He wanted to make love to her.

Badly.

Even right now.

Not good, not a good sign. She was becoming a weakness for him, and a marine did not have any weaknesses.

Riley gripped the door handle tightly and gave himself a mental pep talk. *Okay, go out there and just talk to her as if she were fully dressed. Don't linger; don't make any kind of small talk. Just get the facts, present your case, and get the hell out of there. You'll be in Virginia tomorrow, and if you really set your mind to it, you can find a woman to hook up with, and all of this lust you're feeling toward Grace will be taken care of. End of story. Now march your ass out there, get the information, and get out!*

With a nod of his head, Riley yanked the door open and marched down the path with a determined stride.

And came to a complete halt at the sight before him.

Grace was in the hot tub, and the lighting was soft as it illuminated not only the water, but small lights lining the surrounding garden and twinkly lights laced through the lattice as well. Even though it should have been bright, the lighting gave her the perfect ethereal appearance. He was mesmerized. Transfixed.

And totally screwed.

Her head was thrown back, and he could see the earbuds leading to her iPod. He wondered what kind of music she was listening to. The night was definitely cool, and yet the two heat lamps flanking the hot tub area kept things warm. Riley stepped closer and noticed her eyes were closed. She looked so peaceful that he hated to disturb her, hated the thought of ruining the nightly ritual she clearly needed.

But leaving was not an option. Not only because he needed to talk to her, but also because he simply needed to be near her. Something about Grace beckoned him, and although he was hesitant to think too much about it, he knew this was exactly where he wanted to be.

He took yet another step closer and felt the heat of the lamps warming him. He kicked off his shoes as he watched to see if Grace had noticed his presence. When she didn't move, he bent over and removed his socks. Straightening, he was surprised that she was so deep in thought that she didn't sense he was there. His shirt came off next, and he began to question whether or not this was a smart thing to do.

He unbuttoned his jeans and let them drop.

Softly he said her name, but she didn't move a muscle. Was she sleeping? If that was the case, then it was a good thing he was here. Clearly, she could drown if she was left here by herself. So really, he was *helping* her. He was sure she'd see it that way.

Kicking his jeans aside, he stared at his dark briefs and questioned whether they stayed or went. Peeking over the side of the tub, he confirmed that Grace was wearing a bathing suit.

The briefs stayed.

Riley didn't want to startle her, but he had a feeling that no matter what he did, she was going to freak out a little. With his hands gripping the side of the tub, he made his decision. Swinging one leg over the side and then the other, he slipped into the water and promptly heard Grace scream.

"For crying out loud, Riley!" she cried. "You have *got* to stop doing that!"

"I was standing beside the damn tub for ten minutes, and you never flinched. I thought you were asleep. I figured I'd better wake you up before something happened."

"And you thought scaring me to death was the answer?"

"What was I supposed to do?"

"Oh, I don't know, maybe touch my hand? Say my name? You know, something *not* terrifying!"

"So my being in the hot tub with you is terrifying?" he teased.

She rolled her eyes and pulled the earbuds out before turning and shutting off her iPod. When she faced Riley again, she felt a little more in control. "Why are you even here?"

"I was going for a walk to unwind before going to sleep, and I saw you here sleeping in the water."

"I wasn't sleeping; I was relaxing." She glared at him suspiciously. "And since when do you need to unwind before going to sleep? I thought soldiers were taught how to sleep anywhere."

He shrugged. "I guess I'm getting soft since becoming a civilian."

"It's been six days, Riley," she said flatly. "Seriously?"

He stretched his arms out along the side of the hot tub and relaxed. Grace was sitting directly across from him, and from what he could see, she was wearing a green bikini that matched her eyes.

And she was just as curvy as he had imagined.

"Okay, the truth is that I wanted to talk to you before I left tomorrow."

"About what?"

"My mother and Ben."

"Ah…so you've been observing. Nice."

Now it was his turn to roll his eyes. "It wasn't hard to see. For crying out loud, they do nothing but watch one another. I know Ben is crazy about my mom, but I don't think she's realized how she feels."

"Very astute, soldier," Grace said with a sly smile.

"She doesn't have a clue. Well, maybe a small one, but I think she's a little embarrassed by her feelings."

"Why do you say that?"

"Because we first touched on this subject while she was at the rehab facility. I listened to the way she talked about Ben, and I asked if she had a crush on him. She said she thought she was too old for a crush; I told her she wasn't."

"So then what's the holdup?"

Leave it to a man to be clueless. "Riley, she hasn't dated anyone since your father died. She sees Ben as a friend. I think she's scared to take that risk with him."

"But doesn't she realize how beneficial it would be?"

Grace didn't like the way he said *beneficial*. "Care to elaborate on that one?" she asked.

Taking a deep breath, Riley prepared himself for battle. "All I'm saying is that it would be good for both of them to stop dancing around one another. She'd have someone to take care of her, which is what I've always wanted for her, and Ben would have the woman he's in love with. How can that be a bad thing?"

Grace wasn't an idiot. That was too simple and totally not a guy thing to say. "Okay, thank you for the Miss America answer to our question. Now how about telling me the truth." When he looked at her funny, she simply crossed her arms and quirked a brow at him. "Your poker face isn't always on either, Ace."

"Fine," he said irritably. "If the two of them hooked up, they'd be financially secure for life. You and I both know he doesn't need to work. I'm sure he sold his business for a ton of money, and if he wanted to, he could sit home all day and do nothing."

Grace simply stared at him.

"And if my mother sold the inn, she'd be financially secure as well. The two of them could travel and spend time together and just...finally have a life! Why is that so wrong?"

"You are unbelievable," Grace said with disgust as she rose to her feet. Water streamed off her body, but she paid no attention to it in her indignation. "She has a life, and there's nothing wrong with it. She didn't agree with your career choice, but she didn't demand you leave it. Don't get me wrong. I think she and Ben would be wonderful together, and I am hopeful they'll figure it out. But if they do, it will be to build the life they want together, not the one you expect them to build."

Riley knew she was speaking—he could hear her voice—but all he could do was focus on the body before him, glistening in the moonlight. How could he have thought for one minute this was a good idea? It was one thing to imagine what Grace would look like in a bathing suit—or naked—and another thing entirely to have her body within arm's reach.

He noticed the silence first. He hungrily drank in the sight of her as his gaze slowly rose to her face.

That was one ticked-off redhead standing in front of him. Without conscious thought, Riley reached out, banded one arm around her waist, and pulled Grace onto his lap. She gasped in surprise but didn't pull away.

"You didn't hear one word I said, did you?" she asked, unable to hide her outrage.

Riley was not in the habit of lying, and he wasn't about to start now. "No. Once you stood up in the water, my mind went blank and all of my blood traveled south." To prove his point, he held her more securely against him and rocked his hips upward.

"Oh," she whimpered and hated herself for being so easily distracted by him. Her whole body seemed to willingly wrap itself around him, and Grace didn't have even the slightest inclination to do anything about it.

"I didn't come here for this," he said gruffly as he continued to gently rock his hips against her. "I really did want to talk to you."

Her head fell back, and a small moan escaped her lips. "So...talk to me," she said huskily.

It was Riley's turn to groan. Right now, the only talking he wanted to do was dirty talk, and then he didn't want to talk at all. "Grace," he said slowly, as if it were torture.

She raised her head and met his gaze dead-on. Moaning his name, she took her turn at rocking against him and smiled at the hiss that escaped his lips. "Was there something specific you wanted to talk about?"

Reaching up, Riley fisted a handful of Grace's hair and tugged slightly. "It's not nice to tease, Grace," he said right before his mouth crashed over hers.

It was exactly as Riley had remembered and spent the week fantasizing about. She felt incredible in his arms, and if he had his way, she'd never leave them. He took his turn at nipping at her lip, but she didn't need the prompt. Her tongue was more than ready to meet his. "God, Grace, you feel so good," he growled as his mouth worked its way down her throat and then to the swell of her breasts. The bikini top did little to hide her from him, and without asking for permission, Riley reached behind her, undid the ties, and threw the top aside. Grace gasped as the fabric was pulled away, but the sound turned to one of pleasure when his lips and tongue began to tease her breast.

She panted his name as she continued to rock over him. It would be so easy to simply let go, to remove the last of their clothing and do what they both wanted. But Grace wasn't sure she'd be able to live with herself if she did such a thing. It wasn't who she was. Something about Riley made her completely forget herself. She had no doubt she would eventually sleep with him, but she knew it wasn't going to be here in the hot tub.

"Riley?" she said as she reluctantly put her hands on his head and pulled away from him. "Riley, we can't do this. Not here, not now."

He looked up at her, dazed. "Wait... What?"

Grace scooted off his lap, moved to the other side of the tub, and folded her arms over her chest. "Look, I don't know why this keeps happening, but I know I'm not someone who has sex in my boss's hot tub. I lost my head there for a minute, but it's clear now and we can't do this."

With an impish grin, Riley slid swiftly over beside her. "I like it when you lose your head, and I know exactly why this keeps happening. And you know what?" he asked and waited for her to respond.

"What?"

"It's going to keep happening until we finish what we started."

Grace shook her head vehemently. "It can't, Riley. *We* can't."

"Why?"

She threw her head back and sighed. "You're my best friend's son. You're trying to convince her to sell this place, a place I love. As far as I'm concerned, that's more than enough reason why this can't happen."

He shrugged and moved closer. "These are two separate things, Grace. One has nothing to do with the other."

"Maybe to you, but not to me," she said sadly. "I can't disengage that much. I'm sorry." With as much dignity as she could find, Grace rose from the tub and stepped out, keeping an arm banded across her chest the entire time. Grabbing a towel, she wrapped it around her body while she gathered her things. She looked over her shoulder to where Riley still sat in the tub. He was watching her intently, and it took every ounce of willpower she possessed to not rip the towel off and climb back in on top of him.

"Good night, Riley," she said softly and quickly made her way up the path to the house.

Riley watched her go but stayed exactly where he was. The image of her perfect body was permanently burned in his brain. And the feel of her, the taste of her... Well, that was going to be there as well. Off in the distance, he heard a door close and he smiled. Reaching over, he set the timer on the jets and let himself relax in the warmth of the tub while the water beat on his sore muscles.

Leaning his head back, Riley closed his eyes and smiled. Grace might think this was over, but she was wrong. He had no doubt that if they had been anyplace but a hot tub, he would be making her his right now.

He just had to bide his time for a little bit longer.

Chapter 6

FOR FOUR DAYS, GRACE WALKED AROUND IN A FUNK. SHE did her work; she cooked for the guests. She went for her therapy and treated herself afterward, and yet she felt like something vital was missing. It irked her to no end trying to think what that was.

She hadn't jogged since her knee gave out that day in the park when she'd first met Riley, and in her spare time, she just hadn't felt up to socializing. This funk was seriously starting to grate on her nerves.

All around her, people were chatting and talking about the upcoming holidays, but all she could think about was Riley Walsh in a hot tub. Hot and hard beneath her. She closed her eyes and groaned. Why? Why did she have to stop him? Maybe if she'd just do it, she could move on with her life rather than thinking about him, fantasizing about him, and doing everything but drawing their names in cartoon hearts.

"You okay, Grace?" Ben asked as he came into the kitchen. "You're a little quiet today."

"I'm fine," she lied. "I guess I didn't sleep well last night." She was about to go back to chopping the vegetables she had out for tonight's stew when she noticed Ben was a little off his game, too. "How about you? Everything all right?"

Ben looked around to make sure they were alone. "I've got a date tonight."

"What? With whom?"

He glanced at his feet before looking up and facing her. "Her name is Sharon. I met her at the grocery store."

"Oh, Ben, you didn't... Don't be *that* guy."

"What guy?"

"The guy who goes to the grocery store to pick up women."

He sighed and leaned on the butcher block. "Grace, believe me, I'm not that guy. Unfortunately, I'm a guy who is lonely, and I need more than just hanging around and sharing a meal with a woman who isn't interested in me. It's time for me to put myself first for a change."

"Oh, Ben..." she began.

"I'm okay, really. I guess I kept hoping for things to change, but the reality is that they're not going to. I've done everything but build a neon billboard sign telling Corrine how I feel. I love her, but I can't wait for her anymore. I need more." He looked at Grace with eyes full of sadness. "Does that make me a horrible person?"

She shook her head. "No," she said and walked around to hug him. "It makes you human."

Corrine walked in and placed a glass in the sink. "Everything okay in here?" She looked at the two of them as worry creased her brow. "What's going on?"

Grace carefully stepped aside and busied herself at the sink.

"Ben?" Corrine asked.

Taking a deep breath, he straightened his shoulders and said, "I was telling Grace I have a date tonight."

Shock registered on Corrine's face, but she quickly masked it. "Oh...a...a date. With whom?"

"Her name is Sharon. We met a couple of days ago in the grocery store."

Grace watched Corrine willing herself to stay calm. "I see. Well, good for you. Where...where are you taking her? Dinner? A movie?"

Ben nodded. "We're going to dinner at Mario's. She likes Italian."

"You can't go wrong with Mario's," Corrine agreed flatly. "They do have the best Italian in town." They continued to stare at one another for several moments before Ben spoke again.

"I think we got enough done here today that it won't be a big deal for me to leave early. I'd like to go home to shower and change before I pick Sharon up."

All Corrine could do was nod.

"I'll see you tomorrow, Corri," he said softly. But she didn't say a word. Instead, she watched him leave, and Grace wondered at the pain on her friend's face. Why wouldn't Corrine take the next step? And then Grace wondered if she should be doing the same with Riley.

It took a couple of hours for Grace to finish getting dinner on the stove and setting the dining room before she found Corrine in her room. She knocked gently on the door but wasn't sure if the muffled sound she heard was actually an invitation to come in. Pushing the door open slowly, she scanned the room before spotting Corrine's small form sitting in the corner in her rocking chair.

"I used to rock Riley in this chair when he was a baby," Corrine said. "I used to love sitting here in the middle of the night with him. It was such a peaceful time, just the two of us."

Grace walked into the room and sat on the bed and waited.

Corrine faced her. "Life was so much simpler then. I had my husband, I had my son, and I had my home." She gave a mirthless laugh and looked at her hands clasped in her lap. "Now what do I have? My husband is gone, and my son is here for a short time and wants to escape as soon as possible. He wants me to sell this place, and...I've lost Ben." As she looked up at Grace, her tears began to fall. "I have nothing. It's all gone."

Reaching out, Grace took one of Corrine's hands in hers. "That's not true, Corrine," she said softly.

"It is. It's all gone now. What am I going to do?"

Grace knew she had to choose her words carefully. "Jack has been gone a long time; I know that. And Riley was gone for a long time, but he's back now. It's going to take a while for him to adjust to being home. He may not want to stay here at the inn, but that doesn't mean you don't have him. Who knows where he'll settle down? Now you won't have to wait for him to be on leave to see him or talk to him. You have that freedom."

Corrine gave a trembling smile. "Oh, I hope so, Grace. I hope he'll want me to be part of his life."

"Of course he does! In his own way, he thinks he's helping you by wanting you to sell this place. He just needs to get to know you now as an adult, so he'll understand what this place means to you." Corrine nodded. "And as for Ben?" Grace said as she tugged on her friend's hand. "You know good and well he's in love with you. He's been in love with you most of his life."

"He's out on a date tonight, Grace!" Corrine cried. "How could he go out with someone else?"

"Because he can't sit here with you every day and every night just to be your pal! He's a man, Corrine, and you're a woman. He's been waiting a long time for you, but he feels you're never going to return his feelings. It's not fair for you to expect him to live like a monk."

"I never expected that! He never made a move... never even tried to kiss me!"

Grace laughed. "The two of you are something else. You know that, right?"

"What do you mean?"

"He's afraid to make a move because he doesn't want to scare you, and you're waiting for him to make a move. No wonder nothing has happened."

"Grace, it's killing me he's out with someone tonight."

"I know."

"Do you think it's serious? Do you think he really... likes this woman?"

Grace shook her head. "I think he's just trying something new."

Corrine frowned. "What does that mean?"

"He certainly got your attention, didn't he?"

Nodding, Corrine asked, "So what do I do now?"

Grace gave a wicked grin. "Tomorrow, you go after your man."

"What? Oh no, I couldn't! What would I do?"

"For starters, you could greet him with a kiss."

Corrine blushed from the roots of her hair to the tips of her toes. "But...shouldn't he make the first move?"

"Corrine, it's been what? Twenty years? Clearly he's not going to make the first move. If you don't want him dating anyone else, you're going to have to be the one to do it."

"Oh dear…"

"Trust me, you'll be fine." They sat and smiled. Grace looked at the bedside clock and saw it was time to start prepping to serve dinner. "C'mon. We'll get through dinner and talk strategy afterward." They headed to the kitchen. "Is Riley coming back tonight?"

"No, he called earlier and said he was going to stay a couple of extra days with his friends. He'll be back Wednesday night, so he'll be here for Thanksgiving."

"Oh," Grace said, forcing herself to sound casual. "Any reason for the extended stay?"

"Boys will be boys," Corrine said with a dramatic sigh. "If I had to guess, I'd say he was having a good ol' time going out drinking with his friends and probably making up for lost time with a woman."

Now Grace felt sick and imagined this was how Corrine was feeling a few minutes ago. "And you're okay with that?"

"Grace, Riley is a thirty-year-old man. I don't harbor any illusions of him being… What did you say earlier? A monk?" She chuckled. "I'd say there was something wrong with him if he didn't get out and go a little wild."

Grace slammed a cabinet door with more than a little force as Corrine spoke. "Grace? Are you okay?"

"What? Oh, I'm fine. I didn't mean to slam that so hard." But the slamming continued as she made up the trays of food for their guests.

~~~

Monday morning, Ben let himself into the inn like he always did. The place was quiet. Almost too quiet. There were no cars out in the front, and he thought he remembered hearing Corrine saying everyone was checking out on Sunday. They weren't expecting guests again until the day after Thanksgiving.

Walking to the kitchen, he expected to see Grace. Even on days when they didn't have guests, she was up early and puttering around in there concocting one magnificent dish after another.

The room was empty.

Coffee wasn't even started.

He began to panic. Where was Grace? Hell, where was Corrine? A glance at his watch showed it was just after eight. In all of the years he had known Corrine, she'd always been an early riser. Maybe they went out to start work on the last cottage without him. Walking out the back door, Ben headed down the path to the row of guest cottages. He took pride as he saw them come into view. The grounds looked beautiful, and the cottages each had a fresh coat of paint and looked almost like new.

As he approached the last cottage, he realized this was the last project that would bring him here on a daily basis for a long time. After this, he was really only needed one day a week. The thought of not seeing Corrine every day brought a pain to a region of his heart. She made every day brighter for him, gave him a reason to get up each day.

His date with Sharon had been fine enough, but there were no sparks. For either of them. It was a pleasant evening, but that was it. It was just an evening.

So much for his grand plan to make Corrine jealous. He'd barely made it through one date. He snorted with disgust at himself.

Taking his keys out, he unlocked the door to the cottage and stopped dead in his tracks as the door opened. The entire place was decorated for Christmas. The smell of fresh paint lingered in the air along with fresh pine. He stepped inside, closed the door, and looked around in wonder. How had all of this gotten done over the weekend? He hadn't told his crew to come in.

"I was thinking of doing this in all of the cabins."

Ben turned and felt a wave of shock hit him at the sound of Corrine's voice. She seemed to step out of the shadows. "When... How...how did you get all of this done?"

"I called the boys in over the weekend. Grace and I helped them, and we got this done."

"But...why? You knew I'd be here today, and we had it all planned out. It would have been done by Thanksgiving."

"I was...restless...this weekend," she said coyly. "I needed something to do. All of the guests were out and about, and everything else is done around here, so I decided to take the initiative." Her voice sounded a bit breathless even to her own ears, and she hoped and prayed she could pull this off. Stepping closer to Ben, she gazed into his eyes. "How was your date?"

His blue eyes bore into hers, and his heart was hammering in his chest. She wanted to know about his date? Was she trying to kill him here? All this talk about being restless and taking initiative... What the hell was going on? "We had dinner, and I took her home," he said gruffly, losing himself in Corrine's soft, brown eyes.

"How was the food?"

"Corrine?"

"Hmmm?" she said, a small smile pulling at her lips.

"I don't want to talk about food. Or my date."

"Then what do you want, Ben?" she asked boldly as she stepped closer to him. Corrine held her breath as she waited for an answer. With each second, she was certain Ben could hear her heartbeat.

"You," he finally said. "I want you. I've always wanted you."

And then he kissed her. For the first time in the fifty years they'd known each other, Ben allowed himself to kiss Corrine. He wasn't gentle; he wasn't smooth. He kissed her with all of the passion that had been building his entire life, and the amazing part of it was that she kissed him right back in the same fashion.

Who knew?

Chapter 7

THE DAY BEFORE THANKSGIVING DAWNED GRAY AND dreary, which fit Grace's mood. Riley was due back today, and it had been hell not thinking about him off sleeping with some other woman. She had no one to blame but herself on that one. She could have slept with him—twice! But had she? No…she had to be a stickler about rules and morals. *Idiot*.

And to add insult to injury, she now had to sit back and watch Corrine and Ben. They clearly had worked out their issues, because everywhere Grace went, there they were… kissing, hugging, holding hands. It should have made her happy for her friends, but instead it just made her jealous and pissed off because they had something she wanted.

Grace had never thought herself to be petty, but right now, that was exactly how she was acting and feeling. Walking into the kitchen, she found the two of them there, holding hands while they had their morning coffee. Perfect.

"Good morning," they both said as she walked in, and all she managed was a grunt. "We're taking a ride into town after breakfast. Is there anything else you need for dinner tomorrow?" Corrine asked.

Grace shook her head. "I have everything. If I don't, I'll go to the store."

Ben and Corrine exchanged glances. "Is everything okay, Grace?" Corrine asked.

Pouring herself a cup of coffee, she shrugged. "I don't know. I guess the holidays just get to me sometimes. This is the first time in a long time that I'm spending one with people who are like family to me, and well…"— she sat beside them and cursed the tears that began to fall—"it's going to be so much harder because I know this will be the only one we have together."

"Oh, Grace," Corrine said, and she leaned over to hug her. "What are you talking about?"

"Please," Grace said with a hint of anger as she pulled away, wiping at her cheeks. "You and Ben are together. Which, by the way, I really am happy about. But now that you are, and with all of the fuss Riley's been making, it's only a matter of time before you two decide to go off and travel. Just like Riley said."

"What are you talking about?" Ben asked.

With a huff of frustration, Grace faced her friends. "Ben, we all know you don't need this job. You're here because of Corrine. And, Corrine? You've put your heart and soul into this place, but wouldn't you like a little time alone with Ben?" They both nodded. "See? So the perfect solution is to sell the Snowflake Inn and have a life together. You've both waited long enough for this, and you should enjoy yourselves." If she could have kept the contempt out of her voice, they might have actually believed her. "Damn Riley," she muttered.

Ben cleared his throat. "Um, Grace," he began hesitantly, "I'm sure all that makes sense in your head, but I've got to tell you that you're jumping the gun here a little bit."

She stared at him as if he were speaking Greek. "What do you mean? Are you saying the two of you are going to just stay friends?"

"Hell no!" he said with a laugh. "This is all new to us, and while yes, we do want to have some time to ourselves, that has nothing to do with the inn. You're here now. Corrine can go away on a vacation and not stress out because she knows everything is being taken care of. By you."

"Really?" Grace said with a sob.

Corrine and Ben both nodded. "Really," Corrine finally said. "Oh, Grace, I'm sorry if you've been sitting here thinking we were going to take off on you. To be honest, I still don't know what I'm going to do with this place. With Riley not wanting it, there's no reason for me to hang on to it until I die. I won't will it to him. Eventually I will have to sell it. But I don't see that happening anytime soon."

While Corrine's words should have made Grace feel better, they didn't. The simple truth was that this was all temporary. Grace was tired of temporary. She wanted something real and lasting. She knew better than anyone that there were no guarantees in life, but she was going to do her best to find that for herself.

Over the past couple of days, she had done her research and she knew she would never be able to buy the Snowflake Inn from Corrine. The property was worth far more than Grace could ever afford, and she would never ask her friend to lower the price. So that put Grace back at square one—finding a place of her own where she could grow and settle and find her forever home.

The thought made her sad because she had truly felt this was going to be home. But that just wasn't meant to be. So for this year, she'd have her Thanksgiving and

Christmas with Corrine and Ben...and Riley, but then
it would be in her best interest to move on. It would be
better to cut her losses now than to spend years here and
then be forced to go.

In the past ten years, Grace had learned the fine art of
leaving places that she loved and detaching herself from
the process. Now it was her turn to take control of her
destiny and find her forever place.

She only hoped it was as wonderful and lovely as the
Snowflake Inn.

—∿∿∿—

Riley came back late. It was well after dinner, and he
had planned it that way. The days away hadn't been
all that he had expected them to be. His buddies were
both engaged to wonderful women, and he'd found he
spent most of his time hearing about wedding plans and
houses and building futures.

It depressed the hell out of him.

He had hoped to drink with his buddies, find a woman
to help him get his mind off Grace, and spend a couple
of days in mindless oblivion. No such luck. His buddies
had given up their partying ways, and the only women
he'd met were already married or engaged. So why had
he stayed? Because being surrounded by a bunch of
couples planning their futures was safer than being back
at the inn with Grace sleeping right down the hall from
him. A man only had so much self-control.

Letting himself into the inn, he saw a light on in the
living room and spotted his mother sitting on the sofa
with a book. How many times in his life had he witnessed this scene? His heart ached. This was home. This

was a comforting sight to him. She was always there, always waiting for him to come home. Even when he didn't want her to see him sneak in, she was there.

He smiled to himself. This was a good feeling, coming home to someone and knowing they were waiting for him. In the same moment, he felt a pang of disappointment that Grace wasn't waiting for him, too.

Corrine looked up and spotted him. "Hey, you're back," she said warmly. "How was your visit with your friends?"

He sat beside her and told her how he'd spent his time. "Oh, that must have been terribly boring for you," she said with a laugh. "I'm sorry, sweetheart. Why didn't you come home sooner?"

"I stayed and helped Bobby finish his garage. He wanted it done before the holidays. I figured you had everything under control here, and he really needed the help." It wasn't a total lie.

"You're a good friend, Riley." She smiled and held his hand. "Are you hungry? Want some hot chocolate?"

She knew him so well. "As a matter of fact, I would," he said and saw her eyes brighten. It took so little effort. Why had he been avoiding his mother for so long? She stood and walked to the kitchen, and Riley followed. "So, what's been going on while I've been gone?"

Corrine filled him in on the progress with the cottages and their upcoming guests, and then she broached the subject of Ben. While she left out the more…intimate… parts of the story, she explained that she loved Ben and they were starting to plan their future. "I hope you're okay with it, Riley," she said carefully as she began mixing ingredients for their hot chocolate.

"Okay with it? Mom, are you kidding me? I've been hoping for this!" he said excitedly and wrapped his mother in his embrace.

"Are you sure? I know it's been a long time since your father passed away, but…I'll always love Jack."

"Mom, seriously, I think it's great. Ben has always been part of this family, and I can't think of anyone else I'd want for you."

"You have no idea how happy that makes me, Riley," she said, tears forming in her eyes. "My goodness, I feel like this is all I do lately."

"At least they're happy tears, right?"

She nodded. "I never thought I could be this happy. Just a couple of days ago, I was crying to Grace because I thought I had lost everything, but she showed me I was wrong. Oh, Riley, I don't know what I would have done without her. She's been an amazing friend."

Grace was both the last and the only person he wanted to think about right now. "I'm glad you have her as a friend, Mom."

"I'm worried about her, though."

"Why?" he asked, finding himself worried for her too, even though he didn't know why.

"Well, the holidays are hard for her, and I think that even though she's happy for me and Ben, she's worried about what it all means. She told us how you think that I should sell, particularly if Ben and I are together, and well, she has no one, Riley. She's all alone in the world."

"Mom, you can't keep the inn just for Grace," he said and then realized what a jackass he sounded like and cringed. "Why not sell it to her?"

"She doesn't have that kind of money. This place is

a lot of responsibility. I tried to put her at ease, but I have a feeling that as soon as the holidays are over, she's going to leave," Corrine said sadly.

"Did she tell you that?"

She shook her head. "She didn't have to. I've gotten to know her well enough to know what she's thinking. She's become more detached. We don't talk as much, and some of the sparkle has left her eyes."

Riley's gut clenched. He loved that sparkle. "Why don't you talk to her about it?"

"What would I say, Riley? I can't give her any guarantees. I know she loves this place almost as much as I do. But I've been thinking about it, and I can see now that you were right."

"I was?"

She nodded. "Ben and I want to get married, and while we could live here and run the inn together, we really want to travel and be able to have some privacy in a home of our own. We talked about Grace running the inn, and we even mentioned that to her, but I know her dream is to have a place of her own. She doesn't want to be someone's employee for the rest of her life, and I couldn't ask that of her."

"But, Mom—"

"We'll talk about it more after the holidays. I want Grace to have the kind of Christmas she hasn't had in far too long. I don't want her to worry. I feel a little awkward saying this to you, but I've come to think of Grace like family, like the daughter I never had."

Now his gut really clenched. He had done this. He had put the idea of getting rid of the Snowflake Inn in his mother's head, and because of that, he was hurting

Grace. He had to talk to her, had to make sure she was okay.

"Where is Grace right now, Mom?"

"She went to bed a while ago."

Riley frowned. "You said she never goes to bed early."

Corrine simply shrugged. "She was…different tonight. Quieter. We talked a lot today, and I think she just wanted time alone. I haven't heard a peep out of her in hours. I'm sure she's sound asleep by now."

Coming around the counter, Riley hugged his mother and forgot all about the hot chocolate she had been making for him. "Maybe I should go and talk to her," he surprised himself by saying out loud.

Corrine pulled back and looked at him. "Not tonight, Riley—really. Just let her be for now. She needs her rest."

He wasn't so sure. Corrine poured him a mug of chocolate and then kissed him on the cheek. "Speaking of rest, I need mine too. I'll see you in the morning, sweetheart." Riley watched her leave the room and listened for the sound of her door closing. A lot had happened in his short absence, and while some of it was good, some of it clearly wasn't.

Grace had been honest with him from the beginning about how he would be hurting her by pushing Corrine to sell. He just hadn't realized that until now. Picking up his mug, he headed down the hall to his room but stopped at the door to the basement. He couldn't remember the last time he had gone there; certainly not since he'd been back. Quietly, he opened the door and contemplated talking to Grace. Listening carefully, he found it was very quiet. Maybe his mother was right— Grace was sleeping and he should just let her be.

He was just about to close the door when he heard it. A sob. Taking another second just to make sure, he listened intently and heard it again. Riley closed the door behind him and carefully made his way down the stairs. Fortunately, a small light made it easier to find his way.

Grace's bed was tucked away in the far corner of the room, and for a moment, he could only stop and stare. She was asleep, he was certain, but she was having some sort of bad dream. She was tossing and turning, and every once in a while, she would let out a cry of despair.

Placing his mug on the nearest surface, Riley approached the bed. He called Grace's name softly, but she didn't respond. She thrashed around a bit more and cried out, "*No!*" and his heart jumped into overdrive.

"Grace," he said a bit more firmly, but she didn't hear him. Sitting on the bed, Riley reached over and gently placed his hands on her shoulders. She was wearing a tank top from what he could tell, and her legs were tangled in the sheets.

"Grace, sweetheart, wake up," he said carefully. He watched as her eyes fluttered and opened slightly.

"Riley?" she said quietly, but her body was trembling. "What…what are you doing here?"

"I got home a little while ago, and I heard you crying out. You were having a bad dream. Are you okay?"

Grace pulled away from him and sat up, pushing her long hair away from her face. "I…I'm fine, I think."

"What were you dreaming about?"

She shook her head. "I don't remember."

"Grace…"

"I normally dream about my parents and…the accident. I'm sure that's what it was, but I normally remember it. You must have caught me at the beginning of it." She looked up at him and gave him a weak smile. "Thank you."

"Are you going to be okay?"

She nodded. "I always am," she said with a sigh and then seemed to take in her surroundings. "Is that hot chocolate I smell?"

Riley smiled and stood. "Freshly made." He walked over to where he had placed the mug and picked it up and brought it to her.

Grace shook her head. "No, that's yours. I'll be fine."

He sat beside her. "We can share," he said softly and held the mug out to her.

His blue eyes mesmerized her. She had missed him, and right now it was a nice feeling to have him close by. "Thanks." Carefully she took a sip of the hot beverage and sighed with pleasure. "I can cook a meal fit for a king, but your mom's hot chocolate blows me away."

When Riley pictured himself in bed with Grace—and he pictured it often—they weren't discussing his mother's skill at making cocoa. Grace held the mug out to him, and he took it from her hands, his eyes never leaving hers. He took a sip and then placed the mug on the bedside table. "Are you sure you're going to be okay?"

"You'd think after ten years I'd stop having the dreams," she said with a mirthless laugh. "They don't come as often, and I find I have them more when my life is unsettled or I'm upset."

"What are you upset about?" he asked quietly, moving closer to her.

Grace wanted to look away, she really did, but his gaze held her captive. "I miss my parents the most during the holidays," she said so softly he almost didn't hear her.

"What else?"

She swallowed hard. "I'm upset that this will be my only Christmas here at the Snowflake Inn."

"Why?"

Shifting away from him, Grace adjusted the pillows behind her. "It's just that your mom and Ben are starting their lives together. I'm sure by this time next year they'll have gotten a place of their own and will be enjoying their retirement and freedom."

"That's not a bad thing, is it?"

"For me it is," she sobbed. "I don't know where I'll be a year from now."

Riley lay beside her. "Neither do I," he admitted. "I hadn't planned on being a civilian at this point in my life. I thought I'd be a marine forever. But now? I don't have a job, I don't have a home, and I have no idea what I'm going to do with myself."

Grace rolled onto her side and looked at him. "But you do have a home. *This* is your home. Don't you know how lucky you are? I had no choice but to sell my family home my parents died, and since then, I've been wandering from place to place trying to find someplace to actually call home. They're not easy to find."

He smiled sadly at her. "I'm so sorry, Grace," he said gruffly. "I'm so damn sorry for all that you had and all that you lost."

She tried to shrug dismissively, but the quiver in her voice gave her away. "You learn to deal with it."

Reaching out, Riley wrapped an arm around her and pulled her close to his side. She put her head on his shoulder and a hand on his heart and sighed. Carefully, he kicked off his shoes and socks and tucked her as close to him as she could get with her under the blankets and him on top of them. "Sleep, Grace. I'm here, and I promise there won't be any more bad dreams tonight."

"You promise?" she asked sleepily and promptly yawned.

Riley kissed the top of her head. "I promise."

—⁓—

Grace woke up some time later with a sense of confusion. The light she always kept on was still lit, so it didn't take long for her to figure out what was different.

Riley was sleeping beside her.

She racked her brain, trying to remember why he was here, and then remembered how he had heard her crying out in her sleep. A wave of embarrassment washed over her. *Great. Score yet another point in reasons to run screaming from Grace.* His arm was banded tightly around her, and when she raised her head from his shoulder, he instantly came awake.

"Grace?" he whispered. "Are you okay?"

She kind of liked the fact that his first thought was to see about her feelings, and she just let that warm, fuzzy feeling stay with her for a moment before he said her name again. "I'm fine," she finally said. "I just woke up and realized you were still here."

Riley pulled back slightly and looked at her face. She was so beautiful. Her skin was a little flushed; her eyes had a sleepy, dreamlike quality to them; and she felt so warm pressed up against him. He sighed with contentment.

"Do you want me to leave?" he asked, although he really wasn't sure he wanted to hear the answer.

Grace shook her head. "No," she said firmly, sounding more awake than she had a few seconds ago. "I don't want you to go."

A slow smile crept across Riley's face. "Good." He started to tuck her head back on his shoulder, but she stopped him. "What? What's wrong?"

Sitting up, Grace tugged at the blankets he was lying on top of. "I can't move under there."

He chuckled. "Do you want to move under there?"

"If I didn't, would I have said anything?" she asked sweetly.

Riley wasn't sure if she was just playing with him or if she was serious, so he figured he'd better clarify. "If I'm not on top of the blankets, and you don't want me to go, then that means I'll be *under* the blankets with you."

"That was the plan, Ace," she said with a sassy grin.

Standing up, Riley pulled his shirt up over his head and let it drop to the floor before looking at Grace. His expression dared her to stop him.

She sat up a little straighter and folded the blankets over on his side of the bed.

He reached for the button on his jeans.

Grace fluffed his pillow.

His zipper rasped.

She smoothed the fitted sheet.

Denim dropped to the floor.

Grace reclined against her pillows and raised her hands above her head and smiled when she heard Riley groan.

"You're killing me. You know that, right?"

"Me?" she said innocently. "I don't know what you're talking about." And then she stretched, arching her back so her breasts were firmly outlined in the ribbed tank top she wore.

"That's okay," Riley said, climbing in the bed beside her. "Two can play at that game." He pulled the blankets up and over the both of them. "Oh, should I turn out the light?" he asked.

Grace shook her head. "No," she said a little too quickly. "I mean…um…I usually keep it on."

He wanted to know her reasons, just not right now. He had to clear one last bit of the air before he could do what he had been dying to do for what seemed like ages. "I spent the past few days with my buddies," he began and watched as Grace registered what he was saying. She slid away from him, and he felt the wall come down between them.

Moving closer to her and doing his best to stop her before she completely pulled away from him, he said, "There was no one, Grace. It's you I want. No one else."

"Really?" she whispered.

Riley nodded solemnly. "Really."

"Thank you for telling me that," she said as she reached up, curved a hand behind his neck, and pulled Riley to her. But before he kissed her, she pulled away one more time.

"What?" he asked, barely masking his frustration.

"Why did you stay away so long then?"

He smiled, loving her barely veiled admission that she missed him. "I was trying to show some self-control. But it turns out, I don't have any where you're concerned."

"Oh, I don't know about that. We're still talking, aren't we?"

He gave her a sexy smile that made her purr as he aligned his body over hers. "Not anymore."

Chapter 8

THANKSGIVING CAME AND WENT IN WHAT SEEMED LIKE A flash, and the inn was bustling with activity like Grace had never imagined.

Her days were filled with cooking and decorating and interacting with their guests, while her nights were filled with Riley. They were trying to be discreet because he didn't want his mother getting too attached to the idea of him and Grace together, and although they hadn't actually talked about it, Grace seemed to be taking her cues from him.

While Grace was busy playing hostess, Riley found himself wandering the grounds with Ben and helping to clear a couple of acres for a project Corinne and Grace had come up with—an event barn. Riley wasn't sure he was on board with the idea yet, but the plan was to clear an acre or two and build a barn to hold one hundred to one hundred and fifty people at weddings or parties the inn would host. Ben talked about adding a garden where ceremonies could take place in the spring and summer—a time that was usually slower at the inn. Additions like this would be a way to keep business strong, possibly year-round.

"I have to tell you," Ben began as they walked around marking the land they needed trees cut from, "I love doing all of this stuff around the property, but it sure is nice to have some help. I've been doing this for a long time, and although I get the occasional college kid to help, they're not really interested in what they're doing. It's simply a paycheck."

Riley nodded. "I had to do plenty of things in the service that weren't what I wanted to do, but I had to give it my all."

"But you enjoy working the land out here, don't you?"

Again he nodded. "I missed the mountain air. We spent so much time in the desert that I would often lay in bed at night and try to remember what the air here smelled like. It kept me sane more times than I care to admit."

"There's nothing like this anywhere in the world," Ben said as he inhaled deeply. "If we get the land cleared and graded before we get any snow, we'll be ahead of schedule. We still need to find someone to design the place based on our specs, and I'm hoping to have it done by June."

Riley was impressed with the older man's enthusiasm. "That's pushing it a bit, isn't it? I thought that there wasn't a rush for this."

Ben shrugged. "Well, there wasn't at first, but now…well… Hell, Riley. I want to ask your mother to marry me."

Riley wasn't sure why he was surprised, and yet he was. "O-kay," he said slowly. "And what does this have to do with the barn?"

"I'd like us to be the first couple to get married here. I waited a long time for Corrine, and if it were up to me, I'd marry her on Christmas, but I know she needs a little more time to adjust to our new relationship. I hope you're okay with it too."

"Honestly, Ben, I couldn't be happier for the two of you. I'm just a little surprised, I guess. I always wanted her to find someone to love her, but now that she has, it just feels a little strange."

"I know what you mean. I still walk in the door here every morning and feel a little shocked when Corrine comes over and kisses me."

Riley didn't want to think about that aspect of his mother and Ben's relationship. "I really am happy for the two of you," he finally said. "So what do we need to do to make this whole barn thing happen?"

"Well," Ben said hesitantly, "I really could use someone to work with me."

"Like a crew? Do you still keep in touch with the guys who bought your company?"

Ben shook his head. "I'd like to keep costs down. I was thinking maybe you could help me. I know you've got the skills to do it, and really, I think it would mean the world to your mom to know we built this together for her."

Riley didn't know what to say. That would mean staying here longer than he had originally expected. Even though he had no real plans for his future, and he'd stopped feeling so anxious to escape since he and Grace had gotten involved, could he really stick around that long? Oddly enough, the idea didn't make him break out in a cold sweat like it used to.

"Sure," he said easily, still expecting a panic attack to seize him. "I don't think it will be a problem. I still want to head to Florida for a week to see some friends, but other than that, my schedule is wide open."

Ben's smile widened. He walked over to Riley, and

they shook on it. "Let's get these measurements done so the tree guys can get in here and get started."

—∿∿—

Grace felt dead on her feet. They had a full house, and the guests were a bit more demanding than their usual clientele. It seemed like no matter how much food she prepared, someone always needed something more or had a special request. When the last guest finally left the dining room, she all but sagged to the floor.

"Oh dear. They are a handful, aren't they?" Corrine said as she began clearing the table.

"I didn't think they'd ever stop eating," Grace said, her head still swimming from all of the requests. "I'm going to have to go shopping again tomorrow. They wiped out all of the desserts. Even the ones for the rest of the week! I know they're guests, but we may have to find a way to limit what we offer without coming off as being strict or stingy."

"Either that or bake more," Corrine said with a laugh.

"I may have to move my bed into the kitchen at this rate."

Together they finished cleaning the dining room in companionable silence, and while Grace did the dishes, Corrine set up for breakfast. "Why don't you sleep in tomorrow morning and I'll take care of breakfast?" she suggested.

Grace turned to her and frowned. "Why?"

"Because you put in a long day. You deserve a morning off once in a while. Trust me, the holidays can be hard around here, and from now until after New Year's, it's going to be nonstop. Take the morning, Grace. You definitely deserve it."

The thought of sleeping in was very appealing. The thought of sleeping in with Riley was even more appealing. The only problem Grace saw was that she would have a hard time sneaking him out of the basement if Corrine was already up and taking care of stuff before they came up. Basically, that meant she'd get to sleep in, but Riley would have to leave before Corrine got up.

That wasn't appealing at all anymore.

"We'll see," Grace said. "My body clock doesn't let me sleep in anymore."

When everything was in its place, Grace wished Corrine a good night and padded to the basement. She hadn't seen Riley since before dinner, and all she wanted to do was soak in the hot tub and relax before crawling into bed and sleeping.

At the foot of the stairs she came up short. Candles were lit all around the room, and music was playing softly. The blankets on the bed were turned down, and if she wasn't mistaken, she could smell Chinese food. "What in the world?" she whispered as she stepped farther into the room.

Riley came toward her. "It was crazy up there tonight with that group, and I figured you didn't take time—or rather, you didn't *have* time—to sit and eat your own dinner, so I picked some up for you." He motioned toward the bag sitting on her small bistro table in the corner.

Taking Grace by the hand, he led her to the table. "I wasn't sure what you liked, so I stuck to the basics. We can have a mini buffet." She thought he was going to start taking food out of the bags, but he kept her hand in his and led her over to the bed. "Then, I plan on giving you a relaxing massage to help erase all of the stress and tension from the day."

She almost purred at the thought.

Still walking, he led her over to her dresser, where she noticed her bathing suit was on display. "This is really just for show, because after the massage, I plan on us going to the hot tub and finishing what we started several weeks ago." He waggled his eyebrows at her and smiled when she began to laugh.

"And then…" he said dramatically, "we'll come back here, dry each other off, and"—he led her over to her small refrigerator and opened the freezer—"we'll finish off the night with some cookie dough ice cream."

Unable to help herself, Grace tugged on his hand and pulled him to her as she went up on her toes and kissed him. It didn't matter to her if they didn't eat dinner or do any of the other things that Riley had planned. No man had ever taken such care or been so considerate, and she was simply overwhelmed by his kindness.

This wasn't one of their usual frantic, fast-paced kisses. No, this time Grace wanted to show him tenderness and take the time to just appreciate and explore him. Her tongue lightly traced his bottom lip, and at the same time, as he opened for her, Riley's arm slowly banded around her waist to bring her in close.

Their lips gently sipped at one another and their tongues touched shyly. It was a most erotic form of foreplay.

Riley reluctantly lifted his head. "Damn, Grace," he said, resting his forehead on hers. "I want you so much right now. I was proud of myself for putting all of this together, and you're blowing my carefully crafted attempt at romance to shreds."

He said the words lightly, but Grace knew that he was right. He had put a lot of thought and effort into creating a wonderful night for her, and she needed to let him take the lead. Sighing, she hugged him and rested her head on his chest. "I just wanted to show you how much I appreciate all that you did. This was a wonderful surprise." She raised her head and looked at him. "Thank you."

Smiling, Riley stepped back, once again took her by the hand, and led her to the table where he promptly began dishing out food.

They ate and talked for what seemed like hours. Grace told him about Corrine's offer to let her sleep in tomorrow and asked for suggestions on sneaking him out of the basement so that he could spend the night.

"That's easy. You go up first and distract Mom in the kitchen. I'll come up a few minutes after and go to my room and come out a bit later."

"Done," Grace said, relieved that they had found a solution. Riley told her about his conversation with Ben about the barn. "So you're going to build it with him? Seriously?"

Riley nodded. "I actually enjoy construction. Before Ben sold his business, I used to work with him over my summer breaks. I always imagined that when I came home, I'd work for him. I was a little disappointed that he'd sold the business, but I totally understand why he did."

"Your mother is going to be thrilled you're doing this project together."

"That's what Ben said."

Grace wanted to ask how he felt about staying here at the inn. The fact that he was willing to work on a project that would improve business might mean he had given up his campaign to get Corrine to sell. That would be wonderful for her friend, but it really didn't change Grace's plans. Sure, she might not be in such a rush to leave, but she would eventually. A bed-and-breakfast of this magnitude was out of her reach, but she now knew that she wanted to go in that direction.

It couldn't be around here, because she wouldn't want to be in competition with the Snowflake Inn or Corrine. Who knows? She might head back to New York and see about doing something upstate. She was so lost in her own thoughts that she didn't notice right away that Riley was standing next to her. She looked up in confusion.

Holding out a hand to her, he pulled Grace to her feet. "Before we get too full, I want to make sure you get your massage."

Grace looked at the clock and saw it was nearing nine o'clock. "As much as I love the idea of it, Riley, it's getting late. We can do this another time."

He shook his head. "We get to sleep in tomorrow morning, so we can stay up late tonight." He flashed her a wicked grin before leading her over to the bed.

"I guess you have a point there," she said sexily, leaning in to kiss his neck.

"Uh-uh," he admonished. "None of that." Without another word, Riley began to undress her. His hands moved slowly, seductively, but they were all that touched Grace. When he had her down to nothing but her panties, he instructed her to get on her belly on the bed. She readily agreed. Once she was situated, Riley straddled her thighs and began to work on her back.

This time Grace really did purr. Riley's hands were

pure magic, and it was as if he knew the exact spots that were bothering her because he hit them all. In a matter of minutes, she felt like nothing more than a limp noodle.

It didn't take long for Riley to realize Grace was almost too relaxed. He climbed off the bed and stood beside her. "Okay, now that we've gotten all of those tense muscles loosened up, let's hit the hot tub and soak for a little while."

She whined in protest because she was so comfortable. It was cold outside. Even though she knew that between the heat lamps and the hot water, she'd be fine, the thought of getting to and from the warmth was making her not want to go. "It's cold out there, Riley," she said sleepily.

Leaning down, he flicked his tongue against her earlobe and felt her shudder. "I promise to keep you warm."

The thing was, Grace really wanted to get into the hot tub. Even before she'd found Riley, she had been fantasizing about it all day. So with a sense of determination, she forced herself off the bed and stood before Riley in nothing more than her panties. With her hands on her hips, she looked him square in the eye and said, "Just remember what you promised."

In that moment, he would have promised her anything. Her hair was in sexy disarray and draped over her shoulders to the swell of her breasts. Her skin was flushed, and her eyes had that sleepy look he loved so much. His throat was dry, and his tongue felt like it was the size of his fist. He couldn't have formed a single syllable if he tried, so he simply nodded.

With a lazy smile, Grace began getting dressed again for the walk to the hot tub. When she stood at the base of the steps and looked at Riley, she noticed he hadn't moved. "Well?" she asked playfully. "Are you coming?"

A deep, throaty laugh that was practically a growl came from him as he stalked toward her. "Not yet, but soon."

———∿∿∿———

Much later, they were sitting in Grace's bed propped up on a mountain of pillows and sharing the cookie dough ice cream. "I have to admit," she said after licking the spoon, "I was a little afraid we'd wake the guests while we were out there."

Riley chuckled. "We? Sweetheart, that screaming was all you."

She swatted his arm playfully. "And whose fault was it that I was screaming?"

"That's your big defense? That I made you do it?" She nodded and dug in for another spoonful. "Hey! How about you let me have some of the ice cream?"

Grace shrugged. "I guess you should have gotten two spoons. You snooze, you lose. You know that."

With a lightning-quick move, Riley had the spoon and the ice cream out of Grace's hands. Before she could even react with more than "*Hey!*" he'd put them on the table and had her pinned beneath him. "I didn't want my own spoon," he said lightly. "We were supposed to be sharing." He nipped at the sensitive spot by her pulse on her slender throat and felt her buck beneath him.

"We're both only children, Riley," she said breathlessly as his mouth began to roam to her collarbone and the swell of her breasts. "You know we don't share well." Grace was certain she was trying to prove a point, but as Riley's hands joined the journey his mouth was on, she couldn't remember what it was.

"Is this how I have to distract you to get what I want?" he asked gruffly, quickly returning his attention to the creamy skin of her belly.

She gasped and then settled as he moved lower. "You can have whatever you want."

Chapter 9

THE DEMANDING GUESTS HAD LEFT, AND WHILE EVERYONE was thrilled to have a little more peace and quiet around the inn, it didn't last long. Word had gotten out about the rehab of the rooms, so they had a lot of traffic from curious townsfolk coming through, including the local newspaper that wanted to do a feature story on them. Along with that came the surprising news that Grace's cooking was getting a lot of buzz as well. Soon they were receiving reservations solely for dining. Corrine had contemplated the option but hadn't wanted to commit to it yet. Soon enough, they also were getting a lot more room reservations, and she and Grace both had the sneaking suspicion that they were from food critics coming to check them out.

It was an exciting time around the Snowflake Inn. Corrine sat back and wondered at how she had been managing the inn on her own for so long when suddenly four of them were working full-time around the place — and they were all busy. It did her heart good to have Riley home and to see him taking an active role around the inn. He didn't seem distant and full of resentment for his childhood home anymore.

Out of the corner of her eye, Corrine saw Riley talking to Grace in the kitchen. She smiled. There wasn't a doubt in her mind that Grace was largely responsible for her son's sudden interest in the business — a *positive* interest in the business. Corrine had no idea where any of it was going to lead. All she knew was that right now, at that moment, life was good.

Doing her best to stay undetected, she hid in the shadows and simply watched the younger couple. Riley was smiling at Grace while she talked to him. She was putting together some sort of gourmet potpie while she spoke, and Corrine admired the natural ease with which Grace worked and moved. Looking at Riley again, she realized that a lot of the tension she had noticed in him when he'd first arrived was now gone. He smiled more, laughed more, and was easier in his own skin. As a mother, all she'd ever wanted was for her son to be happy. She wasn't sure if he had been happy in the military, but looking at him, she knew he was now.

"It's not nice to spy on people," Ben said quietly from directly behind her. Corrine nearly jumped out of her own skin, but Ben wrapped his arms around her and pulled her close against him. "What's so fascinating?"

"Look at them," she whispered. "They think they're so clever and secretive, but you can't hide that."

"Hide what?" Ben looked confused. He checked out the kitchen over Corrine's shoulder and saw Riley standing and talking to Grace. Nothing out of the ordinary.

"Oh, for crying out loud," Corrine sighed. "You honestly are going to stand there and tell me you don't see it?"

"Corrine, sweetheart, you're going to have to be more specific."

"Fine," she huffed. "Riley and Grace have gotten... closer."

It took a minute, but finally Ben caught on. "Ooohhh..."

He looked closer at the couple and then nodded. "Okay, now I see it."

"I wish they weren't trying to hide it. I think it's wonderful that they're a couple and that they're falling in love. Maybe now Riley will stay, and eventually he'll want to take over the inn because Grace is here, and then it will go to our grandchildren and stay in the family. And then maybe—"

Ben cut her off. "And that's why they're keeping it a secret."

Corrine turned and looked at him. "What? What are you talking about?"

Ben turned her in his arms and pulled her away from her hiding spot. "Corrine, did you not just hear yourself?"

"What? What did I say?"

"In a matter of seconds you went from wondering why they were being so secretive to having Riley's children and grandchildren taking over the inn. If you come at him with that kind of talk, you'll scare him away."

She wanted to argue with Ben, but unfortunately he was right. She sighed. "I know I can get a little ahead of myself, but…I just want him to be happy, Ben. I was standing there, and I saw the look of peace and happiness on his face, and all I could think was… Finally! My son is finally happy! Is that so wrong?"

Ben shook his head. "No, it's not wrong at all. But if they do decide to share this new relationship, you are going to have to be careful how you react to it. If you get all excited and start planning the future, he's going to shut down again. Is that what you want?"

"No," she said sadly. "But how am I supposed to hide how happy I am for them?"

He pulled her close and wrapped his arms around her. "You share it with me. When you feel like you are just going to burst with excitement, come and talk to me about it. Until you know where this relationship between Riley and Grace is going, you need to reel it in a bit. Okay?"

"Fine," she said with a pout. "I'll do it, but I don't see why I have to pretend that I'm not excited when I really am."

"It's only temporary. Let them figure out where they see their relationship going before you jump in with both feet and share your hopes and dreams for their future. Okay?"

"Fine...for now."

～～～

"I know a lot of people put their Christmas trees up on Thanksgiving, but I'm so glad you didn't do that," Grace said a week after Thanksgiving as they were going through the inn's ornaments and decorations. It was a rare night with no guests, and they'd decided to take advantage of the time to decorate the main house.

"Well, I jumped the gun a little bit on cabin number three, but that was just to impress Ben," Corrine said as she leaned over and kissed that very impressed man.

"And it was well and truly appreciated," he said.

All four of them had gone walking on the property that morning to find the perfect tree, and once they found it, Ben and Riley had cut it down and brought it back to the house to get it acclimated to the temperature before decorating it. Grace had made a batch of chili for lunch and chicken and dumplings for dinner. Now, with their bellies full, they were ready to tackle both tree and home holiday decorating.

Grace had finished her cleanup in the kitchen while the others got everything set up in the living room. The scene that greeted her there hit her hard. It had been so long since she'd had a family Christmas that it was a bit overwhelming. She stood back and watched as Ben and Riley strung the lights on the ten-foot tree while Corrine instructed them on where the bare spots were. Christmas music was playing in the background, and there was a fire roaring in the massive stone fireplace.

Earlier in the week, she and Corrine had baked cookies, and Grace knew that at some point tonight they would all sit and admire their work while eating those cookies and drinking hot chocolate.

Her throat clogged with emotion. In her mind, she could see the last Christmas she'd spent with her parents. It had been an eerily similar scene. They listened to music and laughed as they decorated their tree. Grace remembered how her mother used to love to bake cupcakes; cookies weren't her thing. So every year they made Christmas cupcakes, and the first batch would be eaten only after the tree was decorated.

Her father used to curse as he strung the lights, much like Riley right now. Grace smiled at the similarity. Her mother was lovingly militant not only in the placement of the lights but of the ornaments as well. She had a feeling that Corrine was going to be the same way.

Down in the basement, tucked away in her closet, were three small boxes that held the few ornaments Grace had kept when she sold off everything in her family home. They were ornaments that held special

significance for her, ornaments that represented the love
that they had shared as a family.

Carefully, she tiptoed out of the room and headed to
the basement. She needed a few minutes to compose
herself before joining the others in the living room.
Once in her room, Grace went to the closet and retrieved
the boxes. She had contemplated putting a tree here but
hadn't gotten around to it. For now, it didn't matter that
there wasn't one. For now, it was enough to just unwrap
a few of those precious pieces of her family and to say
a prayer of thanks for the years that they'd had together.
Even though those years had been cut short.

Would they be proud of her? Her parents? Would
they look at the woman she had become and tell her
that she was doing a good job with her life? She hoped
so. Not a day went by that she didn't miss them, but the
holidays were extremely hard. Reaching into the first
box, Grace pulled out the first tissue-wrapped item she
found. It had been years since she allowed herself to
open the boxes, mainly because she never had the time
or a place of her own where she felt comfortable taking
them out.

Sitting on the floor, she gently unwrapped the item
with shaking hands. Inside was a Lenox ornament that
said "Our First Christmas," and below those words was
a picture of Grace as an infant in her mother's arms with
her father beside them. Reverently, she ran a finger over
each of their faces. "I miss you," she said quietly as tears
began to roll down her face.

Hugging the fragile ornament to her chest, Grace
drew her knees up and rested her head on them as she
allowed herself to cry. So many years. It had been so

long since she had seen them or heard their voices or felt their embraces, and right now that was all she longed for.

She never heard his approach, but suddenly there was another embrace, and without questioning it, Grace turned into Riley's arms and continued to cry silently. "Grace? Sweetheart? What's going on? What happened?"

Unable to answer, she did her best to crawl into his lap and just enjoy the feeling of his strong arms wrapped around her. Luckily he didn't push her to talk. He simply held her and rocked her gently until her sobs subsided.

Taking a deep breath, Grace realized she had no idea how long she had been in her room or how long Riley had been holding her. She held up the ornament she had been cradling to her chest so Riley could see it.

"This is me with my parents on my first Christmas. I was three months old."

Not wanting to take something so precious from her hands, Riley looked at it, carefully touched it with one strong finger, and smiled. "You look a lot like your mom," he said softly.

Grace studied the picture and realized he was right. Why had she never noticed that before? "Thank you."

Riley looked around the room and saw the three boxes beside them. Only one had been opened. "Are these all filled with Christmas ornaments?"

She nodded. "They've been in storage for years. This is the first time I've opened them."

"Do you want to bring them upstairs and put them on the tree?"

Now she shook her head. "I promised myself I wouldn't take them out until I had a place of my own, a tree of my own. But tonight"—she stopped and took a steadying breath—"tonight when I came out of the kitchen and saw the three of you working together to decorate, I was just overwhelmed with the need to take these out and see them. To remember."

Riley held her a little tighter. "Oh, Grace…"

"I haven't had a Christmas tree in ten years. I made sure I always worked through the holidays." She wiped at her eyes. "All of my bosses and coworkers loved it because someone else could have those days off. I didn't want to be home alone on Christmas."

"You're not alone this year, Grace," Riley said, his tone deep and serious.

She smiled sadly at him. "I know. But it's still not a place of my own. This…my time here…it's temporary."

"What are you talking about?" Riley was confused. Was she planning on leaving?

"You and I both know that right now everyone is keeping the peace, but once the holidays are over, Ben and Corrine will want to start planning their future, and so will you. As much as I love this place, I need a place of my own where I can grow roots." She scooted off Riley's lap. "Eventually you're going to want to leave, and if you go, Corrine's not going to stay either."

"Then you should buy the inn."

A mirthless laugh escaped before she could stop it. "In my wildest dreams I couldn't even imagine having someplace as grand as this. I have money put aside, but nowhere near enough to own this. Don't get me wrong. I would love to own the Snowflake Inn, but the B and B that I eventually buy will be on a much smaller scale. And I'm really okay with that."

"Grace…"

"Your mother has taught me so much in these past couple of months, and I appreciate all of it. I think she and I were good for one another. But she's got a new life that's just beginning, and I'm realistic, Riley." She reached out and touched his face, looked into those amazing blue eyes. "This was never in the cards."

He knew she wasn't talking only about the inn but also about the two of them, and his chest actually ached. "I thought you wanted to be partners…that the two of you had talked about it."

Leaning in, Grace kissed him. "When you leave, Riley, I won't want to be here."

"Who says I'm going to leave?" His voice was rough with emotion; she was killing him.

"You did. Repeatedly. I'm old enough to know that in the end, everybody leaves."

"So this is what? A preemptive strike? You're going to leave before I do?" Now he was frustrated. What the hell had happened since dinner? All of this was over a Christmas tree? An ornament? He didn't understand. Standing up, he looked at her. "Where is all this coming from, Grace?"

Standing, she placed the ornament in its tissue wrapping and closed the box. Without saying a word, she carried the boxes to the closet and tucked them away. Riley was standing where she had left him, waiting for an answer. "I don't want to argue with you," she said simply.

"Well, that's too bad because that's what's happening, Grace," he said, unable to hide his frustration. "An hour ago we were all laughing and enjoying dinner and planning to decorate for Christmas, and now…now you're not only withdrawing from that but from the inn…and me."

Grace let out a breath she hadn't realized she was holding. "I didn't plan this, Riley. I got overwhelmed by the situation, and when I came here and thought about my parents… Well, it reminded me of what's real and what's not."

"This is real, Grace. What we have is real."

If only, she thought. "I know that. I honestly do. But we want different things in life. I'm twenty-eight years old, Riley. I've been alone and trying to get my head together for ten years. I want…" Now she was getting frustrated. "I want a place of my own! A tree of my own! I want to take those damn boxes out of the closet and hang those ornaments and know they're hanging in my house. I want to look at them without feeling like my heart has been pierced."

"You can do all of that here," he said as patiently as he could. "Bring them upstairs; share them with us."

He didn't understand. Grace knew that he wouldn't, and if she were honest with herself, she didn't fully understand her little outburst either. Riley was right. They had been having a wonderful day, and instead of being upstairs enjoying the festivities, she was having a temper tantrum because, basically, she was afraid. It was a preemptive strike. She needed to start distancing herself from this family, from this place, so that it wouldn't hurt so much when she left.

Riley watched the play of emotion on Grace's face and wanted to do whatever it took to take her pain away. Stepping forward, he carefully pulled her close. "Tell you what," he began. "Let's go upstairs, help with the decorating, eat cookies, and drink cocoa, and we'll put off this discussion until after Christmas." Tucking a finger under her chin, he gently forced her to look up at him. "What do you say?"

"It won't change—"

"Shh…" He placed a finger over her lips. "After Christmas."

Grace didn't see that it would make a difference, but for argument's sake, she reluctantly agreed. "After Christmas."

Smiling, Riley leaned in and kissed her. The kiss was soft and sweet and over almost before it began. "I'm going to head back upstairs and see how Mom and Ben are doing. Why don't you put on something more comfortable?" he asked and then saw Grace roll her eyes. "Like sweats or something," he corrected, "and come upstairs and join us. Mom was singing your praises earlier about the cookies, and if you aren't up there, none of us can have any."

"I'm sure she wouldn't—"

"And you know how much I love cookies," he interrupted. "I've been in the military for twelve years, Grace. By the time any Christmas cookies got to me, they could be used as weapons. Have pity on me."

"Oh, for crying out loud. Dramatic much?" she asked with a chuckle. "Fine, let me wash my face and get changed, and I'll be up in a few minutes."

"You're an angel," he said, placing a kiss on her nose. Turning, he headed toward the stairs but stopped before taking the first step. "I mean it, Grace. You're an angel." His tone was gentler than she had ever heard, and the smile on his face said more than any words could have. "I'll meet you upstairs."

And then he was gone.

Closing the door to the basement, Riley walked determinedly into the living room.

"Is everything all right?" Corrine asked. "Is Grace feeling okay? You were gone for a long time."

Riley looked over his shoulder to make sure Grace hadn't followed him up yet. Turning back to his mother and Ben, he motioned for them to sit on the couch. "She was pretty upset. This is going to be the first real Christmas she's celebrated since her parents died."

"Oh no," Corrine cried. "Maybe I should go and talk to her."

Riley held up a hand to stop her. "Not right now, Mom. I talked to her, and I convinced her to come up and join us."

"Are you sure that's a good idea?"

"I'm hoping it is. Can you both help me with something?" Ben and Corrine looked at one another and then back at Riley. "I want to make this the best Christmas Grace has ever had."

Corrine smiled like the cat that ate the canary, and Ben leaned back on the sofa with a grin of his own. "Whatever you need, son, count us in."

Chapter 10

GRACE WASN'T SURE WHAT WAS GOING ON, BUT SHE WAS pretty sure something was up. The night that they had decorated the Christmas tree and the main house, she had ended up truly enjoying herself. Riley had been attentive and made sure she was included in everything. When she entered the living room that night, he became a different person. He had walked right up to her, taken her in his arms, and kissed her in front of Corrine and Ben!

At first Grace had been too shocked to react, but then she figured if he had made peace with it, then she should too. No one said a word about their kiss, and that in itself had seemed odd. They had ended the night by sitting in front of the fire, eating cookies and drinking cocoa, and Grace felt like she had stepped into a Norman Rockwell painting.

The days that followed had also seemed different. Corrine was asking for Grace's input more and more and leaving her in charge of a few more things. None of it was major, but Grace knew how much her friend enjoyed running her business. She preferred to take care of some aspects of it herself. But suddenly, she was asking Grace to help her with them.

Ben was constantly keeping her up-to-date on the progress with the barn and the garden and had asked her opinion on every decision that had to be made. Grace had wanted to tell him that it really didn't matter if she liked it because she wasn't going to be here when it was done. Unfortunately, the more involved she got in the project, the more she found herself wanting to stay.

And then there was Riley.

Sigh.

Riley had essentially moved into the basement with her. Grace had thought it would be weird, but they'd settled in together perfectly. She hated that everything was going so well, because it was going to make leaving that much harder. Granted, Riley hadn't mentioned leaving once—not even to visit his friends in Florida. All of his conversations about the future were about the barn and the possibility of organizing tours and walking trails and activities for guests.

He worked side by side with Ben all day and then slept beside her every night. The only way Grace could describe life at the Snowflake Inn was…normal. That thought gave her pause because she had been so busy running and struggling just to stay alive that she had forgotten what normal even felt like. But now as she pulled a roast from the oven and looked around the kitchen, she realized that she felt content.

When did that happen?

How did that happen?

And what was she going to do about it?

It was hard to remember why she had wanted to leave, but Grace knew it was getting close to time for her to go. Maybe. Stepping away from the butcher-block island, Grace went to stand by the French doors that led out to a massive deck on the back of the inn. Beyond the deck was nothing but beautiful, wooded property.

A light snow was falling, making the woods look like something off a postcard. She sighed.

How was she going to walk away from all of this? She had spent ten years moving around the country, and no place had ever felt so right or made her feel like she belonged.

The Snowflake Inn did.

Corrine and Ben did.

Riley did.

There was so much uncertainty that Grace was afraid to take a leap of faith to stay and wait to see how it all panned out. There was always the possibility that Corrine and Ben were going to get married and keep the inn. All of the time and effort that Riley had been putting in could show him that this was where he belonged as well, and then he could give up the idea of Corrine selling the place.

Would he still want her if he decided to stay? Would he want to continue their relationship if she decided to stay? And to what end?

If Grace were a different type of person, if she hadn't experienced firsthand the crushing realities of how cruel life could be, she might be tempted to believe in fairy tales and happy endings.

But she wasn't.

For the first eighteen years of her life, Grace had led a perfect life. But then that ended. Tragically. The aftermath had been brutal, every day a struggle to survive. It wasn't a financial struggle; her parents had made sure that she was well provided for. The emotional aspect of losing her family had been harder to deal with. Grace had no one to count on, no one to turn to. Eventually, she'd just stopped looking for anyone to fill that role.

But here and now at the inn? There was hope. There were possibilities. And yet she was still afraid to reach out and take a chance. What if she put herself out there, stayed here at the inn, and then Corrine decided to sell it? Where would that leave her? What if she trusted in the relationship that she and Riley were building, and he came home one day and told her they were through? How would she survive it?

In either scenario, she would be in the same place: homeless with no place to go.

Ah, yes, she reminded herself, *that is why you need to go*.

Grace knew that it would be better and less awkward if she made the decision to leave, rather than have somebody tell her that it was time for her to go. That decision had been made for her at the lowest point in her life. Now when she moved on, it would be on her own terms.

"How's dinner coming?" Corrine asked as she came into the kitchen to collect the place settings for the dining room.

Turning, Grace smiled at her. "I was just letting the roast settle for a bit before slicing it, but other than that, everything is done."

"It all smells delicious!" Corrine began lifting lids off pots and bowls to sneak a peek at that night's menu. "What have we got?"

Walking over, Grace stopped beside her friend and ran through the list. "We've got pot roast, mashed potatoes, carrots, corn, biscuits, gravy, a salad, and an apple pie for dessert."

"Oh, comfort food. It's the perfect night for it. Did you see the snow?"

Grace nodded. "It's beautiful. I didn't realize it was even in the forecast when I did the menu, but you're right. It's the perfect meal for a night like this."

"We've only got a handful of people with us tonight, so if it's all right with you, I'll get everyone settled and served, and then"—Corinne blushed and looked away slightly—"I think I'll head home with Ben tonight. Is that okay? Would you mind terribly handling things here without me?"

Grace knew how hard it must have been for Corrine to ask—and to admit that she was going to spend the night with Ben. Wrapping her arm around her friend, Grace pulled Corrine in close. "I don't mind at all. Like you said, we've got a smaller crowd tonight, and really, we're caught up on everything else."

"I don't want you to think that I'm taking advantage or—"

"Nonsense. I don't feel that way at all. I know that you would never do such a thing. Go and enjoy yourself. You and Ben deserve a little alone time."

"You're sure you don't mind? I can be back to help out for breakfast."

"Don't you dare!" Grace said with a laugh as she stepped back. "You go and spend the entire night with that man, and then make him breakfast in bed or something. I don't want to see either of you around here until at least lunchtime."

Corrine was blushing profusely now. "I don't know about that… Riley might wonder where I am and—"

Grace waved her off. "Don't worry about Riley. I'll

make him help me out around here if I need anything, and believe me, he won't want to know what you're doing."

A small smile crept across Corrine's face. "Oh, I hadn't even thought of it like that." She tried to sound remorseful, but once her eyes met Grace's, they both broke out in a fit of giggles.

That's how Riley found them. "What's so funny?"

Corrine did her best to calm down and answer him with a straight face, but it just wasn't possible. Grace had turned away and began collecting food to bring into the dining room, giggling the entire time.

"Mom?"

Taking a deep breath, Corrine looked her son straight in the eye. "I'm spending the night at Ben's house. I'm leaving you and Grace in charge." The look on Riley's face was near comical.

"Oh…um…" Riley stammered, nervously looking around for Grace. "O-kay," he said slowly. "So…um… when will you be back?"

Grace walked back in and, having heard Riley's comment, decided to be the one to answer. "Whenever she and Ben have thoroughly exhausted one another. It could be days."

And the giggles started all over again.

Once all of their guests had finished eating and had gone to their rooms, Grace and Riley sat down to a late dinner in the kitchen, just the two of them. Leaning across the table, Grace reached for his hand. "So seriously, are you okay about your mother and Ben, you know, doing it?"

His fork dropped loudly on his plate, and Riley

looked up at Grace, his expression stricken. He choked on the food he had in his mouth, and she felt bad about poking at him over the situation. "I'm sorry. That was mean of me," she said, patting him on the back to help him stop coughing.

"That was just cruel, Grace," Riley said when he was finally able to speak. Looking into her eyes, he smiled when he saw that she wasn't the least bit repentant. "I'll admit, that wasn't my favorite moment, hearing my mom talk about spending the night with her boyfriend. To be honest, she never dated. It was never something that came up after my father died, so this is all new to me."

"I can't even imagine. I would hope that it helps that she's with Ben. I mean, you've known him your entire life, so you know he's a good man and he really does love Corrine."

Riley smiled. "He's been there for her—for us—for as long as I can remember."

"It's got to be a little awkward for them. I mean, they've been friends for so many years, and at this point in their lives, maybe they thought it was too late." She shrugged. "I'm just glad they finally stopped dancing around one another and went for it."

"Um…Grace?"

"Hmm?"

"Could we not talk about them…going for it?" Riley put a hand over his stomach. "I know I'm a grown man, but some things don't need to be talked about."

Taking sympathy on him, Grace agreed, and they spent the rest of their meal talking about how plans were progressing with the clearing of the land. "It looked like you were marking a second area today on the east side of the property. What's going on over there?"

"There were some damaged trees in that area. We're removing them before they fall over in a storm and potentially hurt someone."

She nodded. "Smart thinking."

"How are your plans coming for Christmas dinner? Any inspiration?"

A wave of sadness threatened to overcome her, but Grace was able to push it aside. "Well, it's been so long since I've had the freedom to create a holiday meal. I was always working on both Christmas Eve and Christmas Day, and management always told us what we were making, so this has been a real treat."

"Are you going to share the details, or do I have to wait?"

"I'll tell you *some* of the details," she teased. Straightening in her seat, she smiled brightly at Riley. "On Christmas Eve, we are going to do a buffet with the guests. I've got an assortment of great stuff from beer bread and assorted dips to stuffed mushrooms, mini quiches, spicy crab bites"—she stopped and thought for a moment—"and some other fun finger foods. Then we'll take a small break and set up chafing dishes with a pecan-crusted pork roast and a variety of side dishes. And for dessert, we have a multitude of cakes, cookies, and pies."

Riley shook his head. "I don't know how you do it, Grace. I think I've gained about twenty pounds since I've come home. Every day I walk in here and I see all you've created, and you make it look effortless. If I were living alone, I'd be microwaving my meals…or keeping the local diner in business."

"I'm sure after eating nothing but military food for so long, you would have enjoyed just about anything. Don't get me wrong. I love that you enjoy my cooking, but I think you're just easy to please after having to eat such bland food for so long."

Riley stood and silently began clearing the table. Grace gave him an odd look. Had she offended him? Made him angry by criticizing his choice of being in the service? Standing, she helped clear the table, and soon they had the kitchen put back together and all of the items that Grace needed set up for breakfast in the morning.

Finally, unable to stand the silence any longer, Grace placed a hand on Riley's arm. "Did I say something wrong?"

Wordlessly, Riley cupped Grace's face in his large hands. His blue eyes stared intently into her wide, green ones. "No," he said gruffly.

"Then what's the matter? Why'd you get so quiet?"

"I never once regretted my time in the military. It was what I always wanted to do. And then sitting here tonight, talking with you, sharing dinner with you, it made me think about all I would have missed if I had opted to stay in."

She wasn't prepared for that level of honesty with him right now. Her emotions were already all over the place regarding their future, and while Riley was brave enough to open up like that, it made Grace want to run and hide.

"You would have missed having awkward conversations about your mom's sex life," she said, trying to lighten the mood, but Riley wouldn't be swayed.

"I would have missed you," he said softly, leaning

in toward her. "I would have missed out on getting to know you."

There were no words; nothing came to mind. No snarky comeback or sassy retort. His eyes held so much emotion that Grace was getting lost in them. So rather than try to speak, she got up on her toes and gently placed her lips against his. Neither tried to deepen the kiss; it was enough to just lightly sip from one another. Riley's fingers caressed her face while Grace ran her palms up his chest until they came to rest on his shoulders.

"Come downstairs with me, Grace."

She nodded and was about to step away when Riley swept her into his arms. "Oh my," she gasped.

He carried her to the basement door. It was slightly awkward to open the door and then close it again in the close confines, but they managed. Once they were at the bottom of the stairs, Riley carried Grace directly over to the bed and laid her down as if she were the most precious thing in the world.

Staring up at him as he stood beside the bed, Grace could only sigh his name.

"You were wrong, you know," he said and saw the confusion written on her face. "What you said upstairs… You were wrong."

"When?"

"You said that I was easy to please." He pulled his sweatshirt up over his head. "I'm not."

A slow smile worked its way across her lips. She watched as the T-shirt he wore followed the path of the sweatshirt. "Oh, I don't know about that."

Unbuttoning his jeans, Riley continued to stare at

Grace until she began to squirm. "I guess we'll have to see about that, won't we?"

Rising to her knees on the bed, Grace ran her hand over his naked chest, loving the feel of his warm skin against hers. Her fingers traced the many scars he had, and she had to force herself not to think about how they had gotten there. With a wicked smile, she wrapped her arms around him and pulled him close. "I guess we will."

They landed back on the bed, a tangle of limbs as each clamored for the dominant position. Somehow Grace managed to roll Riley beneath her. Straddling his lap, she rose up and pulled her sweater over her head, then peeled away the white lace bra she wore underneath. "How can we find out if you're easy to please if you don't let me…please you?" she asked huskily.

Riley was never one to give up control. That was his to maintain. But as Grace's mouth began a journey from his lips to his throat to his chest and lower, he threw back his head and realized that it was good to try new things.

Chapter 11

For someone who claimed that running a bed-and-breakfast wasn't for him, Riley certainly had a knack for it. After a rather eventful night, he and Grace had gotten up early, and together they had prepared breakfast for their guests. While Grace was busy in the kitchen, Riley had greeted everyone in the dining room and chatted with them until all of the food was on the table.

Then, in a most surprising move, instead of going back into the kitchen to let the guests eat on their own, Riley had prepared plates for both him and Grace, and they sat at the large dining room table and had their breakfast with the guests. Grace knew that from time to time Corrine did that, but since she'd always had the impression that Riley saw guests as an intrusion in his home, his decision to join them was a bit of a shock. Rather than question it, Grace decided to sit back and observe.

Over platters of pancakes and sausage, Riley answered all kinds of questions about the inn, the town, and the military. Gone was the man of few words that she had met, and in his place was a veritable chatter-box! He shared the history of the Snowflake Inn—how his grandparents had built it and opened it to hunters, and how his own parents had converted it to a bed-and-breakfast when they took over.

Grace had often talked to Corrine about the

background of the inn, and while nothing Riley was saying was news to her, it was interesting to hear him say it and to hear the pride in his voice. When had that happened? At what point in time since he had arrived home had his feelings changed?

It was then that Grace realized that for all that she and Riley had shared, they didn't talk a whole lot about him. She glanced in his direction and couldn't help but smile as he told the story of how his mother had made his father take down all of the animal heads mounted on the walls and promise to never hang them back up. Grace loved that story too. But back to Riley…

No, in all of the time that they had been together, they'd talked a lot about general stuff, the day-to-day running of the inn, the barn project, his mom and Ben. Hell, Grace had even shared with him about her parents, but somehow they never seemed to focus on him. Whenever she mentioned his time in the military, he just shut down or changed the subject. Well, that was going to change as of now.

Everyone around the table was laughing, so without knowing why, Grace joined in. Okay, maybe not right now, but later tonight when they were alone, she was going to talk to Riley about *his* life and *his* feelings. If Grace knew anything, she knew that it wasn't going to be easy, and if anything, he was going to pull away and get mad. She smiled when she remembered what she had nicknamed him not so long ago—Cute Angry Guy. The man sitting next to her now did not resemble the man jogging behind her in the park.

She felt Riley's hand reach out, and then his fingers twined with hers. It was a nice feeling. Grace had been really intrigued by Cute Angry Guy, but this man next to her? She was developing far deeper feelings for him.

———∾∾∾———

Corrine did not come home that day.

Or the next.

As much as Grace was outwardly saying "You go, girl!" inwardly, she was getting annoyed because Riley was so distracted by the fact that his mother was shacking up with Ben that she didn't have the heart to have the talk with him that she wanted to. It would be like kicking a puppy at this point.

It wasn't that Riley was upset; it was more like he was out of sorts and unable to figure out what he was supposed to be doing or what his role at the inn was supposed to be. Corrine had always been there. She had never dated after her husband died, and whenever Riley was home, Corrine's presence in the house had been a constant. Clearly that meant a lot to him because her absence was having a weird effect on him.

He wandered around—some would call it puttering— and she heard him sighing. A lot. Without Ben's assistance, Riley was unwilling to take control of the barn project. While he was completely comfortable with the guests and taking care of things around the inn, Grace could tell he was doing that in part because he wanted to take care of things for his mother. She could only hope the other part was that he was really getting used to being here and was making a connection with the place.

When he walked into the kitchen for what seemed like the tenth time in as many minutes, Grace had had enough. "Is everything okay?" she finally asked.

Riley turned and looked at her with confusion. "Sure. Why?"

Here we go. "You're just wandering around and pacing. What's going on?"

He shrugged. "I don't know what you're talking about."

Patiently, Grace put down the wooden spoon that she was using to mix batter for brownies, placed her palms on the butcher block, and looked at him. "Really? You have no idea what I'm talking about?"

"That's what I just said." His tone held a hint of defiance.

"I think it bothers you that Corrine isn't back yet. I think that you're walking a fine line between taking charge of things here and not wanting to step on anyone's toes." She waited a heartbeat and was relieved to see that the sky didn't fall because of her speaking her mind.

Riley opened up his mouth to speak but promptly shut it. After so many years in the military, it had become natural to hear people speak their minds about him, and he had learned to not react. But this was Grace, and unfortunately, she had a point.

"Fine, so I am having a little bit of a hard time with the whole thing," he said begrudgingly.

"But why? I thought you liked Ben."

"I do!" he said a little too loudly and then took a deep breath and began to pace. "I don't have a problem with Ben. I have a problem with everything changing."

Okay, now they were getting somewhere. "Did you really expect everything to stay the same?"

He ran a hand through his hair and stopped. This was the longest his hair had been in more than a dozen years. More damn changes. "I never gave it much thought. To tell you the truth, I had planned on coming here for a couple of days and then leaving. I never meant to stay this long. I wanted to convince her to sell the place so I wouldn't have to deal with coming back here."

Okay, so he was more willing to talk than Grace had expected. "What is so bad about this place, Riley? It's a beautiful home and your mother loves it. Why do you hate it so much?"

Riley stopped in his tracks and faced her on the opposite side of the butcher-block island. "This house may be picturesque and wonderful to a lot of people, but to me this is the place that consumed my parents' lives. Even when my father was alive, we never went anywhere or did anything because of this inn. We never went out of town or away for the holidays. My friends took trips during the summer, but my parents never did. We were always stuck here. When my father died, my mother had to cancel some reservations because of the funeral— three days' worth. That was all the time I was allotted to grieve because there were always guests here."

"Oh, Riley…"

He held up a hand to cut her off. "We had our own part of the house, but I had to watch her put on a happy facade for everyone, and I was expected to do the same. When I acted out in school because I was so devastated by the loss of my father, Mom told me that I needed to get it together because she couldn't take time away from the inn to keep coming up to school." Pinching the bridge of his nose, Riley took a moment to compose himself. "To you, this inn is great and wonderful and someplace that you want to be a part of. But for me? This is the place that took too much of my parents' time from me."

Grace didn't know what she had been expecting when Riley opened up, but it wasn't this.

"In order to not come off like a total jackass, I tried to tell myself that I was concerned about my mother working too hard, and maybe on some level that was true. But the bottom line is that this place holds too many negative memories for me."

Coming around the island, Grace stood before him and took Riley's hands in her own. "Even now? Even now that you and Corrine are making new memories and working on the property together?"

She wanted to ask if her presence had done anything to change his thoughts on the Snowflake Inn, but she didn't think now was the time for that.

"It is getting better, and then that makes me feel guilty too," he said, pulling his hands from hers and going to stand by the French doors and look out at the property.

"Why?"

Riley looked at Grace briefly over his shoulder before returning his attention to the winter wonderland before him. "I was angry for a long time. That was part of what defined me and kept me going. I spent a lot of years being strong and tough, and to find that in a matter of weeks I can be so easily manipulated into changing who I am—"

"No one's manipulated you, Riley," Grace interrupted, anxious for him to know no one was doing that to him.

"Maybe that wasn't the right word," he said hastily and let out a sigh of frustration. "I came home and was forced to stay and take an active role in the running of the place and spend time actually talking to my mother instead of avoiding her. It's made a big difference."

"I'm so glad, Riley," Grace said as she came to stand beside him. She wanted to put her arms around him and hug him and rest her head on his chest and take comfort in hearing his heartbeat, but she was afraid to touch him just yet. There were so many more things to talk about. "So what are you going to do now?"

He shook his head. "I don't know. I think a lot is going to depend on Mom and Ben. He plans on proposing on Christmas and wants the barn done for them to get married on the property." Riley wasn't sure if that was supposed to be a secret or not, but he trusted Grace.

"Is that why he's pushing so hard to get it done?" Riley nodded. "I think your mother is going to love that."

"That's what Ben is counting on."

"What about you?"

He turned toward her. "What about me?"

Grace smiled. "I know you're happy for them, and that shows by how much you're helping Ben to get things done around here. But then what? What are your plans?" She almost hated to ask the question because she didn't want Riley to think she was fishing for a commitment or for him to feel pressured to make some reference to their relationship.

"I never had a plan," he said sadly, returning to the view outside. "My discharge wasn't something I planned. I thought that I was going to be in for life. My injuries… I guess I always thought that I'd recover and go back to business as usual. Then when I realized that I couldn't, all I had was my anger toward the inn, and I knew that it wasn't what I wanted. Beyond that, I had nothing."

"When I was preparing to go to college, I had my whole life planned out," Grace began quietly. "I was going for a four-year degree; then I was going to go to culinary school. I was going to come home for the holidays and breaks and travel with my parents. I had it all mapped out. And then…everything changed."

Reaching out, Riley put an arm around Grace and pulled her close.

"Suddenly, I was afraid to commit to a four-year school. I needed to be able to take care of myself. I had money from my parents' life insurance and the sale of our house, and I got rid of everything in it, but I knew I was going to have to live conservatively in order to make sure I was okay. I was so scared to make the wrong decision."

"You've done an amazing job with your life, Grace," Riley said softly, resting his head on top of hers. "I know it wasn't easy, but you're an incredible woman."

She shrugged. "Most of the time I'm just trying to survive. I had to come up with a new plan for my life, and so far, I'm making it work. Unfortunately, it's a long process, and it can be exhausting at times."

Unable to help himself, Riley turned and pulled Grace completely into his arms and lowered his head to kiss her. His lips were like a gentle caress, and for now, it was enough. When he pulled back, he looked into her big, green eyes and felt like he could stay there forever. "So what's next for you? What's the next step in your plan?"

"I keep surviving. I remember to smile and have fun and not spend every waking moment on work."

"Is working that important to you?" he asked cautiously.

"I want to own my own business. I want to have a

place that is mine that no one can take away from me. I need to remember what it's like to have a place where I belong, and then maybe I'll be able to relax."

Riley let those words sink in but wasn't ready to respond. So he simply held her, and together they watched as fresh snow began to fall.

—⁓—

Later that night, after all of their guests had gone to their rooms, Grace and Riley sat in front of the large stone fireplace in the living room and enjoyed the fiery warmth of it. They were wrapped up in each other in companionable silence, just relaxing after a long day.

Grace wanted to stay like this forever. In the warmth of Riley's arms, she felt a peace she hadn't felt since she'd lost her parents. "Riley?"

"Hmm?"

"You never answered my question earlier."

"Which one?"

"I asked you what your plans were for your future. I know you said that you didn't have any when you were discharged, but what about now? Are you going to stay here and work the inn with Corrine and Ben, or are you planning on leaving?"

Riley looked at her, his expression serious. "Part of that is going to depend on what my mother and Ben decide to do."

"What do you mean?"

"What if they decide once they get married that they don't want to run the inn? What if they want to travel and enjoy their retirement?"

"You could run it," she suggested shyly.

He chuckled. "I can't cook." He kissed the top of her head and pulled her a little closer against him. "I think the guests would get tired of instant oatmeal for breakfast and frozen pizza for dinner."

Grace found herself laughing too. "You would have to hire people, obviously."

"I don't know. If you weren't here, you'd be a tough act to follow. No one would be able to do what you do or replace you." Gone was the teasing tone of only seconds ago; his voice was more gruff and serious.

She could only hope he wasn't strictly referring to her cooking skills, that some part of him knew there wasn't another woman who would take care of him and love him like she did.

Wait a minute… Love him? *Love him?* The thought came to mind so easily that it made her heart race. All this time, Grace knew her feelings for Riley were strong, but to love him… That wasn't something she was prepared to admit. Besides, at this point, from what she understood, Riley wasn't asking her to stay. He seemed to understand her need to find a place of her own and knew that it wasn't here with him or the Snowflake Inn. Part of her wished he would ask her to stay, to tell her that this place would be theirs and that they would make it work together.

But he didn't.

It would be a lie for Grace to say, even to herself, that she wasn't hurt. Here she was, finally figuring out that she was in love with Riley Walsh, a.k.a. Cute Angry Guy, and all he was willing to say was that no one could replace her. Not the most romantic declaration, or really, any kind of declaration for that matter.

Maybe this was for the best. Grace knew that she planned to leave, and while her heart was definitely going to break, at least she knew now—or thought that she knew—that there would be no scene when the time came for her to move on. They would probably part as friends, and hopefully Riley would remember her fondly.

Grace imagined that she'd keep in touch with Corrine and would probably invite her and Ben to come and visit wherever she settled, but talk of Riley would always bring a pain to her heart. He was going to forever be known as the one who got away.

"You got awful quiet there, Grace," Riley said, breaking into her thoughts. "What are you thinking about?"

Why it is that you don't love me…

"I was thinking that I really wish there was a fireplace in my apartment." It wasn't a total lie; the thought had crossed her mind a time or two.

"Really?" he asked, his tone conveying his disbelief.

She nodded. "I was thinking how nice it could be if we had one downstairs, where we could lock the door and"—she rolled over so she was facing him—"make love in front of it. I've never done that before."

Slowly, Riley rolled Grace beneath him. Before he could let his weight fully settle on her, he kissed her softly, deeply, and then rolled off her until he stood next to the sofa. "What are you doing?" Grace asked, confused by his abrupt departure.

"The cool thing about old houses," he began as he walked across the room toward the entryway, "is that there are a lot of hidden features nobody really notices." He got to the archway between the living room and the entryway and pulled at the wall molding. "Pocket doors," he said simply as he pulled one out from each side and then locked them together. Once that doorway was secured, he walked toward the back of the room where a swinging door led to the kitchen. On most days, the door was kept open so people could come and go, but Riley closed it and then slid the small bolt at the bottom of it into the hardwood floor.

Then he slowly walked toward the sofa, toward Grace.

Sitting up slightly, Grace watched his every move. She loved the way Riley walked. Every muscle in his body moved with ease, and there was something very sexy about that. When he was standing in front of her, he held out a hand and pulled Grace to her feet. Pulling her in close, Riley cupped her face in his hands and leaned in and kissed her. This time not so slowly or so sweetly. This time it was all heat and passion and need.

Grace got up on her toes and pressed her body as close to Riley's as she could possibly get while his tongue traced her bottom lip. She gasped as she felt the proof of his arousal pressing against her belly, and that one little movement allowed Riley entrance into her mouth to tease her tongue with his.

She lost track of time, had no idea how long they stood there, holding one another while they made love simply with their lips, but suddenly Riley pulled back. "Stay there," he said, his breath ragged. Turning from her, he walked over to a large ottoman in the corner of the room and lifted the top from it. Inside were several blankets. He took the first one out and laid it on the floor in front of the fire, then put a second one nearby. Next, he pulled several pillows from the sofa and placed them on top of the blanket.

When everything was where he wanted it to be, Riley walked over to Grace and stopped in front of her. Without a word, without asking permission, he reached out to the hem of her sweater and swiftly pulled it over her head. He bent and kissed her throat, nipped at her pulse, and reached up to cup her breasts. He loved to touch her, to kiss her, and standing here in the firelight with her only seemed to heighten his desire for her.

Taking a cue from Riley, Grace boldly reached out, pulled his shirt over his head, and ran her hands over his chest. He was all finely chiseled muscle, and as her hands roamed, they always stopped right above his heart. She loved to feel it beating beneath her almost as much as she loved how hot and hard all of his muscles were.

Looking up, she stared at the raw desire banked in his eyes. It mirrored her own. "Make love to me, Riley," she said huskily. "Please."

Sweeping Grace up into his arms, a move that he was coming to enjoy more and more, he carried her over to the blankets and laid her down. Kneeling beside her, he peeled her jeans from her body before joining her there.

"You are so beautiful," he said reverently as his hands skimmed her body from her face all the way to her toes.

Grace had no words, no response. The emotion that she heard in Riley's voice made her quiver. She reached out and ran her hand across the strong line of his jaw, enjoying the roughness of a day's worth of stubble there. Whispering his name, she cupped a hand around his nape and gently guided him forward. When their lips were merely a breath apart, Grace felt like she was going to burst with the love that she was feeling. The anticipation of the kiss, the touch of his hands, and Riley's lovemaking left her breathless.

But he didn't kiss her, didn't touch her. Carefully, Riley rolled away until he was naked beside her and then pulled the second blanket over them. Only then did he roll Grace beneath him and kiss her.

And then, well into the night and until the fire had nearly died out, he made love to her and said with his body what his words hadn't said earlier.

Chapter 12

IT WAS THE WEEK BEFORE CHRISTMAS. GRACE AND Corrine had been baking up a storm, and reservations were filling up for the New Year. A constant bustle of activity was going on at the Snowflake Inn, and Grace was loving it all.

Something had changed the night she and Riley had made love by the fire. She couldn't quite put her finger on it, but she felt as if the two of them had become closer and even more intimate since then, if that was even possible.

When Corrine and Ben had finally come back the following day, they also seemed different. They seemed more at ease with one another, and Grace was certain if she asked Corrine, her friend would tell her she saw the same in her and Riley. Love was in the air at the Snowflake Inn, and as wonderful as it was, it was also bittersweet.

Without saying a word to Riley, during her free times throughout the day, while he was out working with Ben, Grace would go to her apartment to search online for bed-and-breakfasts that were for sale. She wasn't particular about where the property was located; all she knew was that she didn't want to be in competition with Corrine. She had found several properties that looked interesting, but none she was willing to travel and see just yet. If and when that time came, she would deal with it. For now, however, it was her own little secret.

It wasn't that she was in a hurry to leave—far from it. The newfound level of intimacy that she and Riley had was going to be even harder to leave. But she was a realist. Riley hadn't professed his love, and his life was seemingly up in the air right now. He might not know what he wanted, but Grace certainly did. She had worked hard toward her dream for ten years, and it was finally within her reach. Once she found the perfect property, she was going to move quickly to make it a reality.

Leaving the Snowflake Inn and Riley was going to be the hardest thing she had had to do since saying good-bye to her parents and selling their home. Grace had never wanted to face that kind of heartache again, and to be fair, she never thought she would have to. Meeting and loving Riley was something she hadn't planned on, but now that she had and knew how it was going to end, Grace still couldn't say that she regretted it. What was the old adage—it's better to have loved and lost than never to have loved at all? She could fully understand that now. She would rather walk away having loved him than to have never had this time together.

The phone rang in the distance, and Grace figured that Corrine would get it. By the fourth ring, she found herself running across the kitchen to pick it up.

"Thank you for calling the Snowflake Inn. This is Grace. How can I help you?"

"Grace?" a male voice said on the other end of the line. "You're the cook at the inn, right?"

It was an odd greeting for sure. "I'm sorry, who's calling?"

"This is Matt Handler. My wife and I spent a couple

of days there a few weeks back with some friends. Do you remember me?"

Grace rolled her eyes, thankful that he couldn't see her. He was part of that demanding group who had eaten her out of house and home. "Yes, Mr. Handler. I do. What can I do for you?"

"Well, I was hoping that I could speak to the owner. Corrine Walsh, wasn't it?"

"Yes, that's right. Let me see if I can find her for you. Hold on a moment." Placing the call on hold, Grace called out to Corrine, who came fluttering into the room looking a little unkempt. A quick glance in the direction she had come from and Grace saw Ben coming too. A sly smile crossed her face when she faced her friend. "You have a call," Grace said, grinning now from ear to ear.

"Who is it?" Grace explained who was on the phone and chuckled as Corrine had the same reaction. "I hope he's not calling to make another reservation. I don't know if I could handle that group for a second time." Doing her best to compose herself, Corrine took the call.

Meanwhile, Ben came into the kitchen and helped himself to a cup of coffee and some of the home-baked cookies Grace had cooling on the counter. "Who's on the phone?" he asked. Grace got him up to speed. "What do you think he wants? If he wanted to make a reservation, he could have just talked to you."

Grace was just about to comment on that when she heard Corrine say, "Let me put you on hold for a moment while I take this call in my office." Without looking at either Grace or Ben, Corrine hung up the phone and left the room.

"That was odd," Ben said. "In all the years I've been hanging around here, she's never taken a call in her office. She's pretty much an open book."

"What could that guy want that would require her to need a little privacy?" Grace wondered out loud. Riley walked into the kitchen, saw the looks of confusion on both Grace's and Ben's faces, and asked what was going on. Ben explained it all to him, and Riley sat beside him and joined in the contemplation.

"If it was just a reservation," Riley said, "she could have done that right here. What in the world could he want?"

Together they huddled around the butcher-block island while Grace continued to roll gingerbread cookies and made small talk to pass the time until Corrine came back into the room. It took a lot longer than any of them were expecting. Twenty minutes later when she returned, three pairs of eyes were watching her.

Corrine took in the anxious expressions and almost laughed. "Well, that was out of the blue," she began.

"What did he want?" Ben asked, standing from his stool and indicating for Corrine to take it. She waved him off and walked over to pour herself a cup of coffee.

"As you know, Matt Handler was part of the demanding party from a couple of weeks ago. It seems," she said, stopping to take a sip of her coffee, "that he and his friends would like to buy the inn."

She said it so matter-of-factly that it didn't register with Grace at first, but once it did, she stopped what she was doing. "Wait. What? They want to buy the Snowflake Inn?"

Corrine nodded. "He started out by telling me how

much he and his friends had enjoyed their stay, and that owning something like this was what they had often talked about. After staying here, they knew this was the place for them."

"But…" Grace began hesitantly, "it's not even on the market. Why would he call and make an offer on a property that's not for sale? There are tons of B and B's on the market. Just twenty miles from here, there are two of them comparable to the Snowflake Inn. The properties aren't as large, but—"

"How do you know that?" Riley interrupted.

"Oh…well… You know, I…" she stammered.

"It doesn't matter," Corrine said. "He said that he was taking a chance by calling and making an offer and wanted to see if it was something that I would consider."

"And?" Ben asked. "Are you?"

Corrine shrugged. "I don't know. He made a very compelling presentation. I was kind of impressed with how he put it all out there. I'm glad it was all over the phone, because I think if he had come here and done it in person, he would have been very persuasive."

Riley was still looking at Grace as he listened to his mother. He knew that Grace wanted to own a place of her own, but he hadn't thought she was actively pursuing that right now. How could she? Did their time together mean nothing to her? Was she planning on leaving here and him as soon as she found someplace better?

The thought of Grace leaving him hurt more than Riley would have thought possible. Didn't she know how much she meant to him? He'd thought they had been getting closer. Didn't she feel it too?

"So what did you tell him?" Grace asked Corrine even while she was feeling the intensity of Riley's stare.

"I told him it wasn't something I was considering right now, but I'd like a couple of days to think about it and talk to my family." Corrine looked at the three people before her.

Grace placed the last tray of gingerbread in the oven and set the timer. Quickly, she cleaned up her work space while Corrine talked about some of the specifics that Matt Handler had presented to her. Grace did her best to not involve herself in the conversation. This was between Corrine, her future husband, and her son.

Her family.

Grace wasn't part of that.

When everything was in its place, she cleaned up imaginary spots on the countertops and waited for the timer to go off on the oven. Once the cookies were out, she placed them on the rack, and only then did she turn her attention back to the others. "Excuse me," she said softly to Corrine, "I'm sorry to interrupt, but if you wouldn't mind putting those away with the rest of them once they're cooled, I would really appreciate it."

"Are you okay?" Corrine asked, concern lacing her voice.

Grace nodded. "I have a bit of a headache, so I'm going to lie down for a little while. Everything is prepped for dinner, so if it's all right with you, I'm going to head downstairs."

"Of course, of course," Corrine said. As Grace went to walk by her, she reached out and placed a hand on her arm. "Are you sure you're okay? Do you need anything? Some aspirin? Tea?"

"I'll be fine. A nap should do the trick." Exiting the room as quickly as she could, Grace didn't let out a breath until she was safely in her apartment. Part of her was shocked that Riley hadn't said anything to her or tried to stop her. She thought of how he'd sounded when he questioned her about knowing of other B and B's that were for sale. He had not sounded pleased.

Unable to help herself, she stopped at her desk and booted up her laptop, then went immediately to her search for properties for sale. It looked like she was going to have to step up her search and find a place of her own sooner than she'd thought. Scanning the now-familiar pages on the site, she begrudgingly added three potential inns to her list of favorites.

None of them were in North Carolina.

Sighing, she stood and walked across the room. Kicking off her shoes, Grace crawled into the bed. The headache wasn't a total lie, but her need to escape the kitchen and the discussions about possibly selling the Snowflake Inn were what really prompted her to walk away.

With a sigh, she curled up on her side. The possibility of Corrine selling the inn had always been there, ever since Riley had come home. But knowing there was a genuine offer for the place—even though Riley had dropped his campaign to push Corrine to sell—left Grace conflicted.

A tear rolled down her cheek. In a perfect world, she would have been partners with Corrine by now and be safe in the knowledge that this inn was her home. Grace couldn't imagine finding another place like the Snowflake Inn. From the first moment she had seen it in person, she had felt a connection. While Riley and Corrine and Ben had added to the appeal of the inn, the structure itself had screamed home to her.

And now it was all going to go away.

With the promise of a new life ahead of her, Corrine would probably give this offer serious consideration. She'd be a fool not to. If Grace were in her shoes, she certainly would.

Even though Grace knew that she was planning to leave, it still hurt to think of someone else taking over this particular inn. She couldn't imagine anyone but Corrine running it.

That wasn't completely true.

She could imagine herself running it.

With Riley.

Sigh.

Closing her eyes and wiping away another tear, Grace did her best to relax. All of the deep breathing exercises in the world couldn't stop her from wondering what they were talking about upstairs. She snuggled deeper into her pillows and forced herself to take a deep, cleansing breath and to relax.

Maybe it would work.

Maybe she could count backward from one hundred.

Maybe someone could shoot her with a tranquilizer dart and put her out of her misery.

Maybe... Oh, the heck with it. She tried counting back from one hundred, and amazingly enough, it was having the desired effect. The last thing Grace remembered was the number thirty-eight when she felt Riley curling up behind her. She purred sleepily and moved a little so their bodies were perfectly aligned.

"Hey, sleepy girl," he whispered. "How are you feeling?"

At that moment, she was feeling pretty darn fine. "Mmm…good," she sighed.

Wrapping her in his arms, Riley held her close. When he'd first come down the stairs, he could see that Grace was sound asleep. He didn't want to disturb her, but on the way across the room, he'd caught sight of her open laptop, which hadn't gone into sleep mode. He stopped in his tracks when he saw the real estate page open and the list of potential inns that Grace was looking at.

She was really planning on leaving.

Unwilling to go there after the day he was having, Riley simply closed the computer and walked over to the bed and crawled in beside her. Maybe if he held her close, he could will her to not leave.

"Mom is handling dinner tonight so that you can have a break," he said, gently placing a kiss on her temple.

"She didn't have to do that," Grace protested quietly. "I just needed a little rest."

"Well, now you can have a little more of a rest."

"That sounds good." She snuggled even deeper against Riley, and suddenly rest wasn't what was on her mind. It didn't take long for her to realize that Riley wasn't exactly taking the hint. Carefully, she rolled over in his arms and began planting tiny kisses along his throat and up to his jaw, and still he didn't react. "Riley?"

Shifting slightly, he looked at her, his expression intense. "I just want to hold you," he said simply.

There had been many times over the last weeks that they had lain in this very bed wrapped in each other's arms, but this was the first time that Riley seemingly did not want anything more than that. Grace smiled against his chest and thought that it was a very nice way to spend the evening.

———~~~———

Three days later, Grace was running around the inn in preparation for the soon-to-be-arriving guests who would be with them through Christmas. All of her baking was done, the inn was decorated inside and out, and now it was just a matter of getting the rooms ready.

Corrine had asked if Grace could help put the final touches on each of the rooms, and she was more than happy to do that. Gift baskets were put in each room, along with information packets telling guests about the area, should they want to go sightseeing. When she had completed that task, Grace had put fresh flowers in each room, and with a sense of accomplishment, she headed back to the kitchen to prepare the stew that she was going to serve for dinner that evening.

The sound of Riley's and Corrine's voices stopped her.

"Are you sure about this?" Corrine was asking.

"Absolutely."

"How long are you going to be gone for?"

"Only a couple of days. I'll be back for Christmas Eve. You can count on it."

"It's been a long time since we've been together for Christmas," Corrine said, and Grace could almost hear the smile in her voice. "You have no idea how much it means to me that you're here."

"Me too, Mom. Me too."

"I still don't understand why you're going to talk to

Matt Handler in person. I thought things like this were done through lawyers and by fax and all that. Isn't that supposed to be one of the wonders of technology?"

Grace felt sick. The decision to sell the Snowflake Inn had been made, and no one had bothered to tell her. She wrapped her arms around her middle and tried to fight off the wave of nausea that overcame her. How could they do this? Right now? At Christmas? It was true she hadn't made it a secret that she was planning to move on, but to not even tell her was hurtful. Grace thought she and Corrine were better friends than that. And Riley? Well, she would have thought he'd share this information with her too, especially after all of the conversations they'd had about the inn since they first met.

All of this just reaffirmed Grace's decision to leave. She couldn't count on anyone but herself. Not her friend. And not her lover.

"Technology is well and good," Riley was saying, "but I just want to handle this personally."

"And all of the other stuff? You took care of it?"

What other stuff? Grace wondered. *What else have I been excluded from?*

"It's all under control."

"So you're leaving in the morning?" Riley nodded. "Does Grace know?"

"I was planning on telling her tonight after dinner. The two of you have been working so hard to get everything ready for Christmas that I just…I didn't know what to say," he admitted.

"I'm sure you'll figure it out."

Grace had heard enough. She wouldn't let either of

them know she had heard their conversation, but for now she still had a job to do, and no matter how much her heart was breaking, she was going to do it.

"All the rooms are ready!" she announced brightly as she walked into the kitchen. "I wouldn't say no to a couple more poinsettia plants for the stairs, but other than that, everything looks wonderful." Smiling at them both, Grace walked over to the refrigerator and began taking out the ingredients she had prepped for dinner. "Beef stew tonight in homemade bread bowls. I think they're going to be a big hit."

"That sounds fabulous," Corrine said with a smile. "What can I help you with?"

Riley watched the two women he loved as they worked together, and he was filled with pride. He was happy. He hadn't thought that would be possible after his discharge, but somehow these two amazing women had healed him and made him realize there was more to him and his life than his career in the military.

And as soon as he took care of business, he was going to make sure that one of those women in particular knew exactly what she meant to him.

Chapter 13

CHRISTMAS EVE DAY DAWNED GRAY AND SNOWY. GRACE was sluggish when getting up because she hadn't slept well, again, without Riley. He had flat-out lied to her about where he was going, and if she hadn't heard his conversation with Corrine, she would have been none the wiser about it. She didn't correct him or argue with him when he said that he was going back to Virginia for a few days to visit the friend he had seen when he first came home.

"He's getting married soon. He and his fiancée just bought their first house, and I'm going to help them move," Riley had said that night when they were alone. Grace had wanted to yell and scream and demand to know why he was lying to her, but instead she had smiled and said, "That's very nice of you. I'm sure they appreciate the extra help so they can be in their new home for Christmas."

She made herself sick.

Now with fresh snow falling, Grace worried Riley wouldn't be back in time for dinner or might not make it today at all. Had he only been in Virginia, she would have worried less, but knowing that Matt Handler lived in Delaware and this winter storm was covering the entire Northeast, Grace had her doubts. She guessed Riley had flown since his truck wasn't here, but she didn't bother asking.

In the kitchen, Grace was making homemade cinnamon rolls and Belgian waffles for their guests' breakfast. Corrine came and went from the kitchen while everyone was being served. "I cannot believe it's Christmas Eve already!" she gushed as she put more orange juice into a ceramic pitcher. "This is the first Christmas I've had with Riley in more than ten years!"

Grace was happy for her friend, she truly was, but right now she just didn't have it in her to be enthusiastic about anything. It was going to be a long day, between keeping things festive for the guests and finishing all of the cooking she had to do. Added to that was her worrying about Riley making it home safely. It was on the tip of her tongue to ask Corrine if she had heard from him, but Grace didn't want to open that dialogue.

Riley had called her every night while he was away, but the conversations seemed to be forced—at least Grace felt she was forcing her end of it because she knew he was lying to her.

Corrine left the room and came back five minutes later. "I actually had calls this morning from people looking for reservations for tonight! Can you believe it?"

"Some people are procrastinators," Grace commented dryly.

"Mmm…I suppose. This is the first year I've been booked to capacity for Christmas in I don't even know how long. I forgot how much I love it."

"I always worked on Christmas Eve and Christmas Day in restaurants. It's nice to have a smaller crowd this year." Grace meant to keep her tone light, but somehow her words came out sounding a bit depressed. Before she knew it, Corrine was at her side, hugging her. For a moment, Grace just stood there, unable to react. But when Corrine spoke, it was almost her undoing.

"I am so sorry for all of the years that you lost, Grace. I can't even imagine what it must have felt like for you. Even though Riley was overseas, I had the inn and Ben to share the holidays with. But I want you to know I love the fact that you're here, and while I know that no one can ever replace your family, I would be honored for you to be part of mine."

No words had ever had a more profound effect on Grace. People often expressed their condolences over the loss of her family, and over the years, many friends had tried to include her in their family plans on the holidays, but never had anyone expressly asked her to be part of their family.

Grace didn't know what to say. If she had, she wouldn't have been able to because she was so overwhelmed with emotion. Corrine hugged her a little bit tighter, and Grace found herself returning the hug with just as much strength.

"I knew from the moment I met you that we were going to be friends," Corrine said and then pulled back so she could look at Grace's face. "But it wasn't until you came here and helped me with my business and encouraged me in my relationships with Ben and Riley that I knew you meant just as much to me as they do."

"Corrine…" Grace began, her voice a little shaky. "You don't know what this means to me."

"Yes, I do because it means exactly the same thing to me. You are the daughter I never had, and I can't thank you enough for sticking with me during one of the lowest and darkest times of my life." She wiped away a tear that fell from her eye. "I mean, I know it wasn't as traumatic as when I lost Jack or when Riley was first stationed overseas, but while I was recovering from the surgery, I felt totally lost and alone. Your friendship gave me the strength to get up each day and to get better."

"And you encouraged me to stop having my own pity party and to leave a dead-end job to see what else is out there." Grace didn't want to ruin the moment by talking about Corrine selling the Snowflake Inn, but there didn't seem to be a way to avoid it. "And even though this isn't going to get to be my forever place, working with you has been such a blessing."

Corrine opened her mouth to say something but instantly closed it. She pulled Grace in for another hug instead. "Now," she began, taking a step back, "how about we get the breakfast crowd cleared out so we can move on with the rest of our plans for the day?"

"Sounds good to me."

By four o'clock, Grace was getting nervous. There had been no word from Riley, and the snow was falling pretty heavily. Their guests had been positively ecstatic at the sight of the snow and the thought of a true white Christmas, but Grace didn't see it as a reason to celebrate. Not if it meant Riley wouldn't be there to spend Christmas with them.

After she and Corrine had cleaned up the breakfast dishes, they immediately began preparations for the big dinner. There were going to be thirty people around the massive dining room table, so while their guests went out to explore the town and frolic in the snow, the two women were busy making sure they were all going to have a magnificent Christmas feast.

Lunch was not included for the guests, so Grace and Corrine had just eaten sandwiches while they were working. Once everything was prepped and in its proper place, they each retired to their rooms to relax until it was time to finish cooking and begin serving hors d'oeuvres.

Since she was going to spend most of her time in the kitchen, Grace had quickly given up the idea of buying herself something fancy to wear. Instead she had chosen a long, black wool skirt, a green twinset that matched her eyes, and black boots. She was going to put a little curl in her hair just to be festive, and while she was getting ready, she realized it had been a very long time since she had put a lot of thought and care into her appearance.

She usually dressed for comfort and practicality. Getting dressed to spend time with friends, even though she was doing the bulk of the cooking, was a new experience. One she found she liked.

A quick glance out the window showed the snow was tapering off and the sun was going down, and still Riley wasn't back. Why wasn't anyone talking about it? Why wasn't Corrine more freaked out? Since this was her first Christmas with him in years, Grace would have thought she would be upset at the thought of him missing it.

With nothing left to do, Grace went back up to the kitchen and pulled out an apron to cover and protect her outfit. Corrine stormed into the room not long after, looking a little disheveled.

"Is everything all right?"

"I just hate it when guests get difficult."

"Why? What's going on?"

"The guests in cottage number three don't want to come in for cocktails and appetizers. They want something brought out to the cottage, and then they'll join us for dinner."

Grace walked over and placed a reassuring hand on her friend's arm. "Okay, that's not a catastrophe. Maybe they want to have some quiet time, or maybe it's part of their holiday tradition. Whatever the reason, I'll make up a tray and bring it out to them."

"It's not part of the package, Grace," Corrine chided. "If we start making all kinds of exceptions, then it will make things more difficult. As it is, most bed-and-breakfasts only do that—breakfast and provide a bed. I already offer more than most, and it just upsets me when people take advantage."

"I agree. It's not very considerate, but this is why people love coming to the Snowflake Inn. Because we take care of them." Grace looked around the kitchen and began making up a tray. "Everything is under control here. I've got my list up on the board showing when the hors d'oeuvres go into the oven, and really, it's not like I'll be gone long. So if you don't mind manning the kitchen, I'll take the food and maybe a bottle of wine out to our guests."

"Please be careful, Grace. Ben has been clearing the paths and the deck all day, but it can still be treacherous."

"No worries," Grace said absently as she made up an assortment of food to take out to the cottage. Most of the appetizers that she had planned weren't heated yet, so she went with a variety of cheese and crackers, fruit, beer bread, and dips instead. Walking into the pantry, she found a large wicker basket and artfully arranged the food in it along with some plates and silverware, and then carefully placed the wine and two glasses in with it.

"I think this should do nicely," she said to herself as she closed the basket. Quickly, Grace made her way out of the kitchen and to her room to grab her long wool coat. Running back up to the kitchen, she stopped to catch her breath (that's what happens when you stop going for morning jogs because you have a sexy man in your bed!) and did a final check to make sure she hadn't missed anything.

There were footsteps out on the deck, and Grace quickly turned, hoping to see Riley. But there stood Ben, shaking snow off his boots before he came in. Maybe she could ask him to deliver the basket since he was already covered in snow…

"Hey, Grace! Whatcha got there?" He motioned toward the large basket. "It's a little cold for a picnic."

She laughed. "Apparently our guests in cabin three wish to have a private cocktail hour and requested that we bring some food to them."

"And Corrine agreed?" he chuckled.

"I had to convince her it wasn't a big deal and that I would take it out there to them. But since you're still kind of snowy, I don't suppose you'd mind…" She let the implication hang out there in hope he'd catch on.

"Normally I'd do it in a heartbeat, but I can't quite feel my toes. I should have come in about an hour ago, but the paths needed to be taken care of. Plus," he said as he leaned in close and lowered his voice, "I have a big question I want to ask Corrine before all of the guests come down for dinner."

"Oh my goodness! Now? Really?"

Ben nodded. "I hate that I even waited this long. I wish we were someplace romantic and that I didn't have to rush it."

"That's not going to matter to her. She's just going to be thrilled."

"I hope so," he said distractedly. He looked around for any sign of Corrine.

"I think she's up front, talking to some of the guests," Grace said as she pulled on her coat and took her gloves from her pockets. "I better get moving so I can get this food over to the cottage and be back in time to get the rest of the food in the oven." Picking up the basket, she flashed Ben a smile. "Wish me luck!"

"Luck?"

"That I don't slip in the snow!" she teased. "My name may be Grace, but I certainly am not graceful." She winked at him and walked out the back door.

The scenery took her breath away. Her breath was visible in front of her as she carefully made her way across the deck and down the steps. Ben had done a fabulous job in clearing the paths and salting them to make sure they weren't slick. It was just her luck that the cottage where she was heading was all the way at the end of the path, the farthest from the inn. By the time she was walking up the front steps, her cheeks felt frozen.

Taking a moment to catch her breath, she raised her hand to knock and was shocked by who answered the door. "Riley? How... What...what are you doing here?"

Taking the basket from her hands with one of his,

he used his other hand to lead Grace into the cottage. Wordlessly, he placed the basket on a nearby table and then turned to rub her hands in his to warm them up before helping her take her gloves off.

"I don't understand what's going on," Grace said, appreciative of the fact that she was out of the cold.

"What's in the basket?" Riley asked instead of answering her inquiry.

She let out a huff of frustration and pulled her hands from his. "Seriously? That's all you're going to say?"

"It's just that I'm really hungry," he said simply.

"So you're not going to explain what you're doing here in this cabin until I tell you what's in the basket?"

"Basically."

Anger and frustration warred within her. She tore her coat off and threw it on a chair before turning to the basket. She opened it and began taking food out and placing it on the table. "We have a bottle of wine," she said as she banged it down on the table, "two glasses, a plate of assorted cheese and crackers, some beer bread, bacon dip, spinach dip, grapes, strawberries, some plates, and silverware." She slapped the cover of the basket down and faced him with hands on her hips. "Your turn."

He chuckled as he slowly walked toward her. Knowing that he was pretty much risking his safety right then, Riley cupped Grace's face in his hands and leaned in and kissed her. He just wanted to feel her lips beneath his, but he knew instantly that she wasn't ready for him yet. Reluctantly, he pulled back and then led her over to the small love seat in the corner of the room. When they were both seated, he held one of her small hands in his and faced her.

"I didn't go to Virginia."

"I know."

Riley was shocked. How? When? "Who told you?" That was clearly the wrong thing to say, based on the look she gave him. "I mean, how did you know?"

"I heard you and Corrine talking before you left. So is it a done deal? Did you sell the inn to Matt Handler?"

He couldn't help it; Riley burst out laughing.

Grace promptly pulled her hand from his. "What's so funny about that?"

Riley took a moment to compose himself. "Nothing. It's not... Well, all right, it's a little bit funny."

"Care to share the joke?" she snapped.

"Okay," he began seriously, "here's the truth about what's going on. I did go to see Matt Handler and his friends, but that was so I could turn them down in person. I didn't want them to keep calling and pressuring Mom into accepting their offer."

"Wait... What? I thought that you wanted her to sell the inn. I thought that she wanted to sell the inn so that she and Ben could travel."

He shook his head. "At first, that was what I wanted, but one night, when you had gone to bed early, Mom and I talked, really talked. I explained my issues with the inn and with her when I was growing up. She was pretty devastated, but now, looking back on it all as an adult, I realized she was doing the best she could in a really horrible situation. I didn't make things easy on her, and she was doing everything she could to keep our lives together."

Unable to help herself, Grace put her hand back in his. "I'm glad that the two of you finally found a way to talk about it."

"It's like a big weight has been lifted."

"But I still don't understand. I heard you talking to her about lawyers and documents and faxes…"

"No good ever comes from eavesdropping, Grace," he chided lightly.

"I wasn't eavesdropping, exactly," she said shyly. "I was heading into the kitchen, and that's where the two of you were. I didn't want to interrupt your conversation."

"I'm teasing, Grace." He looked into her face and smiled. "The paperwork was for something completely different, and we'll get to that later." Rising, he walked over to the table and opened the wine and poured them each a glass.

"I still don't understand why you're here in the cabin, and why Corrine sent me here when there's so much to do for dinner."

"Please, my mother has been doing Christmas dinner for guests for over thirty years. She can do it with her eyes closed. You prepped everything, and she's going to finish it up."

"But why?"

Riley handed her a glass of wine before sitting back down. "Because I wanted to be alone with you. I wanted us to have a little time with no interruptions and no responsibilities."

"Why?" she whispered.

"I don't talk a lot about my feelings, Grace. I never have. When I met you, you challenged me, and you forced me to admit to the things that were bothering me. Plenty of people have tried, but I always resisted. Something about you, though, made me want to open up." He placed his glass on the end table beside him and let out a breath. "When I'm with you, I feel more things than I ever have before. I grew up in this house, and yet I don't ever remember feeling as content as I do now, when I'm here with you."

"Riley…"

"No," he said, softly cutting her off. "I need to say this. When I saw you walking out of the inn when I first came home, I was drawn to you. When you fell in the park and I helped you to your car, I wanted you. And when you stood up to me that first day I was here at home, I fell in love with you." Carefully, he dropped to one knee in front of her and pulled a small box from the drawer in the end table. Flipping the top open, he revealed a beautiful marquise diamond set in a braided platinum band. "I love you, Grace. I want you to be my wife, have a family with me, and…help me run the Snowflake Inn."

She sighed his name as tears welled in her eyes. One of her hands was trying to steady her rapidly beating heart, while the other reached out and cupped his stubbled jaw. "Yes," she whispered and then gasped as he placed the exquisite diamond on her finger.

They both moved as one, leaning in toward one another to seal their promises with a kiss. Riley rose on both knees and gently ran his fingers along Grace's jaw and throat as his lips coaxed hers open and his tongue touched hers. After that, all semblance of restraint was gone.

"I missed you so much," she said between kisses.

"I missed you too," he said, and then silenced her with another kiss. His hands fisted in her long, red hair, and he gently tugged so that he could kiss her more thoroughly. "I hated leaving you."

"Promise you won't ever again." She sighed as his mouth traveled along her neck and he lightly bit her.

"I promise," he growled, frustrated by their positions. He rose to his feet and then scooped Grace up into his arms and strode toward the bedroom. She let out a gasp of surprise.

"The tree..." she said in awe, and Riley stopped in his tracks. Grace fidgeted in his arms until he put her on her feet. Walking across the room, Grace felt as if her heart might explode in her chest. It wasn't possible...

"Riley?" she whispered, her voice shaking. "How... When did you do this?"

Coming to stand behind her, Riley carefully wrapped his arms around her middle and held her trembling form. "I wanted to surprise you."

There, on a freshly cut tree, were all of her family ornaments. Grace reached out and touched each of them reverently. "I can't... I never thought... For so long, I wanted a tree of my own to put them on. I promised myself that when I found a place of my own, I would take them out."

Gently, Riley turned her toward him, his strong hands on her shoulders. "This is your home, Grace. That's what the documents were for. Our names are now listed as the owners of the Snowflake Inn. It's yours, sweetheart. You're home."

It was more than she ever could have dreamed of, more than she had ever imagined possible. "It's real? This is really happening?"

Leaning in again, Riley kissed the woman he loved. "Welcome home, Grace."

Epilogue

Christmas Eve, One Year Later...

"YOU KNOW, THIS ISN'T THE FIRST TIME WE'VE DONE THIS. It shouldn't be this difficult."

"Who are you kidding? It's never easy. There are too many chances for things to go wrong."

"Way to stay positive..."

Corrine had heard enough. "You know, the two of you big, strong men are acting like a couple of babies."

"What?" Ben asked. "How do you figure that?"

"We had our wedding here back in June when the barn was barely finished. We had never hosted anything like that here at the inn, and everything went off without a hitch. You and Riley set everything up like pros. Now, here you are six months later, and it's like you're all thumbs. What's going on?"

"It's not me," Ben said defensively. "It's Riley. He's a nervous wreck!"

"I think that's a bit of a stretch," Riley said, hating the slight tremor in his voice. "I just want everything to be perfect for Grace. She's having a hard enough time with the fact that she doesn't have any family here and that her father isn't alive to walk her down the aisle. I need everything to be just right."

Corrine stepped forward and hugged her son. "As

long as she sees you standing at the altar waiting for her, everything is going to be all right."

"I wish it were that simple, Mom."

"It is. Trust me. I've done this twice, and I know what I'm talking about." She walked out of her son's embrace and right into her husband's. "It's natural to be nervous on your wedding day, but when all is said and done, it's the two of you that matter. It's not the decorations or the guests; it's that the two of you love one another and are starting your lives together."

"I know you're right, but I can't help but want to take away all of her pain and anxiety. I don't want her to focus on anything sad today."

"Sweetheart, it's only natural for her to focus on the two people she loved the most in this world and who can't be with her on the biggest day of her life. There's nothing you can do about that. What you can do is love her and support her and make every moment from this point forward wonderful for her."

Riley smiled with renewed confidence. "I can do that."

Corrine nodded. "Good. Now, you two finish setting up the chairs while I attend to the bride." She was almost out the door when Riley caught up with her.

"Listen, Mom…" he began hesitantly. "I know I don't say it very often, but I just want to tell you that I love you."

"Oh, sweetheart, I know that you do."

"I'm sorry for all of the years that I stayed away. I never should have done that to you. You were always there for me, and I feel like I let you down."

She reached up and cupped his cheek. "Don't you

ever say such a thing to me again!" she gently scolded. "You have never let me down. No mother could be prouder than I am. You grew up to be an amazing man, Riley. And as much as I hate all of the years that we missed together, it has made this time that we have now that much sweeter."

"Thanks, Mom."

Corrine smiled. "Now, is there anything else that you need?"

"Grace," he said simply. "You make sure that she's okay and that she hasn't changed her mind, because I can't imagine my life without her."

"Me either, Riley. Me either."

And on that Christmas Eve, in a barn on the property of the Snowflake Inn, a family was born.

Keep reading for a sneak peek from Samantha Chase's Shaughnessy Brothers series

This Is *Our* Song

THE SOUNDS COMING FROM HIS GUITAR SEEMED ROUGH even to his own ears. Disgusted, Riley Shaughnessy put the instrument aside and raked his hands through his hair. Head lowered, he stared at the ground in defeat.

"Something's got to give, Ry."

Riley didn't need to look up to know his manager Mick was standing in the corner of the room. The man was like some sort of ninja—you never seemed to see or hear him coming or going, and yet there he was.

"Yeah, I know," Riley said quietly.

Stepping farther into the room, Mick stopped and sat down on the sofa opposite Riley's. "We've all been patient. We've given you time. This album has been at the halfway point for far too long. You need to finish it."

Riley's head snapped up and his eyes narrowed. "You think I'm not trying, Mick? For crying out loud, I've spent every minute of every day trying to come up with something—anything—to make it happen! I...I can't seem to get what I want from here"—he pointed to his head—"to there." He pointed to the guitar.

"Maybe it's time for us to bring in someone to write the music for you and you just...you know, sing it."

For a minute, Riley felt like he was going to be sick. It wasn't an unusual suggestion and in the past, when he was still playing with his band, they had done it. But this was his solo project—his chance to prove to the world that he had the talent to stand on his own. The rest of the guys were doing well with their solo work; Riley didn't want to be the lone failure.

"No," he said firmly.

Mick relaxed against the sofa and looked at him with what could only be described as pity. "Dude, you need to know when to call it a day. No one's saying this is a bad thing. We're just trying to speed up the process a bit. You wanted some time off, we gave you some time off. You wanted to do this solo crap, we were happy to let you do it. But now? Riley, come on. You're asking too much. The label is getting antsy and you're not giving them anything to work with. Take the gift. Take the damn songs, record them, and let's wrap this thing up. Maybe once you get on the road and tour a little bit, you'll get your muse back."

If only it were that easy.

The look on his face must have conveyed that because Mick sighed and leaned forward, his tone a little gentler.

"Look, Riley, I get it. I do. I know what you're trying to do here and I think it's great. And no one was cheering louder for you than me. But it's not happening the way we thought. No one's going to think less of you because you're using some songs written by other people on this project."

"I think you're wrong," Riley said a bit defensively. "Just like the people from the documentary—"

"Man, you have got to let it go!" Mick snapped.

"It wasn't even that big a deal! Quit harping on it and move on!"

"I can't!" he shouted and jumped to his feet. "I was on top and everything was going freaking great, and then this documentary comes along, and the next thing I know, rumors are starting to swirl that I'm not relevant enough or talented enough or...whatever the hell else people were saying! It's not so easy to pick up and dust that shit off!"

Slowly, Mick stood and walked over to Riley. "Okay, you're right. I'm sorry." He paused. "The thing is, the label is going to cut you loose if this project isn't wrapped up in the next three months."

"What?"

Mick nodded solemnly. "I did everything I could, Ry. I really did. They're tired of waiting."

"There's got to be something...something I can do to show them I'm trying—I'm really working hard at this because I want the album to be a success." Damn, he was almost begging and he hated it. "Mick, there has to be some sort of goodwill gesture to show them I'm good for this."

"Well...there was the other songwriter..."

Riley shook his head vehemently. "No. Something else. There's got to be another option on this one."

"Dude, you're killing me."

Riley was about to say the same thing when Mick's phone rang and he stepped away to take the call. This whole thing was a nightmare. His whole life, he'd never had a problem writing songs. Whether it was rock music, ballads—he'd even written a couple of country music songs—but nothing was coming to him for this particular album.

For so long he imagined how he wanted this project to go and once he'd gotten the green light, the first few songs flew out of him and then…nothing. And Mick could say whatever he wanted; the documentary was a big deal and the rumors about him that went around afterward—like how he was the least talented of his own band—had seriously affected Riley's self-esteem.

He sighed and walked over to the window looking out on the city. His house on the hill had become his prison. Even though it had a great view, it still felt as if the walls were closing in on him. He was afraid to go out—didn't want to risk hearing people talk about him. Hell, he'd even taken a break from seeing his family because for some reason, his insecurities seemed to be right at the surface whenever he was around them and they were all starting to call him out on it.

It sucked.

Out of the corner of his eye, he saw Mick heading for the door. He put whoever he was talking to on hold and looked at Riley. "I'll be back at three. We'll finish up then." And then he was gone.

Shit. Now what? He basically had a few hours to either come up with six songs to complete the album or admit defeat and take on someone else's music. No, that wasn't an option. He needed to get his head straight and figure out what to do. He needed…

His phone rang and when he saw his twin brother's face on the screen, Riley nearly sagged with relief. Before he could say hello, Owen was talking.

"As a scientist, it's hard for me to accept this twin telepathy, and yet I found myself driven to call you because I felt you were really sad. Are you okay?"

Riley smiled and sat on the couch and relaxed. "Come on…you mean to tell me after all these years you doubt the telepathy thing? I would have thought you'd be anxious to run experiments on us."

"I don't know if it would really prove much. We know each other so well there's hardly any science involved. We're siblings, we grew up together, why shouldn't I know what you're thinking? Besides, the whole twin telepathy thing is less common in cases like ours."

"Wow, did you just oversimplify something, Owen?" Riley asked with a chuckle.

"I am capable of doing it from time to time."

Even as fraternal twins, they were as different as night and day. Where Riley had always been an extrovert, Owen was an introvert. Riley was a singer and a performer, Owen was an astrophysicist. He was scary smart and it tended to make him socially awkward, but there wasn't another human being alive who understood Riley like his brother.

"So you felt compelled to call me, huh?"

"I did," Owen said simply. "I was in the middle of teaching a class and you were just there so strongly—it was almost as if you were standing right there."

"Sorry about that. How did the rest of your class go?"

"Oh, they're still in there. I gave them some work to do and stepped out into the hall to call you."

"Owen Shaughnessy!" Riley mocked. "Now you're telling me you ignored your job because of this telepathy? That tells me you really are beginning to believe it's a thing! Come on. Admit it!"

Owen groaned. "Are you going to tell me why your

negative thoughts and feelings are interfering with my life or am I supposed to guess?"

"You tell me. Can't you read my mind?" Riley couldn't help but tease.

"So they're still giving you a hard time about the album."

Damn. "Okay, now you're freaking me out."

"It really wasn't that hard a conclusion to draw, Riley. This is hardly new information. Why are you still struggling with this? Music comes as easily to you as breathing."

"It used to. I don't know, Owen. It's like I can hear the music off in the distance and I just can't reach it. Like it's behind a closed door and no one will let me open it."

"Have you thought about talking to a therapist?"

"Hell no. The press would have a field day with that."

"So? Seems to me if it helped unlock the music, it shouldn't matter if the press finds out. It's all for the greater good."

Riley stopped and considered his brother's words. "What's going on with you? What... Why... You're not talking like yourself."

"I don't know what you mean," Owen said.

"Bro, normally you would have quoted all kinds of statistics about mental blocks and therapists and named a couple of renowned doctors and scientists to back up what you're saying. But you're not. What gives?"

Owen sighed loudly. "You know, sometimes there is no pleasing everyone. I get criticized when I talk like a scientist and then I get criticized when I don't. Honestly, Riley, I didn't expect it from you!"

Uh-oh. Something was definitely up with his brother. "Okay, okay, you're right. Sorry. And for the record, I wasn't criticizing. I was merely making an observation."

"Whatever."

Riley burst out laughing.

"What? What's so funny now?" Owen demanded.

"Nothing," Riley said, instantly sobering. "Nothing at all. Look, go back to your class. I'm just trying to work this stuff out. Mick came to me and suggested using someone else's songs to finish the album. The label's getting pissy and basically everyone's losing faith in me. They gave me three months to finish things up."

"Okay. So do it."

"Seriously?" Riley asked with a bit of frustration. "You—who knows me better than anyone—thinks I need to quit?"

"I don't see it as quitting. I see it as moving on from a project that has proven not to work. We do it all the time in the labs. You test a theory and when it doesn't work, you move on. You wanted to try this solo project and you did. It's not working for you so stop forcing it."

Now Riley growled. "You know, I think I liked it better when you said stuff I couldn't understand. This getting right to the point is kind of hurtful."

"I'm sorry!" Owen said quickly. "All I meant is—"

"Don't. It's okay. You're saying what everyone else has. And coming from you? Well, that tells me what I needed to know. It just doesn't make me feel like any less of a failure."

"You're not a failure, Ry. You're a gifted musician. No one says you can't try again in the future. You just need to let this project go."

Emotion clogged Riley's throat and he nodded silently. And just as he suspected, his brother knew it.

"You're going to be okay, Riley," Owen said softly.

Normally Riley would agree simply because his brother was rarely wrong.

Only right now, he was having a hard time keeping the faith.

―――≈―――

As promised, Mick was back at three o'clock sharp. The man was a stickler for keeping a schedule. Well, he normally was. He'd been a little more than frustrated with Riley's lack of one lately.

As soon as Riley got a glimpse of his manager, he knew something was up. It was written all over his face. "Okay," Riley began as soon as they sat down. "Out with it."

Luckily Mick wasn't the type to play dumb. "I spoke to Rich Baskin earlier—that's who called when I was here."

Rich was the head of Riley's record label, and it was all Riley could do just to nod.

"I told him you really weren't on board with using outside writers to finish the album."

"And what did he say?"

"What do you think he said? He's pissed."

"Great."

"However," Mick began, "he is willing to give a little."

Riley's head shot up and for the first time in what seemed like forever, he felt hopeful. "Okay. How?"

"Do you know Tommy Vaughn?"

Riley's eyes went wide. "Of course I do! Who

doesn't? The man is right up with Jagger, Mercury, Lennon, Bowie… I mean, the guy is a rock god. Why? Is…is he one of the song writers? Does he want back in on the music side rather than writing about it?"

"Okay, so you're aware of his magazine."

Reaching over the side of his sofa, Riley pulled a copy of *Rock the World* magazine. "Aware of it? I subscribe to it!"

"That's good," Mick said. "Because you're going to be in it."

Riley pulled back and frowned. "What do you mean?"

"Look, I don't play dumb with you, don't do it to me." Mick paused. "Tommy wants to do a huge piece on you—possibly multi-issue. He doesn't do it very often. He's got someone lined up to work with you. Rich wants this. So if you're hoping to get back in anyone's favor, you're going to do this."

"Mick, you know how I feel about interviews. Especially right now!"

"Then you're going to have to get over it. Fast. Because if this deal doesn't happen, they'll pull the plug on the album even sooner, and think of the lousy publicity that is going to cause. 'Riley Shaughnessy cut loose because he didn't want to talk and couldn't write any songs.'"

"That was pretty low," Riley sneered. "Even for you."

"I'm not here to candy coat it for you. I've been doing it for too long and now look where we are." He shifted in his seat. "You never asked for much and you were never complicated to work with—you were certainly never a diva—so when you started to struggle, I let it slide. Well, I'm done with it now. It's time for some tough love. You need to stop with the pity party and get your ass back in the game." His phone beeped and Mick looked at it and stood. "I've got another appointment to get to. You're gonna get a call from the magazine. Take it and be thankful." And he headed for the door.

"Mick—"

"I'm not kidding, Riley," Mick interrupted. "Everyone's done playing around. We want an album from you, and we wanted it six months ago. Don't turn into a diva on me now. Do the interview. Hell, who knows, maybe talking to someone—even a magazine reporter—can be…what do you call it? Cathartic. Yeah, I think that's the word. Maybe you'll finally get out of your head and get the music down like you need to." With a pat on Riley's back, Mick walked to the door. "I'll talk to you in a couple of days. Think about it—but don't screw this up."

Riley stood and stared at the closed door for a solid five minutes before he could force himself to move. When he did, it was to go back to the couch and collapse.

He'd sworn he wouldn't do any interviews until the album was done and he knew it was perfect. Now what was he supposed to talk about? How he couldn't write? Couldn't play? Couldn't sing?

Yeah, the fans would love that.

Unfortunately, he knew he was screwed and there was no way out. So he'd give the interview—a super-ficial one. No one said it had to be deep and meaning-ful. And it wasn't written anywhere that he had to be sincere or enjoy it. The label wanted this? Fine. He'd do it. But Riley would do it on his own terms, not theirs.

Jumping to his feet, he almost felt like some sort of

evil genius. He'd say all the right things and smile at all the right times. They could take their pictures and think they were getting a glimpse into the real life of Riley Shaughnessy.

But they wouldn't.

They never would.

There was a time when Riley loved these times—the interviews, the press tours—they were always fun. Now it sounded and felt like a chore—one more thing to piss him off and make him resentful toward the talent that had deserted him.

He walked back over to the window and looked down at the city. Somewhere out there was some reporter thinking they'd struck gold by getting the chance to sit down with him. He had a reputation for being a great subject. Well, news flash, that guy was gone and no one had seen him in about a year.

God, he was sounding morbid.

Maybe it would work for him. Maybe—rather than being a phony during the interview he would be just...difficult. Morbid, depressing, angsty. Or maybe just indifferent.

Well shit. Now he was more confused than he was a minute ago.

There was only one thing for certain right now: He honestly felt sorry for whoever Tommy Vaughn was giving this interview to.

"Change of plans."

Savannah Daly looked up from her laptop to see her boss standing next to her desk. Before she could inquire about what plans specifically, Tommy continued.

"You are interviewing Riley Shaughnessy."

Normally Savannah enjoyed a good challenge, but this was not one she was willing to take on. "You promised me the story on Coldplay. I've been researching and planning the whole thing for a month. I've talked to their people and I'm scheduled to go on the first three California stops of their upcoming tour with them—which starts in two weeks! I don't have the time to deal with Riley Shaughnessy."

"Like I said, doll…change of plans. Blake's taking the Coldplay story. I need you on Riley's." Tommy Vaughn was a rock and roll legend back in his time, and now at the age of sixty-two, he ran one of the biggest music magazines in the business. At six-foot-four, he wasn't someone you would say no to.

Or at least you *shouldn't* say no to.

Savannah chose to ignore the memo. "No," she said firmly. "You promised me Coldplay. This was going to be my big piece. The cover!"

"Riley's story will be even bigger, I guarantee it. You'll still get your cover…it will just be after Blake's Coldplay one."

She let out a very unladylike whine. "Come on, Tommy," she pled. "What's the point in giving me your word if you're just going to take it back?"

He leaned in close. "Sweetheart, I didn't give you my word. I offered you the story, you accepted. There's nothing written in stone and you know it. Now, you can sit here and whine and complain and do the damn piece, or…" He paused and straightened. "You can pack your stuff and go back to cutting hair at the local salon for all those soccer moms who seem to be everywhere. Your choice."

She couldn't believe it. He was threatening her? Seriously threatening to fire her if she didn't take this stupid story? Unable to simply accept it, Savannah took a different approach. "Can I ask you something?"

"Sure."

"Why me? Why do you think it has to be *me*—specifically—who writes this story? You have dozens of reporters on staff, some who are real fans of the guy. Why would you think I'm the right fit?"

Tommy studied her for a long minute before sitting down on the edge of her desk, crossing his arms over his chest. "Savannah, when you and I first met, you were a journalism graduate who was paying her bills cutting hair, do you remember?"

Seeing as how it was only a little over a year ago, she did. Rather than give him a snarky comeback, she simply nodded.

"That day we were doing a story on some local band who had recently hit it big, and you happened to be one of the stylists on the set of the photoshoot. You weren't even supposed to be there, but their usual stylist got the flu and you were called in. I remember watching you. You weren't starstruck and you didn't get overly chatty with the band, you just did your job."

"Tommy... I don't..."

He held up a hand to stop her. "When the guys walked away for the shoot, you and I stayed back and talked. It didn't take long for me to realize you had a good head on your shoulders. You weren't some naive chick and you weren't easily impressed. I was the guy there to write the story, but you were the one who essentially gave me the interview."

She looked at him quizzically. "What do you mean? You never said—"

"I was there—just like you—because someone had called in sick. Another reporter was supposed to do the interview so I was there with very little prep time and wasn't sure what exactly I wanted this piece to say. But you," he said with a smile, "you seemed to hone in on these guys and figured out their personalities pretty quick. And you were spot-on. Had I not talked to you, I would have looked at them as four morons who happened to get lucky. What I had by the end of the interview was a pretty deep piece showing a side of a band no one had explored before." He shrugged. "*That's* why I hired you."

"Riley Shaughnessy has done dozens of interviews over the years, Tommy. Believe me, you're not going to find anything deep about the guy. He's a pretty-boy rock star. That's it. You ask me? *He* got lucky."

"You don't think he's talented?"

Now it was her turn to shrug. "It really doesn't matter what I think. Obviously millions of people think he is."

"But you don't," Tommy concluded. "This is why I want you on this story."

"Because I don't like the guy?"

"Because you won't be easily swayed." He looked around the newsroom and lowered his voice when he focused on her again. "Riley Shaughnessy is one of those stories you have to be careful about who you send in there to do it. Some of the girls on staff? They're going to go and flirt and write some bubblegum piece more suited for a teen magazine. Some of the guys on staff? They'll go in there and make it a pissing contest and then

I've got a story that is off-balance." Then he smiled. "But you? You'll go in there and try to figure him out because it's what you do. You want to write a story that makes people think and will show off your skills. And you know you're not going to get that if you write fluff."

"So basically you're saying I'm the only writer on staff who can be trusted to write a story on this guy?" She shook her head. "Uh-uh. I'm not buying it. You can try and stroke my ego all you want, Tommy, but I don't believe you."

With a huff, he stood and motioned for Savannah to follow him. When they reached his office, she stepped inside and watched him as he shut the door. "A year ago, Riley got turned down for some legends of rock documentary. Word around town is it messed with him. He can't finish his album, he's in a funk."

"So he's pouting," Savannah stated.

But Tommy shook his head. "I think there's more to it. I think it's something deeper. The guy's been spewing out hits for years. Technically, he's too young to be considered a legend and he didn't really belong in the documentary—you know it. I know it. Hell, even his record label and agent know it. So what's his deal? Why the retreat?"

"Like I said, he's pouting. It's ego. He wanted something and he didn't get it. End of story."

"No, Riley Shaughnessy was a publicity machine. The guy knows how to work the paparazzi, reporters, the late-night talk show hosts…everybody loves him. Then a year ago, he just clams up? I'm telling you, there's a bigger story here and I want you to get it. Call it ego stroking or whatever you want, but you and I both know you're the only one on this staff who is going to give this piece the kind of in-depth attention it needs."

"But…but…Coldplay. Chris Martin…"

Tommy patted her on the shoulder. "I'll still get you backstage for one of the shows, but Blake's doing the piece, Savannah. That's final."

She crossed her arms and frowned.

"Now who's pouting?"

"I can't believe you're doing this to me," she grumbled.

"Hey, it's not like I'm sending you on tour with some boy band or something."

Just the thought of it made her stomach clench. She'd been there, done that, and had the heartache to prove it. Not that she'd ever share that bit of information with Tommy.

Or anyone.

"You might as well be." She sighed and sat down in the chair closest to him. She took a minute to get her thoughts together. "Okay, say I decide to take this on."

Tommy's bark of laughter almost shook the walls. "Seriously? Did you just make it sound like there's a possibility you won't?"

Savannah shrugged. "Maybe I miss cutting hair."

"Yeah, okay. And I miss eating ramen noodles ten times a week. Cut the crap, Savannah. You and I both know you're going to do it."

She acted as if he hadn't spoken. "If I agree to this piece, how do you propose I get Riley to agree to an interview? He's been turning down people left and right for a year. I heard he turned down Ellen! And you really think I'm going to be the one to convince him to sit down for a conversation? You're crazy!"

Tommy smirked as he slowly walked around his office and sat down behind his desk. Then he took his time getting comfortable and folding his hands in front of him. "Sometimes it amazes me how little you think of me."

She rolled her eyes.

He held up a hand dramatically. "No…no. It's all right. Let me enlighten you on how I make things happen. For starters, I know *everyone* in this business. Everyone. Secondly, Riley's people are just as anxious to get him back out in the spotlight as his fans are. So much so they're guaranteeing he'll agree to this interview."

"You mean…"

Tommy grinned. "They're probably breaking the news to him as we speak."

"He'll never agree to this," Savannah said hopefully.

Tommy shook his head at her. "We nailed the exclusive. You've got an all-access, monthlong pass to work with Riley Shaughnessy."

"*A month*? Tommy, I'm writing a piece for the magazine, not his autobiography."

"Yeah, well…from the way I understood it, Riley may be a little gun-shy so this isn't something you're going to accomplish in a couple of sit-downs. Hell, for all I know, you may get enough information to make it a multi-edition story, and I'm okay with it. But we've got a basic timeline. All you have to do is reach out to him." He handed her Riley's number.

Stuffing the paper in her pocket as she stood, she glared down at him. "You know, you can be a real jackass sometimes, Tommy."

He stood and chuckled. "Only sometimes? I'll take that as a compliment."

Dread filled Savannah as she walked to the door. Turning around, she pleaded one last time. "Come on, Tommy. Seriously. Someone—anyone—else would do a better job on this story. Please reconsider."

He leveled her with a hard stare. "I hear there's a sale on hair dye at Walmart this week. You won't even need a coupon. You interested?"

Heat crept up her cheeks at his implication. She was screwed. There was no way out of this nightmare of a story no matter what she tried to do. Without another word, she walked out of Tommy's office. She wouldn't give him the satisfaction of seeing the defeat in her eyes.

Back at her desk, she sank down in her chair and sighed. In the past year, she'd done more than her share of lackluster interviews. It was supposed to build character, Tommy had told her. Only she had hoped by building her character, she'd start getting the assignments she really wanted. Better yet, she'd get first choice of incoming assignments.

No such luck.

While she knew she owed a lot to Tommy Vaughn— hell, she probably *would* still be cutting hair if it weren't for him—it didn't mean she had to like him.

And right now, she didn't.

The decision to stay and work or leave and vent warred in her head. Tapping her keyboard, she watched her computer come back to life and immediately began a Google search on Riley. Instantly there were dozens, if not hundreds, of pictures, links, and blurbs about him. Not that it was surprising, but Savannah wasn't one who subscribed to the motto of more is better. Her first hit went to Wikipedia.

Riley Shaughnessy is an American singer-songwriter, record producer, philanthropist, and actor, best known as the founder and front man of the rock band Shaughnessy. During his career, he released four studio albums with his band, which to date have sold over fifty million albums worldwide, making them one of the world's bestselling music artists. Currently Riley is embarking on a solo career.

"Bor-ing." Savannah sighed and then clicked through photos of Riley throughout his career. Tall, lanky, dark hair...all things she normally found very yummy in a man. So why did it make her almost want to sneer when it was this particular man? He had the look—the sexy grin, the earring, and probably had a tattoo. She snorted. "Typical rock star."

She skimmed the rest—four brothers, one sister. Mother dead, father alive. Grew up in North Carolina. No marriages. Just the basics.

With Riley doing his solo thing, Savannah did a quick search to see what the rest of the boys in the band were doing with their time. "Hmmm," she began, unconsciously reading out loud, "Matt 'Matty' Reed is writing the music for a Broadway musical and starring in it. Not bad."

Scrolling down a bit, she continued. "Dylan Anders, the partier of the group, has been popping up onstage with various other artists...drunk. Lovely." *Scroll, scroll, scroll.* "And last but not least...Julian Grayson." She sat back and almost smiled. "Just got married and has a baby on the way. He's taken up photography in his downtime and has no musical plans at the present." She nodded with approval. "Good for him."

Okay, maybe this assignment wouldn't be the worst thing…

"Hey, Van," Blake Jordan said as he sauntered by her desk—using the nickname he knew she hated. "Tough break about the Coldplay story. I promise I'll give Chris and the boys your regards."

Once he was out of sight, she flipped him the bird. "Bite me."

Now she was even more ticked off than she had been five minutes ago. Knowing she wasn't going to accomplish anything here, she closed her laptop and packed it up—along with a few other items—and made her way out to the parking lot. The sun was shining as she fished around in her oversized purse for her sunglasses. Sliding them on, she hastily combed her long black hair out of the way and trudged to her car, cursing Tommy, Blake, and Riley Shaughnessy the entire time.

Once she climbed into her Jeep, Savannah secured her computer bag and purse and then pulled a clip out of the glove compartment and clipped up her hair. Driving such an open vehicle had become a love-hate relationship. Deep down, she loved her Jeep. It was her to a T. It just wasn't conducive to her long hair. Luckily hers was pin-straight and it didn't matter if the wind blew it or she clipped it up or threw a baseball cap over it, it was still going to look the same. And really, doing all those things was for her own safety—she'd learned relatively quickly that long hair, wind, and open sides on a vehicle were not a good combination.

Never let it be said Savannah Daly needed a ton of bricks to fall on her.

Pulling out onto the main strip, she began to drive aimlessly. It seemed too early to go home, but there wasn't any place in particular she wanted to go. With a muttered curse, she forced herself to just drive for a while—to enjoy the sights and sounds of the city. Not that downtown L.A. was anything spectacular, but it had the potential to be a good distraction.

An hour later, traffic was becoming more of an issue and Savannah decided she'd pretty much cooled off enough. She could go home and think about this new assignment without feeling an immediate urge to strangle someone. The next right turn would lead her to the freeway, which would—in turn—take her home. Her stomach growled loudly and she cursed again. "Yeah, yeah, yeah…I was supposed to food shop yesterday," she said.

Knowing that shopping for groceries was even less appealing than doing research on Riley Shaughnessy, she stayed on the road and opted to find someplace to grab takeout.

"All the usual suspects," she murmured as she flew by restaurants and cafés. Did she really want to go home and eat? Shaking her head, Savannah knew at this rate with traffic, any food she purchased would be cold by the time she arrived at her home. That left a sandwich or salad to go or dining alone at the restaurant of her choice.

Suddenly, the thought of a sandwich became really appealing. No need to go for anything fancy. She could grab a sandwich and maybe hit the beach. She'd driven far enough that she was minutes away from Hermosa Beach. "Okay, for once, my aimless driving has paid off." Slowly, she drove through town and found a place to park. Grabbing her bags, Savannah felt at peace. The sun, the sand, the surf…and a sandwich. Not a bad way to spend the early evening hours. She was thankful for the currently cool California weather.

With so many places to choose from and her stomach getting more and more vocal, she found a small bar and grille with outdoor seating facing the beach and opted to go there. A burger was just like a sandwich, wasn't it? And sitting at a table was a bit more civilized than the sand. The hostess led her to a table for one, and Savannah smiled and got herself situated. It was tempting to take out her laptop and do some work, but she opted to go with just taking out her phone and checking email.

She ordered her dinner and a drink and was happily scrolling through her inbox when someone slammed into the back of her chair, nearly causing her to drop her phone. There was no apology and Savannah turned around and glared at the culprit. The guy had his back to her and essentially had his chair right up against hers. Seriously? Was this guy for real?

Unable to help herself, she nudged her chair back with a little more force than was probably necessary and waited to see if he'd acknowledge her now.

He didn't.

He wore a baseball cap pulled low over his eyes and a newspaper opened to the point where it was practically a wall; Savannah decided the guy was clearly a jerk. Rather than getting into a fight with him, she moved her chair around to another side of the table— and found herself still looking out at the beach. Smiling, she went back to her phone, pulled up the camera, and took a couple shots of the sun on the water. Yeah, it was beautiful and peaceful. There was a light breeze that felt glorious and…

There was a newspaper in her face.

"You have got to be kidding me!" she snapped as she peeled the paper from her face, crumpling it up. It didn't matter if the wind blew and it was an accident, this guy was seriously messing with her peaceful evening and she was done playing nice. "Hey!" she said as she tapped the guy on the shoulder.

He looked up at her, but between the sun and the cap basically shielding his face, Savannah had no idea what the guy looked like.

"Seriously, you bang into my chair, your newspaper blows in my face, and you can't be bothered with an apology?" she demanded, hands on her hips.

"Um…sorry," he mumbled and took the crumpled paper from her hands and turned back to his table.

"That's it? That's all you have to say?"

Without turning around, he said, "You asked for an apology and I gave you one."

Well damn. He had her there. "Oh yeah… Well… fine. Just…keep your crap on your table, okay? I'm trying to relax over here." When he made no further comment, Savannah went back to her seat. Within minutes, her meal was in front of her and she felt all the tension leaving her body—a good burger could do that for a girl.

And the fries were damn near orgasmic.

She let out a little moan of pleasure and noticed Mr. Personality was staring at her. She saw he hadn't ordered any food yet. The waitress had inquired several times, but he continued to send her away.

His loss.

When she looked over and saw he was still staring, she put her burger down and stared back. "Problem?"

He shook his head. "I was just wondering what it was you ordered that had you sounding like that."

"Like what?"

"Really?" he said with what sounded suspiciously like sarcasm.

Rolling her eyes, she motioned to her plate. "Bacon cheeseburger—pepper jack cheese, avocado…the works. And fries." She picked one up. "These are the culprits. They're so good they should be illegal."

He chuckled. "I don't think I've ever heard someone describe French fries that way."

"Trust me."

"I guess I'll have to," he said and for a minute, he just sat back and smiled at her.

"Look…um… Can you turn around? You know, go back to your reading? You're starting to freak me out. And besides, didn't your parents ever tell you it's rude to stare?"

He laughed again. "As a matter of fact they have. But I wasn't a very good listener."

"So it's a lifelong problem?"

"Tell you what, you let me have one of your moan-inducing fries and I'll go back to reading my paper and leave you alone."

"Is that a promise?"

He nodded. "Scout's honor."

Somehow she couldn't envision this guy ever having been a Boy Scout, but whatever. Watching him warily, she picked up a fry and held it out for him. "One fry and then you turn back around so I can eat without an audience, right?"

He nodded again when suddenly the wind picked up, and in the blink of an eye, Savannah's napkin blew off her lap. She bent over to reach it at the same time he bent over to help her. Their heads bumped and with a startled "*ow*" coming from both of them, Savannah reached up to touch her head. On the ground was his baseball cap. Out of the corner of her eye, she saw him reach for it. After she had her napkin safely back in place, she realized she was still holding the French fry.

"Hey, aren't you gonna…" She looked up and gasped.

Staring back at her was none other than Riley Shaughnessy.

About the Author

New York Times and *USA Today* bestselling author Samantha Chase released her debut novel, *Jordan's Return*, in November 2011. Although she waited until she was in her forties to publish for the first time, writing has been a lifelong passion. Her motivation was her students: teaching creative writing to elementary-age students all the way up through high school and encouraging those students to follow their writing dreams gave Samantha the confidence to take that step as well.

When she's not working on a new story, Samantha spends her time reading contemporary romances, blogging, playing way too many games of Scrabble or solitaire on Facebook, and spending time with her husband of twenty-five years and their two sons in North Carolina.

Saving Jake

Blessings, Georgia

by Sharon Sala

New York Times and *USA Today* Bestselling Author

—∿∿—

There is always *hope*

After eight years in the Marines, Jacob Lorde returns to Blessings, Georgia, with no plans other than to hole up in his empty house and heal what's left of his soul. But with a charming next door neighbor and a town full of friendly people, keeping to himself is easier said than done.

as long as you can come *home*

Laurel Payne understands far too well what Jake is going through, after witnessing her late husband experience similar problems. She's in no hurry to jump into another relationship with a complicated guy, but their attraction is undeniable—and perhaps exactly what both of them need.

—∿∿—

Praise for *I'll Stand By You*:

"An amazing story by a true storyteller." —*RT Book Reviews*

"Sala hooks you from the first page." —*Fresh Fiction*

For more Sharon Sala, visit:

www.sourcebooks.com